ZOMBIE

DOMINATION

Tales of Undead Terror

ZOMBIE DOMINATION

Tales of Undead Terror

by

Bruce S. Larson

ZOMBIE DOMINATION
Tales of Undead Terror
by
Bruce S. Larson

This and other fine fiction...
Published by
World Line One Press

ISBN: 978-0-9856841-9-8

CONTENTS

ACKNOWLEDGEMENTS

Cristopher DeRose. First rate first reader. First rate author. If you like this book, thank Cris. It was his inspiration that started the undead ball rolling. If you like good fiction, check out his books.

FOREWORD

What can anyone say, or scream, about our current zombie fascination? The word *RUN!* comes to mind. At least if you don't wish to become one of the flesh-seeking horde. But in a way, we all are. We populate our media with zombies and watch them devour the living. We like it. We like zombies, a lot. In some stories in this book, humans have run to the stars and colonized other planets. And it's still not far enough to escape the undead, brain-hungry masses bringing carnage and apocalypse. It seems no place is ever safe from them. So stop running. Sit down. Give your brain to this book. Shuffle in your seat as the plague spreads with each page. The zombies are here. They're everywhere. Let them in. You know they will like you. A lot.

Bruce S. Larson
Shambling onward
2016

BLUE EMPIRE

Once, everyone considered her beautiful. Eyes in gym showers and the few lovers she allowed the pleasure of her body had admired her naked form. Now she stood naked again, but in front of a stranger and separated from him by a thick, clear security wall next to a reinforced metal hatch. She bared her teeth. The act was not defiance, but from the growing hunger slowly replacing all sensations. Complex thoughts were lost to her. Her shapely body was the same temperature as the cool cell. She desired the warmth in the man called Toolie. She would swallow it with his skin, organs, and blood she craved to tear from his nervous, twitching form.

Toolie lost his arousal to sudden fear as the naked zombie lurched at him. He was safe with the prison cell's hatch closed. Inside it, the zombie opened and closed her jaw as if biting something. Toolie knew she wanted to bite him, or parts off him. Her skin has still smooth, almost glistening, but it became more pallid with each minute. Her eyes were darkening from blue to bloody from rupturing veins or something else red. Toolie knew she was fresh infected. He could not see where she was bit or pricked. Maybe she was surprised in the shower, or slept nude and forgot to lock her door. Somehow she got the plague, died, and then went looking for meat. The plague was spreading deeper into the city. Some zombies were solitary roamers like feral cats. They were rarely seen but dangerous when found. The lone biters were hideous reminders that a horde of undead shifted and drifted ever closer.

A police net team caught the former young woman, but the government didn't want more test subjects. New orders said kill them all. Toolie was supposed to haul her by the leash, smash her brain, and then dump her in the burn pit. Such was the life of a police operations engineer. The job gave Toolie access to every dark police building and lonely holding cell. Such access was worth something to some people. It was easy to sell access with most of the armed officers fighting every undead thing clawing closer to downtown. Toolie kept reminding himself to carry his large wrench with him, just in case he needed to crush a zombie's head. That might not drop the zombie, but it made it thrash and spin which bought time to run. He intended to earn and scam enough to buy a ticket and skip town before someone put a gun in his hands.

"Wow! She's a beauty!"

The voice came from behind Toolie. He jumped.

"Now, Toolie, you should be afraid of her, not me." Naslock smiled. It was a sharp, narrow smile under a sharp nose and cutting stare. His face held no curves.

Naslock was tall and straight like a long knife. His back-up thug, Shims, was even bigger. Drugs and grafts pumped Shims' muscles impossibly round. His body was too vast for his skull. The armor padding in his expensive Action Attire suit made the effect worse. Together, his body and clothes caused his head to appear as a tied knot on an upside-down, cloth balloon.

Shims wasn't sleek like the clothing ad models. The ads read: *Worlds change. Be ready for anything in Action Attire!* Most times, a world changed from zombies. People ran from them as crazed rabbits fled rabid wolves. This world, Camponon, had no rabbits or wolves. At least Toolie had never seen them in a park. Flying, spider bats in the trees, yes. Warm, fuzzy rabbits, no. Most zombies looked like walking wolf victims. Blood and swallowed parts of victims dripped out their guts and torn skin. Zombies were more vicious than rabid wolves. Or bunnies. Zombies were in the park and your building. Maybe they were your roommate or spouse. Bummer that, Toolie thought. Bummer, too that he could not afford nice Action Attire.

Toolie was glad his head was proportional. Shims was no natural thing. But Naslock was more dangerous than a rabid zombie. He was a hands-on racketeer. Maybe because zombies ate his men. His smaller men. Still, Naslock's stare suggested things more threatening than being crushed by the inflated Shims. It felt like a needle through Toolie.

"Well, you did good." Naslock said. He looked at the naked zombie. "But let's wrap this quick. Being on police turf, even empty, makes me slightly nervous."

"I thought you'd paid everyone off around here." Toolie said as he turned back to stare at the monster in the cell.

"I did." Naslock sighed. "Then they were eaten."

"Pay off the new bosses." Toolie shrugged.

"Problem, there." Naslock said. "They have other, apocalyptic concerns, currently."

Shims bobbed his seemingly small head in a slow nod of agreement.

"And, surprise, surprise!" Naslock continued. "Not everyone is corrupt like us, Tools."

"Look, I'm not corrupt. I just want out of here." Toolie said with a entreating tone and expression.

"And you're willing to bend your morals to do that. Good for you!" Naslock smiled wide and looked at Toolie. "That's what creates opportunity. For me."

"I'd have thought apocalypse was opportunity for you." Toolie said without looking back at Naslock. He preferred to make eye contact with the hungry zombie.

"You might think chaos is good for otherwise questionable business. Truth is you need stability for commerce. At least in the long term. But right now my garbage trucks are busy."

Shims' head bobbed again.

"Bodies?" Toolie asked.

"No. Quarantine violating transit." Naslock nodded to himself thinking of his cash profits.

"Here I was saving up for a shuttle ticket." Toolie droned.

"Good luck with that. And good luck cutting into her." Naslock pointed to the zombie who flinched. "You should have shackled her."

"What?" Toolie shouted and finally looked at Naslock. He then looked passed him to see if they were still alone. He caught

3

glimpse of Shims whose eyes stared down at him from atop a small planet of expensive weave.

"Look, I'm not getting within a centimeter of that clear wall!" Toolie waved his hands. "You go in there and do whatever you want!"

"Not my style." Naslock flicked his fingers at the zombie, and then looked at his manicured fingernails. "But it does bring a few ideas to mind. Right now, go get a seal-suit and a knife. Or just a knife."

"You said you just wanted to see one close but safe!" Toolie took a step back from Naslock. He moved closer to the cell. He jerked away as the zombie's hands struck the clear wall near him. She left an odd slick on the glass-like barrier.

Naslock chuckled. "That's what I said. I lied. Business strategy. Now get me what I want."

"I did that." Toolie pointed at the zombie who bit at the extended finger. "There you go. A zombie. Now I want what you to pay me."

"Come on, Toolie!" Naslock raised his palms to the air. "Where's your curiosity?"

"Where my cash?"

"I'll pay you with sex." Naslock smiled and nodded as if the deal was sealed.

Shims bobbed his head. Toolie thought he might be smiling above the Action Attire summit.

"I don't walk that way, man." Toolie stepped back from Naslock and eyed the chamber's exit.

"Not me, you fool. From my prosties. You get your choice. Of more than one." Naslock winked. His eyes darted to the zombie who now focused on him. He stepped back from the clear wall.

"Yeah?" Toolie looked off considering the offer. He became aroused again.

"Yeah." Naslock gave Toolie a practiced, softened smile. "See, you want something and I can give it to you. Commerce, my friend. Commerce."

"But it ends tonight. That thing should be ash." Toolie jerked his head toward the zombie. "I don't want an outbreak in my zone. So have a look. Then we burn it. Fast."

"Take a deep breath, Tools." Naslock put his hands on his chest and inhaled. He solicited Toolie do the same with a slow nod. "Look beyond tonight. What you see now is a liability, a plague. What I see is untapped economic potential."

"What I see is part of the apocalypse. Death!" Toolie felt regret overtake all his other sensations.

"Can't say there is no market in that, either." Naslock mused and looked back at the zombie.

Toolie felt the cold against his sweaty hands and perspiration soaking his armpits. He had brought a zombie into a clean zone, violating quarantines, ethics, and reason for untaxed cash and a chance to save his own skin. He realized Naslock didn't bring the cash. Toolie thought he could still save himself. But he had to get free of Naslock and Shims, and then burn the hissing evidence in the cell.

"Look, let's go." Toolie said. "There is no way you can sell something, anything to a zombie. They'll just bite off your face. Or worse!"

"I don't intend to sell anything to zombies. That's nuts. I intend to sell the thrill of, well, of whatever anyone will pay to do to a zombie. Some living people might bite them for a change, or worse."

"Who the hell would want to suck or screw a zombie?" Shock overtook Toolie.

"No one here." Naslock shrugged, and then smiled. "I want to build an empire, so I create markets. Markets are people. Here, zombies are well known. I need a place where their scare is just a news vid or mind clip. Some place where gnashing dead are unknown in person."

"No place like that in the world." Toolie said and thought he should just run.

"No place like that on *this* world." Naslock cocked his left eyebrow.

"Another colony?" Toolie shrieked. "Are you insane?"

"Just sociopathic." Naslock said and aimed his penetrating smile at Toolie. "Just like a lot of bureaucrats. The kind of bureaucrat that writes permits for personal economic benefit."

Shims bobbed his proportionally small head with enthusiasm. Toolie hoped it would pop free and roll down his expensive suit.

"No way they--anyone would let you take biters off this rock. No way!" Toolie said and stepped towards the exit.

"In a way your own brain is dead." Naslock sighed with feigned disappointment and turned his body square with Toolie. "Of course you don't tell them what your long game is. You lie. Just like I lied to you."

"What?" Nervous tension strangled Toolie's voice. He saw Naslock's face completely relax with no faked emotions or expression. It was colder than the zombie who pressed her once comely form against the clear wall as she tried to push through it.

"Another reason I want off this rock." Naslock said in dead monotone. "I'm a business man, but also a killer. One of those jobs is going to catch up to me. Time to move. Because of that. And the plague."

"Okay. But--hey! You don't need to kill me." Toolie bent at the waist with his palms extended before him. He stepped to the side of Shims and closer to the exit. "Just pay me--but hey! You don't even need to do that. We're good! Good!"

"Glad to hear that. Really." Naslock spoke with a chipper tone as he breezed by Toolie and Shims and then closed the chamber's exit door. "Now go in the cell and kiss the zombie. Or I'll beat you to death. You're choice. Either way, it's a good night to be me."

Toolie dropped his jaw. He knew even if he had his big wrench that he would have dropped it, too. The last thing he saw was Naslock's narrowed eyes over his pointed nose and widening smile. The last thing Toolie felt was an impossible number blows in such a short time. They felt sharp until his flesh became kneaded, bloody welts. He didn't think Shims' fist would feel sharp or that he could even move fast. Then the punches became dull as he hit the floor. The last thing he heard was his own screams when he realized Shims had dragged his body near the cell and opened the hatch, and then the zombie started to rip open his back.

Hunger drives zombies. That hunger can ravage a planet's population as zombies ravage living flesh. Humankind now lived on many planets. Undead apocalypse followed to some. Other planets still awaited a human invasion. One such world spun far from Toolie's screams. A man very different from him, Shims, and especially Naslock, looked at his new world. His name was Vyk Reis. His profession was peacekeeper. Duty drove Vyk Reis.

Vyk arranged for early waking from a long, artificial peace spent inside plastic, glass, and steel. Now he looked out a starboard viewing portal that faced planet side. He wanted a live view of his new home. However, his own image caught his attention. He stared at the reflected, transparent likeness of himself. Internal improvements to his body had completed while he slept between planets. They were supposed to be discreet. Yet, his re-gen or the nano-installs had tweaked his iris color from brown to grey. That annoyed him. The emotion was lost as his eyes focused on the planet. Vyk saw a blue world without oceans. It was a massive, round sand dune. Vast drifts visible through the white clouds were all variations of blue, from light shades to deep hues. A spectrum of the one color painted the hemisphere.

The ship that brought Vyk and a waking multitude was the *CFS Mabon*. CFS stood for Colonial Foundation Ship. Vyk thought Colonial *Franchise* Ship might fit better. Yet the CF did provide his job. Vyk could feel the tops of his feet press against his anchored boots. Gravity began to ebb as the ship stopped its spin to deploy the important cargo. The *Mabon* had traveled from the inner stars of the federated colonies to this frontier planet only just made habitable. Or at least given a breathable atmosphere, Vyk noted. Loud metallic tones reverberated through the huge vessel as enormous locking arms released their cargo. A loud *CLANG!* sounded. Vyk felt swayed in the microgravity. He flexed his toes in his boots stuck to the deck. His compact, athletic form stayed as rigid as the ship's alloy frame. Although he had to pull his head back to avoid hitting the viewing portal.

Vyk imagined the ground on the blue world as being loose under his boots. Still, it was a clean world. No plague. No marauding hordes of the dead tread the blue soil. Other colonies had gone dark. This world was free of zombies and other darkness humans brought with them. For now.

The blue planet had no official name other than stellar coordinates and the focus group approved tag of Opportunity 80-8-18. Once a colony was established, it could petition for indigenous name recognition. Vyk played with the name Cerulean One in his mind. He saw other names float down to the blue sands. They were huge, brightly colored logos emblazoned across corporate transit cubes. The cubes left the *Mabon* for the planet's sands. They had advertised their companies with bright, happy hues between stars but to no one. Or so it was thought. At least nothing registered on the sensors while Vyk was in suspension.

Vyk wondered if aliens needed the cubes' services. Their logos proclaimed shelter, food, and appliances for what food becomes after you eat it. Vyk read *READY 'BODES. A solid roof at a reasonable price!* A cube for *FAST FLUSH! Go in peace. Anywhere. Any world!* followed it. Then a cube with *BRINKERS! Great meals for pioneers!* cube sailed downward.

Not all goods and services came in prefabricated stores. Vyk knew darker markets would follow. That's where Vyk and his officers came in. He was this blue world's CEO. He smiled at the initials. His abbreviation stood for Chief of Enforcement Operations. He was the planet's lead cop. His assigned duties required enforcing both corporate dictates and civil codes. His real duty was to keep the peace for the people. Others would ensure that ores, fees, and local product flowed back to government and corporate concerns. To do his job, he had weapons, a small force, but mostly his cold stare. He used it to eye the rock below him that would be his beat. That was, after all the commercials cubes had touched down. His shuttle couldn't launch until they had landed.

"Cee-*Eff*-Ess," Vyk muttered.

Interstellar distances away, Naslock rarely muttered. It would take away energy from his scheming.

"Christie! Christie! Christie!" Naslock chirped as he and Shims entered an illegal laboratory inside a bare loft. "How's it going for my favorite little blackmailed PhD? Or is it MD? Screw it. Let's just say Doc."

Christie looked at her central screen displaying numbers from monitors on all her glassware, thermocyclers, hexifuges, and burners. She couldn't allow sudden shock from unannounced gangsters to distract her. She kept her back to the men and kept working to prevent an explosion that would scatter them in charred pieces across the street below. Once she achieved a balance, she would turn and participate in the intimidation session.

"Christie?" Naslock stared at her back and the bright, striped pattern that showed through her threadbare lab coat.

"Shut up. I'm working." Christie spat. She entered another command on her tablet, and finally turned.

Shims stopped his approach and lowered his arms. Christie glared up at the giant through goggles pressed across pale skin.

"Well now, that's better." Naslock smiled. "Group hug?"

Naslock smiled and raised his arms to Christie.

"No." Christie said. "I delivered early. What now?"

"No room for social calls, Doc?" Naslock feigned a hurt expression and shrugged. "It's a freebie. A bonus!"

"Hug me with cash." Christie breathed. It seemed like a sigh, but she was testing the air for chemicals. "That type of bonus might even out the cuts I take by selling to you, wholesale."

"Man, you are bold, little cooker. Biochem smart, but maybe stupid in some ways. So, careful." Naslock reached out his right hand and finger-flicked Christie's goggles.

"Making drugs is cheap, but the chems are not free." Christie adjusted her goggles.

"Now you're cutting me, sweetheart. I pay better than any black racket." Naslock stepped close to Christie. "I mean, today any kid can whip up narc with a toy store chem-kit and tap water. It cuts into my business. A lot of my business. A little more water with added spit and they can mutate Fido. No spit and it's free boner pills for dad. Add more spit and a Fido hair and now dad becomes mom."

Shims jerked at the thought.

9

"You got kids, Shims?" Christie asked as she slid sideways from Naslock.

"No." A deep rumbling voice rolled down from the Action Wear summit. "I don't think so. I hope not."

"Don't worry. Messing with genomes is a little more complicated than that." Christie said and looked at Naslock. "And my stuff is much better than your imaginary imp with oedipal issues. If you want the latest and greatest cheap thrill, you know I give it to you. With the genetic hooks that ensure repeat customers. I just want what's fair."

"And a little more." Naslock smiled somehow in straight lines on his angular face.

"Same as what you pass on to your customers, Nas." Christie said.

"True. But my real reason for our association, the Docile Project." Naslock stopped smiling and stared at Christie. "I got you a sample. Is it--well?"

Christie looked over at a small refrigerator. She took a breath and answered. "Ongoing."

"So is the plague." Naslock grated. "I want a product, Christie. One I can use before a zombie is biting into that chem-kit brain of yours."

Naslock raised his finger to jab Christie's head but she preemptively flinched. Christie considered her fate. She didn't fear zombies. She didn't fear Naslock. Christie was afraid of a world with all her comforts trashed and her skills and intelligence worth nothing. Even the scheming Naslock types needed some society to manipulate. In an apocalyptic world, people like Shims would be the new kings. Everyone else would be a slave. Or a zombie. She thought her work on the Docile Project might stave off apocalypse. Naslock could unwittingly pay for saving the world, and others. But she was good at math. She could see that as time and plague marched on, a zombie or Naslock was more likely to kill her than finishing the project. Especially because she wasn't exactly working on what Naslock wanted. Still, she would keep working. Naslock was probably not good at calculating exponential plague growth. And she might surprise herself and succeed.

"I'll get it done," Christie said.

"Do so. Quick. Or I'll do you. Actually, I'll have Shims do you." Naslock looked up at Shims with a sinister grin. "You'd like that. Right, big guy?"

Shims response was only a slight shrug that still moved a glacier-sized amount of Action Wear suit.

"Tough room." Naslock said as he turned to leave. "All I want to do is build an empire. That's all."

Shims followed his boss. He was impossibly quiet for a living avalanche.

Right after they left, Christie turned and tapped her tablet to stop the timed release of toxic gas that would have killed them all. Christie didn't have a death wish, just spite for anyone who would kill her.

An astronomical distance away, Vyk Reis left the *Mabon*. The franchise cubes had landed. Azure dust was settling around them. Vyk sat in the shuttle cockpit. The pilot sat behind him and the copilot likely had wide eyes under his dark face shield when Vyk switched off the autopilot. Vyk held the ship's controls steady. Any atmosphere could send a sudden, shearing surprise among clouds or in clear skies. Vyk stayed in control. His emotions were typically clipped back just as the length of his shorn, gray hair. He felt that color matched with his uniform and now his eyes. It was also close to some lighter shades of blue on the planet's surface.

The thought he was going to set foot on a new world, a still largely alien world did stir his excitement. His mouth nearly curled into a smile. He was partially remade to improve his abilities. He wondered if that brought him a kinship with the altered planet. He had genetic coding and machine elements with patent numbers inside him. However, he wore a uniform, not a company logo. Yet a partnership of civil and corporate concerns recreated the blue world and provided his position. Nevertheless, he was a human being, not a licensed property. Both civil and corporate executives knew his psychological profile. They must consider his desire to protect people a greater asset than liability.

Vyk wondered if most people assigned to the new colony also respected life. Many had come from worlds overrun by the dead remade into ravenous monsters. He hoped that odd combination never walked the blue sands that sped beneath his shuttle. Soon his ship would swirl the blue dust with its landing jets. Then the grains and the ship would become still as Vyk's boots touched ground and he went to work. For now, he enjoyed the sensation of speed and peace.

Worlds away on Camponon, peace was lost. The zombies surged. Their mass raged with a unified purpose to kill and eat the living. Naslock thought that if zombies could chant, it would be *Kill! Eat! Kill! Eat! Kill! Eat!* He repeated the imagined chant in his own mind, but there was loud noise and shouting around him. Toolie paid with his life to show Naslock a zombie. Now zombies overran the city. Hordes of them were mere meters away. Naslock and Shims ran to save their lives or else become ripped meat like Toolie.

They ran from the city streets into a corridor of crysteel barricades. Each interlocked section was a meter wide and two meters high. An electrified line ran along the top. No zombie had climbed to taste the voltage. The crysteel looked too thin. But worse, it was transparent. Rotten or ripped faces, snapping jaws, and bloody eyes with no skin for lids pressed against the barricades. They looked to rip and devour those running in the corridor. The zombie growls and hiss didn't drown the cries of their victims behind the pulsing mass of undead.

When safe on another world, Naslock would exploit people. Only in more subtle ways than killing and eating their brains and entrails. Shims had no large brain, but Naslock needed his massive body. Naslock's held a secret tucked and shielded carefully inside his own. Units of police roamed to counter attack zombie breaches. Drones flew the perimeter with canisters of acid. Naslock was more afraid of a drone crashing and spewing acid than zombie bites. He hoped no cop recognized him or Shims, either. His man mountain would protect him. Naslock had paid well for his loyalty. But Naslock figured one look at Shims and the evacuation officials would shove a rocket engine up his ass make him a shuttlecraft. His size was not much smaller than the flying busses with delta wings and plasma drives.

They ran with a crowd and hit a dead stop at a constricted arc of the corridor. The flow to safety became a crush of sweat and cursing. Police pressed shields against a gap in the crysteel plates. The zombies weren't completely mindless. Their surging weakened the interlocking of the plates. The police fell back. Zombies broke through.

"Help us!" one officer screamed to Shims.

Several animate corpses crawled over the collapsing police line. Shims acted, but to save himself and Naslock. He turned and became a human bulldozer. He pushed the people nearest the flailing zombies into the monsters' arms and teeth. Naslock pushed through the thinned crowd to continue down the corridor, and then ran.

Naslock was a blur as he ran by a young woman named Sooz on the ground. Her boyfriend Mitt cradled her head and shoulders on his lap. Sooz saw the name 'Janeck' on the patch stitched to the paramedic's red jumpsuit as he opened his med-kit beside her. Sooz looked at Mitt with frightened eyes. He smiled at her through tears.

"It's good I got here in time." Janeck said to Mitt. He held up an injection gun.

"It's good. All good." Mitt said to Sooz.

"I just want you to be okay," Sooz said as tears rolled from her eyes.

"I will. I promise." Mitt nodded as he pulled his grief contorted face into a comforting smile.

Janeck reached down to inject Sooz. His head suddenly pitched forward and struck Mitt who fell back from Sooz. Shims snatched away the injection gun from the limp Janeck. His expensive jacket was a zombie casualty. He pressed the injector against his left shoulder above bleeding wounds and pulled the trigger.

Mitt recovered and screamed. "You monster! You can't do that!"

Shims ignored Mitt and tossed the injector aside. Sooz reached for Mitt as he bolted up and attacked the massive, selfish man. Shims lifted Mitt and threw him at a gap in the buckling barricades. Sooz screamed as zombies yanked Mitt's upper body into their horde. Mitt's legs kicked. Blood spurted across the outside of the thrusting barricade. Shims fled down the corridor. Mitt's limp legs vanished through gap. Sooz kept screaming as she stood and stumbled to the splash of Mitt's blood. Janeck recovered and instinctively grabbed her from behind.

"He's gone! He's gone!" Janeck shouted.

Sooz said nothing. Janeck looked at her eyes. Their whites were now smeared red as blood and infection pooled in Sooz's head and brain. Janeck pushed her away. He gripped the back of his head that bled from Shims' punch. He staggered to his med-kit while keeping watch on Sooz. The gap in the barricade became wider. Flailing zombie arms grabbed at Sooz. Police in heavy armor with assault rifles charged in. They formed a line between Sooz and the splitting barricade. Janeck jolted from deafening noise and dropped a bandage as the police opened fire. Sooz shuffled toward the carnage of blasted zombies outside the bullet-perforated crysteel beyond the police. She was oblivious to the sharp, violent gunfire. Then a rifle muzzle pointed at her.

Far ahead, Naslock ran with the fleeing crowd toward an air and spacecraft port. The crysteel barriers ended at the lane between two vast shuttle hangars. Naslock felt a moment of self-hate realizing his crimes had made him rich but not rich enough to escape through a nice concourse to a nice ship with a nice cabin steward handing him a cocktail while the masses screamed on the tarmac. He didn't scream, but he was among the masses. Many were honest, working class people. Others were unwitting, former customers of his many markets. The hangar lane opened to a makeshift evacuation zone. Across a wide field of tarmac sat every manner of orbital and interplanetary ship. Interstellar vessels were en route, or so everyone hoped. In this hour, apocalypse reigned.

Beyond the ships, the flaming city lit the horizon as a belt of orange. The evening drew darker. Black smoke blotted out appearing stars. Distant screams seemed to echo off the dark clouds. Streaks of launching ships leapt out from the belt of fire and burning buildings. They appeared as ascending comets. Four pierced the smoke clouds. One ship flipped and arced back to the city and collided with buildings. A massive, white star flashed for an instant in the city. Then a glowing mushroom cloud rolled up behind burning skyscrapers. Screams rose across the refugees on the tarmac. Naslock used the moment of shock to push forward.

Salvation was beyond a gauntlet of pushing, twisting, and jabbing. Naslock was practiced at sliding through crowds to escape pursuers. That skill and deft thumbs to eyes worked to advance him quickly. The crowd spilt into lines running to ships. People remerged into several, smaller masses in front of ship-deployed ramps, rolling stairways, dangerously propped gangways, and ladders threatening imminent collapse. Armed officers controlled ship entry. Frantic medical personnel scanned each accretion of the terrified. Behind them, cleared people thinned into a near orderly flow up each access and through the ships' hatches.

Naslock snaked to the ramp of a commuter shuttle. Sudden light split the clouds with a deafening roar. More ships maneuvered to land beyond those on the evacuation field. Heat and the smell of ionized air from their descending engines washed over the crowds. Cheers accompanied the touchdowns. Naslock attempted to step on the ramp. A rifle barrel slapped his face.

"Get scanned!" The officer with the rifle shouted.

"Look, I'm inoculated!" Naslock screeched.

"That's crap!" The officer rose the butt of his rifle.

"It's okay." A medical tech behind Naslock said reading his scanner's readout. "He's clean!"

Naslock bobbed around the officer's rifle and grabbed the ramp's railing. A man in a dark brown suit jacket with a ripped back seam bolted ahead of him.

"Hey, boss!" A familiar voice boomed over the crowd drone and stunned Naslock. "I feel kinda funny!"

Naslock turned. He looked at the massive and now battered Shims with genuine surprise.

"You know him?" The officer asked Naslock.

"Never seen him." Naslock shrugged and headed up the ramp.

"Hey!" Shims yelled.

Janeck staggered to the ramp. He threw a blood-soaked wad of gauze at Shims and shouted at the huge man. "You! You damn well aren't getting away!"

"It's everyone for himself!" Shims bellowed. "I want to live. Do you?"

"You won't live!" Janeck barked. "That injection was nerve tox. I can't believe you're still moving. But you won't be. The toxin locks up your nerves so you can't move after becoming a biter."

"What?" Shims grabbed Janeck's jumpsuit and lifted him off the ground.

Behind them, the med-tech and officer bolted up the ramp. A brief scream left the gathered crowd and the people fled towards the other ships.

"You're dead, freak!" Spit flowed from Janeck's mouth as he shouted. "You just won't be a walking zombie!"

Shims opened his mouth to shout into Janeck's face. Instead, Janeck screamed. Shims' eyes lit with shock as the man was torn from his powerful grasp. Arms and teeth of zombies pulled him down. Shims started to scream. Only a short screech left his mouth as his body tightened. His face locked in terror as zombies ascended his mountain-like body and then began to tear it down as red, spurting strips.

In the shuttle, Naslock's screamed "let's go!"

The med-tech and officer swung the shuttle hatch closed from inside. Instantly, zombies pressed against the hatch and scraped teeth against its portal. The ship began to rumble as its engines started. The shuttle rose among a sea of clinging zombies. The aft engines blasted a mass of undead into spinning torches and ash. Others fell back into the sea of animate dead or spattered against the tarmac as the shuttle gained altitude. Its nose pointed skyward as it sailed towards space. The last, clinging zombie slid into the plasma wake.

Time and space seemed to collapse when the human mind fell into deep sleep. It was standard for long space flight. For some, both travel and suspension was a forced necessity after their planet's apocalypse.

Vyk heard the drone of conversations, questions, and complaints at kiosks inside a large cube dubbed *the gates* that processed immigration. It was supposed to be a temporary structure for the *Mabon's* colonists. It served again to process unplanned refugees from a fallen colony. An express evacuation ship, the *Chatham*, remained in orbit. Such ships carried many people and little supplies. They were stripped-down and engine-amped people haulers used only in apocalyptic emergencies. People from the *Chatham* filed from its landers and into the echoing cube. The destruction of their world still dazed them. Humanity settled Camponon generations ago. People were born and died never seeing the inside of a space faring ship. Some never saw Camponon as a colony of another world. Now, the planet's apocalypse made many of its citizens sudden, unintentional pioneers. Families had been broken apart. Loved ones were lost in horrific ways. It was all fresh in their minds, no matter how long they slept or how far they traveled between stars. For many, waking over the blue world with no name seemed as an afterlife with no future.

Even more refugees were still aboard the orbiting *Chatham* in the purgatory of extended suspension. The blue world didn't have resources for them all. Not yet. Others more fortunate had already walked through the gates. They were former officials, dispossessed captains of industry, or people holding enough clout or credit in interstellar accounts. Vyk considered the people he watched now to be the ones who would do the work and make this blue world survivable. Nevertheless, he looked them over to find any questionable characters.

His black and grey uniform distinguished him from the various colors and styles in the lines and crowds. More distinct was his assault rifle slung on his back. It was thick, heavy, and obviously capable of killing something big and heavy, or several things attacking. Some of the colonists had witnessed armed officers shoot hordes to pieces. The pieces were once people, perhaps family. When shot they were ravenous, clawing undead. Soldiers and police fought the zombies so others could escape. Now those survivors saw people with guns on this new world. CF theory held that survivors willingly traded amenities for greater safety. Vyk figured they were glad just to be alive. He would work to continue their chance at life.

The doors opened to allow more people in. Inside Vyk's head, he felt the nasal filters deploy too late. The mucus flowed to roll out the dust entering his sinuses. The combination trapped air and caused pressure to build. A headache followed. Internal nano-ports release the drug endopren into his blood. Vyk's system had become drug tolerant to the pain reliever, but he didn't want the upgrade. He'd been altered enough.

What most people noticed about Vyk was his stare. The detail of eye color was forgotten when they quickly looked away. Details were Vyk's concern. Details such as law, commerce, and respect for life. Legislatures, corporate boards, and people generated that triangle of details. Vyk tried to find stability among the three points, or else bring enough force to impose order. But force had limited and temporary effects. Social tolerance held order for longer spans. Vyk's tolerance was a critical detail for his colony already under stress. Vyk's force was undermanned before they touched blue dust. Now the CFA sent even more evacuees from fallen Camponon. The *Chatham* was an express ship made for apocalypse. However, express actions frequently led to lapses or lies in the details.

Vyk's second in command, Lieutenant Artemis Caine looked over the *Chatham's* list of refugees. She felt a familiar presence and stare. Caine looked up from the sheet hologram projected from her wristband across her opened left hand. She met eyes with her boss, CEO Vyk Reis.

"Ships manifest, Artie?" Vyk asked spying the list.

"Yep." Caine said. "I'm looking at some refugee profiles that have curiously missing data. Have a look." Caine raised her palm to Vyk.

"Send me," Vyk said.

Caine tapped air where the send button appeared in her projection.

"Okay. Got it." Vyk's eyes moved as he read a screen only visible to himself.

Caine observed Vyk. She knew he was reading the *Chatham's* manifest displayed by biotechnology. "Boy, so nice of the CF to give you all the new toys."

"You want them?" Vyk asked while reading.

"I want your job, more." Caine smiled.

"One day. One colony." Vyk said.

"Right now I'll settle for more data on the *Chatham* relokes I flagged."

Vyk figured *relokes* meant relocated people, but didn't let on it was new jargon to him. "Their details are slim. Not all files have been loaded. We'll need to compile data, here. We'll start with interviews of your selected targets."

"I'll get right on it." Caine said.

"No. For now, keep an eye on this crowd. I'll conduct the opening rounds."

Caine sighed. Vyk smiled. He left the gates cube and headed into the rows of tents erected for the overflow of refugees. Caine had done a fine job in flagging persons of interest. Vyk chose one Peter Gillen for his first interrogation. Vyk reached Gillen's tent. He observed Gillen through the semi-transparent tent walls. Gillen read from an old-style, solid screen. Vyk tapped the security feeds installed in all CF-supplied equipment. Even in the warp of the micro-camera's lens on Gillen's screen, his face seemed to have no curves. Vyk determined he was alone and, as he should be, unarmed. Vyk walked in, unannounced.

"Hey!" Gillen jumped from his small table as Vyk entered. A dark-brown suit jacket with a ripped back seam fell from the chair. "And, wow! What a gun!"

"It's a defensive weapon, Mr. Gillen. No cause for alarm."

"I'll try not to make you defensive, officer--?"

"I'm Commander Vyk Reis. I'd like to speak with you."

"Roger, that, Vyk. How can I help you?" The man's sharp features snapped into a practiced smile. In his own mind he chanted the thought: *Gillen, Gillen, Gillen. My Name is Peter Gillen.*

"You registered a significant credit balance from Camponon." Vyk only stated the fact and then waited to see Gillen's response.

"Um, yes." Gillen looked to his left as he considered what information Vyk truly sought. "I was told there were no intake taxes, here. Unless there's been a coup?" Gillen winked.

"No. The provisional civilian authority is still in place. I simply wanted to meet you. Your fortune makes you a comparatively wealthy person among the refugees, and among assigned colonists. Do you have any associates that came here with you on the *Chatham*?"

"The *Chatham*?" Gillen gave an entreating shrug with his question.

"Your ship. The one that brought you here from Camponon." Vyk noted Gillen's posture and attitude were false attempts at looking compliant. The use of Vyk's first name was a passive attempt at making them equals. Vyk sensed Gillen was not used to being deferential. Instead, Gillen seemed to prefer manipulation to cooperation. That, and his registered wealth in two accounts with wildly different balances, didn't match with his listed occupation of social worker.

"Right! I thought it was called *Chadwick*." Gillen smiled and nodded. "I sort of left in a rush. Zombie apocalypse. It's a cliché now, I know. Anyway, no. I'm looking forward to a fresh start, here. No need to worry about me. I've always been a solid citizen. Trust me."

"I would imagine," Vyk said with his own version of a faked smile. That was his eyes opened wider than their usual narrowed stare. "I'd expect nothing short from a social worker."

"So I guess you're wondering where all my other cash came from." Gillen said and took in a breath as he prepared to launch into an explanation.

"Thank you for your cooperation, Mr. Gillen." Vyk said. "I'm sure we'll meet again."

Gillen's eyebrows pitched back in surprise with his mouth still open as Vyk turned and left his tent.

In the immigration cube, Caine heard the high tone for incoming communication above the crowd din. She brought her wrist unit to her ear.

"Boss?" Caine queried and then heard Vyk's reply.

"Good work, Artie. We have a live one."

To the sleeping refugees still on the *Chatham*, time was nearly meaningless. On the surface, time allowed the colony to begin building infrastructure and expand as Single City. Beneath the veneer and within certain minds, time allowed plans to be refined and enacted. Time allowed for change. Ethics determined if some change was a benefit or an abomination. Some changes served the greater good. Others widened profit margins. Some changes seemed more alien than a world of endless blue wastes.

Vyk looked at a certain prostitute and felt shock. He brought her to the central security cube under her protests. Her profession was legal. Vyk thought her appearance was bizarre. Her eyes were clear and her mind active, but her body was that of a famine victim. Even with the rationing caused by the unexpected population increase, food was not so scarce to cause starvation.

"Look, I'm tailored to look this way!" The prostitute waved her twig-like arms in front of her narrow torso. "It's my niche market. I make good money like this! I have my own Fast Flush cabinet in my apartment. My *own* apartment!"

"Fine," Vyk grated. He pushed aside jealousy from still having to share the communal toilets with his officers. Some activities done as a group did not foster camaraderie.

"I still want to meet your boss," Vyk continued as he sat her down in the plastic chair beside his desk. Unlike the woman in question, Vyk had to squeeze through his cramped, metal walled office. "Holo him."

"Yeah, yeah, okay." The woman bobbed her narrow face with sunken cheeks. She looked at her bony wrist and tapped her com-unit with needle-like fingers.

Vyk watched her and suppressed a shudder. The hologram's projection bubble popped on over the small desk. Vyk sighed, but was not surprised that the smiling face of an alleged, former social worker appeared. Peter Gillen was the woman's Colonial Economic Council approved pimp.

"Vyk!" Gillen beamed. "We do meet again. Nifty!"

"Look, boss, I didn't--" The prostitute began.

"Oh, I know, Reedy." Gillen said in the bubble. "I'm sure Vyk here is just concerned for your well being. I think he's like that. Tell you what, commander good-man--Vyk. Have Reedy see your med-tech. She'll check as healthy."

"I told him that!" Reedy cast a stare of bright eyes in a gray face at Vyk. "I'm burning daylight and client time!"

"Fine. Go." Vyk droned.

Reedy got up and flew from Vyk's office like a piece of string in strong wind. Vyk wondered if she would need a med-tech if someone merely bumped her. He thought about her job and what physical stress it might have. He felt nausea.

"Okay, then." Gillen said.

"She can leave, not you." Vyk stared at Gillen's head in the bubble. "How does a person go from being a social worker to running alters as prostitutes?"

"Easy transition, really." Gillen said. "I worked with people on the street and saw what worked on the street, if you get me."

"So you learned about human vice and decided to exploit it." Vyk grated. "A one-eighty in ethics, isn't it?"

"I see your point," Gillen nodded "But this is a new life, a new world. I guess I'm going from one way of servicing the public to another. But, physical entertainment is all legal." Gillen winked.

"Most. Not all." Vyk scrutinized Gillen's expressions on the hologram. "Why would you alter someone to such an extreme?"

"I didn't." Gillen raised his hands into the projection field as if in defense. "She did it to herself."

"So you exploit her self-mutilation." Vyk narrowed his eyes.

"No, I provide benefits and base pay. She provides me with a loyal and active employee in our legal, mutually beneficial enterprise. I get people think sex, any sex, is a dirty deed. But my business is all legal. You, especially Vyk, must respect the law."

"I do, because I respect human life, Mr. Gillen. I have to, in order to defend it."

"Hmm, Commander. I sense an unspoken accusation, there. It's a little stinging. And maybe presumptuous about my character." Gillen looked to the side and shook his head. "Look, Reedy is quite alive. Quite active. Quite well paid. If she's not your type, fine. But she's also not your concern. She, and me, haven't broken any law."

Vyk spoke immediately after Gillen finished. He hoped to make him falter. "Do you have any workers and associates from Camponon working for you here?"

"Um," Gillen paused. "Didn't you ask me that before?"

Vyk knew he had asked that question when he met Gillen in his tent. He was certain the man was now working at what he did before Camponon's apocalypse. Vyk hoped that Gillen being among his shifty peers would slacken the man's defenses. Unfortunately, Gillen was a well-practiced liar.

"So," Gillen continued with a renewed smile. "You seem to have quite the interest in prostitution. Did you have Reedy call me because you're looking for a career change?"

Vyk only glared.

"Bad joke. Sorry." Gillen's shoulders pitched as he shrugged where he sat.

"There are codes for such employment," Vyk said. "Age restrictions. Wage minimums--"

"Yes, Vyk!" Gillen threw his hands into the projection field again. "Look, I know. I follow the codes. The law. Trust me."

"I trust procedure. Did you file the correct change in colony status from public service to private enterprise?"

"Of course," Gillen's smile ebbed. "All the boxes were checked in all code forms. I have all the authentication numbers."

"Transmit them." Vyk said.

"Fine. Sure. One second." Gillen said slowly. "You got them? I'm sure there's a copy in your own files."

A stream of numbers rolled under Gillen's projected head. Vyk heard a shift in Gillen's tone from ingratiating, to annoyed, to restrained aggression. Vyk suppressed a smile of his own. With more time, Vyk felt he could pry the man's real identity from him. Plus, whatever he was hiding. Vyk was certain Gillen was doing something outside the law.

"All right, Mr. Gillen." Vyk spoke in deep but calm tones as he focused on the man and ignored the stream of numbers. "Thank you for your cooperation. You're free to go."

Gillen's right eyebrow cocked and his image vanished.

The number on the hatch-like, plastic door corresponded to the name Kathy Norland. Unlike some emergency evacuees, the CFA was certain about the woman's identity. Biographic records were cross-referenced with her willing submission to DNA sampling. It all confirmed Kathy Norland's identity. It was all a lie.

The woman who lived in the stand-alone apartment node came to the blue sands of Opportunity 80-8-18 aboard the *Chatham*. She had stolen the Kathy Norland identity from hacked files. She reconstituted Kathy's DNA from medical records, and expertly placed it where necessary. The old Kathy was now a starving zombie, or ashes on burning Camponon. The new Kathy was a good, if not brilliant scientist.

On the new planet, her comforts were less, but her skills and intelligence built a career. Inside her small home sat a coveted example of her growing success. Back on her now dead home world, sanitation was a public service. Here, if you didn't want to be public when using sanitation, you paid a private business. The new Kathy was happy to pay for such privacy. She caressed the *FAST FLUSH* cabinet's door with its credit slot on the handle.

"Hey-yo, old friend!" The voice sounded from behind in the dark. It was horribly familiar. She flicked on the lights as she spun.

"Who the--?" A familiar, angular face and penetrating stare over a fake smile looked at her from her only chair. "Oh, crap!"

"Literally. Nice throne, *Christie*." Gillen stood holding a small, colorful box. "Look on the bright side, I'm not a rapist."

"We'll see." Christie said as she backed away. She dropped all pretense of her new identity.

"Christie, please! Did I ever--?"

"I don't know who or what you did when you weren't threatening me. Or how. How about Shims? Did he--?"

"He's dead." The man currently known as Peter Gillen shrugged.

"Oh. Sorry."

"I'm not." Gillen shook his said. "I'm saving a fortune by hiring local talent. They have no clue what to ask for, so they take what I give them. And some freebies from the prosties."

"How about the cops? Are they looking for you, here?"

"I'm Peter Gillen, now. A legitimate business, man. Respected." Gillen took one hand from the box, pulled on his shirt collar, and made an exaggerated smile.

"I doubt it. But I'm sure you're in business."

"I see so are you." Gillen raised the bright box emblazoned with the words *FIDO'S BIG FUN KIT, make a rock come alive!* He tossed it to Christie.

"This new gig is working for me." Christie caught and then cradled the box. "New world. New life. Don't rape it!"

Gillen waved his hands. "Like I said, I'm a--look, just shut up and listen. I'm here. You're here. We have unfinished business."

"Nope."

"Yup. Unless you want this new, blue world to know you're a convicted killer. Multiple bodies, right Christie? You little death witch."

Christie stayed silent. She dropped her head and looked at the box. A mournful sigh left her.

Gillen watched her. He could press her, but he needed to bring her under control and not inflame her emotions. Threats and force usually worked, but they had limitations. Manipulation was a better tool in the long game. That game might collapse if he didn't play Christie right. If she rebelled, he would have to kill her to guard his secret. Then finding another sick genius would take more time. He needed to act before the sleepers on the *Chatham* woke up. He would play Christie with softer tactics. For now.

"So, tell me about this racket." Gillen pointed to the box. "It's making money."

Christie made a deep sigh. "Yeah. Damn thing is, I thought of you when I named it. Fido."

Gillen smiled. "Well, I am a bit of a dog."

"It's simple brilliant." Christie said looking at her product with a slight smile of pride.

"How so?"

Christie took a breath and began a keyed-down version of her sales pitch. "What do all kids want? A pet. But what's rationed? Food. What do you have a lot of, here? Rocks. So, make a pet that requires no food. Take a rock. Put my engineered algae on it. Chose a color. Boom. Now it's a rock you can pet."

"And it moves?" Gillen raised his sharp eyebrows.

"For extra."

"I like the way you think. Always did."

25

Suddenly, Christie threw down the box. Small vials scattered across the floor and a rock bounced up and over Gillen, who jerked back.

"I'm not doing drugs, Nas! No way!" Christie screeched. "I'm legit here and making it! Kathy Norland! That's who I am!"

"Okay!" Gillen raised his hands in mock surrender. "Stay with me. I won't ask you to do drugs. To make them or take them. But you will restart the Docile Project. I still have the last sample sewn in--"

"I have samples." Christie said in a dead, flat tone.

"What? How did you get them through the scanners?"

Christie simply stared back and pitched her head slightly left.

"Well I guess if shields are equal, you have more places to hide things." Gillen shrugged. "So, we're in business, again."

"No." Christie breathed.

"Oh, yes." Gillen's big smile made him look like a shark tasting blood. "Remember what I have on you."

"Kathy Norland has no past."

"But little, little Doc Christie does. And that's you. You wouldn't sell too many rock pets if the kiddies' moms and pops knew you were a serial killer."

"That's a long time ago. I did an experiment. To help people." Christie took a shallow breath.

"But they died."

"Yeah," Christie took several shallow breaths and dropped her head to her chest. She then raised it and glared at her tormentor. "But why risk what you've got? Revealing anything from Camponon fingers you. It could end you, here. Even if you rat and kill me."

"In time your rocks might earn you enough to buy influence and power, not just your own private toss throne." Gillen pointed at the *FAST FLUSH* cabinet. "But I have it, now. I own people who will do the fingering for me. So if you don't want my finger or anything else in you, like through your skull, take Docile 11 and make Docile 12. And you'll start, now." Gillen put his finger between Christie's blinking eyes. "Look, it's a challenge. Be a pioneer. It's what we are on this blue pile. Pioneer sounds better than refugee. Or mass murderer."

Vyk preferred to walk a beat. His biotech allowed him to keep up on forms and read files while he patrolled. On this world, pounding pavement meant treading on plated walkways over crunching sands. The sound was louder than the din of Single City. Its noises were similar to frontier towns on many worlds and in past eras. Many plates under his boots were CFA tablet screens supplied to the colonists. Preferring newer technology, and perhaps wanting some measure of privacy, most people had turned them in. The durable, flat units made adequate walkway tiles. Vyk regretted the loss of them for intelligence, but appreciated not sinking to his ankles in indigo gravel. He did not appreciate the meeting he later endured in his office.

He thought of Reedy, the prostitute. He considered the man now seated before his desk as being much the same kind of professional. Carlis Maui smiled with his mouth but accused with his glare. He represented a collective of small businesses with an unusual request. During the period of interim government, Vyk regulated non-corporate, off-world commerce. He was the customs cop for small business. There was typically no such market because shepherd corporations dominated off-world commerce. But most early colonies didn't have a manned ship on extended mission in orbit like the *Chatham*.

"All we want is to make money while we can, Commander. And the *Chatham's* crew has a lot of it and wants to spend it."

"And I support your entrepreneurship, Mr. Maui, but I simply cannot redeploy officers and assets to oversee the flow of people and materials between Single City and the ship."

"But you don't have to. Our consortium will oversee everything."

"And it will all be perfectly legal with all taxes collected, I'm sure. Nevertheless, it would be inappropriate for me to allow unsupervised traffic between the *Chatham* and the surface."

"What are we living under? A police state?" Maui raised and dropped his hands.

"For now, yes." Vyk replied. "Especially when it comes to small markets in orbit. Plus, if you want the crew's credits, you'll get them as they rotate for shore leave."

"Some. But exporting to the ship is a bigger boon. We can charge more."

"That's fair?" Vyk knew he shouldn't be surprised by Maui's exploitive statement, but his eyebrows still pitched up.

"That's business." Maui shrugged.

Vyk took a breath. He wondered if the real issue was commercial access to the crew, or access to the ship.

"My request is actually just a formality," Maui said. "We fully intend to execute this trade, Commander."

"Doing so without my customs approval would violate CFA protocols. It would be illegal."

"I'll take the issue to the committee." Maui said with a sharp tone.

"Go ahead, sir." Vyk gave a slow nod. "They are bound by CFA law, as well."

Maui dropped his smile. He stood up and walked out.

Lt. Caine stepped in while watching Maui walk away, and then turned to Vyk. "He'll try going over your head."

"I'll go over his," Vyk said. He sat up straight and rigid. "There's a way to lock this down. I'll get the ship's captain. He's the law on the *Chatham*."

"And without a committee or council," Caine said.

Vyk nodded at Caine and then looked ahead and tapped his left temple.

Gillen ran through his bordello. Tents taken from the surface sat rebuilt inside a larger cube to create at least the illusion of rooms. He charged down a hall of plastic sheeting and dodged fleeing customers. He clenched a small, oval case in one fist. Those who didn't hide their faces from Gillen saw his creased by an odd smile of glee. Yet the customers were afraid. They had heard screaming and someone get called a killer.

Gillen punched through a plastic curtain made slick from human condensation. Beside a battered cot, Reedy knelt by another plump, blonde woman lying motionless on the cold floor. Red marks ringed the dead woman's neck. Reedy held her right fist to her bony chest and rocked back and forth while crying.

"That the guy?" Gillen pointed to a man with a ball gag in his mouth held down by two of his thugs.

One thug, Loco, had motion tattoos of trains on his face, chest and arms. The man they held down bled from several small pressure cuts on his cheeks and brow.

"Yeah," Loco replied.

"Why is he still alive?" Gillen asked.

The man struggled against the pinning thugs.

"Reedy wanted to beat on him." Loco said as a train engine puffed steam clouds on his left cheek.

"Looks like she did," Gillen smiled. "As much as she could. Now drag Donut's killer over to Doc Rock. She can use him in her lab."

The train tattoos rolled and puffed steam as Loco and his partner stood and yanked up the struggling killer. They hauled him through the wet curtain as he kicked and grunted through his ball gag.

"Kill him, then drag him, morons!" Gillen yelled out after them.

"Gills, save her! She's still warm!" Reedy beseeched Gillen. "I heard they can do rejuve even if you bleed out. You just gotta be warm. Save her, Gills! Please!"

"Let's see how this works." Gillen said and removed a narrow cylinder from the oval case.

"What is that?" Reedy asked.

"Something a friend gave me," Gillen wiggled the cylinder. "A doctor friend."

"Will it help her? Is it meds?"

"Sort of," Gillen shrugged.

"Then shoot her up!" Reedy bolted to standing.

"I intended to." Gillen dropped to a knee beside the blonde Donuts. Blood had begun to pool from under her body.

"Do it, Gills! Do it!" Reedy pushed on Gillen's shoulders. Blood from her hand smudged his shirt.

Gillen turned to Reedy and yelled. "Okay. Cool off!"

"Do it! Hurry!" Reedy screamed.

Gillen paused. A thought occurred to him. A dark thought. He considered how Reedy looked compared to the pump corpse, and how that could help hide the experiment he was about to try.

"Gills!" Reedy screeched.

Gillen turned and struck Reedy on her bony left hip with the tip of the cylinder. A sharp pop sounded. Reedy jumped back with a red spot where and Gillen's injector shot something into her body. Reedy looked at him in shock.

"So, Reeds," Gillen said, and stood. "It could be time to renegotiate your contract. Let's see how this works."

Vyk enjoyed walking. It was about the only thing he enjoyed about his meeting in motion with Executive Oversight Chairman Fukuda. They walked the promenade leading to the so-called Capitol Building. It was a large meeting cube topped with a metal dome. The unique, cushioned walkway to the Capitol muffled the crunching sound of the areas groomed, light-sapphire sands beneath its marble plates. It was a typical, bright day. Vyk thought he heard birds chirping over Single City's din, but it was only an imposed memory from past planets. Vyk didn't feel he was making an imposition on the man who had been his ally. Yet, he might as well be walking on the sand for traction.

"I appreciate your position, Commander." Fukuda said.

The Chairman rarely looked directly at Vyk. His secretary Olong kept watch on his boss as he trailed him and Vyk.

"With respect, it's not a position, Chairman." Vyk said. "It's an enforcement issue. An effort to avoid exploitation."

"But it feels as though your probes are preemptive, and too focused on certain individuals. Perhaps unfairly."

"Sir, we must look into possible crimes. That's not preemption. That's investigation."

Olong's sharper voice chirped from behind them. "Isn't that mere semantics, Commander?"

"No," Vyk turned his head to answer Olong. He turned back to Fukuda. "And no action will be taken if these individuals and their activities clear. I simply request all CFA files on Camponon refugees be released to government servers. Law enforcement on Camponon had compiled data on convicted criminals. I just want to make sure those people are not repeating those crimes, here."

"We have to treat the issue of the refugees with great care." Fukuda said and gestured with his left hand while still not looking at Vyk. "We need to ensure a smooth integration of Camponon's people and the originally selected colonists. This is more complex than planetary engineering. People need to adapt more psychologically than to differences in gravity and atmospheric pressure. We are building a new society with more unknown factors than anticipated. Many refugees are still suspended on the *Chatham*. We want them all to feel at home, as one. Eventually. We don't want fractionalization on our colony."

"So far, sir, the people are becoming one society quite naturally." Vyk said. "The gift of a mutual frontier."

"The gift of strong civilian oversight." Olong shot from behind.

Vyk paused but said nothing in reply to Olong. He continued to address Fukuda. "I only want to ensure the continued peace, Chairman."

"So trust us, Vyk." Fukuda smiled, but kept looking forward as they approached the Capitol's doors. "If something does occur, you'll have my full support."

"And the Camponon files, sir?"

"Like I said, we need to treat the refugees--"

"Sir," Vyk cut in. "Information on bad actors is no threat to the hardworking people from the *Mabon* or the *Chatham*."

Fukuda stopped and turned to Vyk. "Just a quick piece of advice. Don't interrupt me. And here's a free second piece. You used up your influence on the customs issue. You had the Captain's support above, and mine on the surface. But the Captain gives orders and his crew complies. I have to negotiate and compromise for accord. If I back you so quickly again, I'll be seen as your stooge, and inflexible. So before you need political help, think on what you need most, especially when we switch to open elections. If I get voted out, do you think your own job is safe?"

Fukuda walked on.

"You have the Chairman's answer, Commander. Good, day." Olong said as he stepped around Vyk and followed Fukuda.

Vyk watched the two men disappear through the only set of ornate and automatic doors on the colony. He found himself clenching his jaws, hard. He blinked as blue dust stung his eyes. Useless endopren released into his system.

Pathetic, lost causes. One inspired the career of Artemis Caine. Lt. Caine looked through the thick crysteel portal. She felt shock, some fear, but mostly contempt for a useless fate. She worked to prevent such ends to human life. She could not prevent the fate of the woman sealed away in the bio-lock chamber. Years and vast distances did not separate Caine from the memory of her first, failed cause. She could still recall the beige, not blue sand caked to weakened limbs.

Those limbs belonged to slider monkeys. They were nothing like true primates. Sliders were a large, crustacean lifeform that survived planetary reengineering and human habitation on Caine's ocean planet. They lived among kelp and rising rocks where they clambered sideways. From a distance they looked vaguely like submarine orangutans. Slider monkeys had stout, dark brown to red bodies with several small limbs down their banded sides. They used their two large, paddle limbs just below their head to reach between kelp stalks, and to propel them through the clear, tropical waters. Sliders seemed to enjoy swimming with people. They entered open water when people swam nearby to join the swimmers in groups. Caine had loved to swim with them. Vyk's stare reminded her of their unblinking eyes.

People considered it bad luck to eat sliders on Caine's home island. Yet some islands had stands and large boilers going to feed tourists. Caine's family visited one such island in her childhood. Her parents shunned the local slider monkey stall. That was not enough for young Artemis Caine. She recruited a boy visiting from her island and a local girl to save the sliders doomed for tourist plates. They stole the vat holding the live sliders and ran with the sloshing mass as fast as they could. It was not fast enough. The boy and girl dropped their holds and ran off. As the owner and other adults closed in, young Artemis dumped out the vat. She thought the sliders would scamper across the sand and find liberation in the surf. But the crustaceans just flailed their paddle limbs and kicked up sand in a pathetic, failed escape.

Caine didn't want things to be pathetic. If the rules said she couldn't help slider monkeys, she would find those she could help. Her goal slid into keeping peace to preserve life. Years and an academy course later, she had the skills for the task. She lived longer than a normal, planetary life because of sleep years between worlds. Physically, she was still young. Mentally, she was still ambitious. Caine wanted to earn the top spot of colony commander for personal satisfaction. Then she would ascend to the top spot on the CFA Council. Overseeing all of the colonies could change many unjust rules, help a lot of people, and save slider monkeys.

Caine wondered if what she saw in the bio-lock chamber meant her new planet's fate was beyond saving. She looked through thick crysteel at Reedy. The name described the woman well. *Bony* was the only other, less pleasant option. Caine knew Reedy was not her original name. She had reinvented herself from Mara Kuen. Some people had paid well for the pleasure of her attention. Caine had looked at her with disgust when they first met. She overcame that and tried to offer compassion. That disgusted Reedy. She wanted no one to treat her as a pathetic, lost cause. She said her life was her choice. Deal with it. She then resumed her charge out of the precinct cube. Caine wished she had followed.

Caine struggled to understand the path Reedy chose when others existed. Life was strange. And life was no longer something Reedy could understand. She was dead. Worse for the colony, she had somehow been infected with the undead plague. Reedy was a zombie. But a very strange sort of zombie.

Vyk entered the observation room outside the bio-lock chamber. His face stretched with shock.

"A zombie!" Vyk vibrated with the words.

"Yes," Caine said in a low, resigned voice.

"I'm glad you used quiet code," Vyk said. "Was she part of a pack?"

"No, Reedy was alone. And what is weirder is that she's quiet. Docile."

"A lifeless zombie?" Vyk said and then shook his head. "Any other signs of outbreak?"

"No. The med-tech and responding officer have been quarantined."

"Who were they?" Vyk asked and stared at Reedy who just stood in the chamber and looked on with waxy, dead eyes.

"Officer Palden and Med-tech Grecka," Caine answered. "So far, both are okay."

"So far," Vyk droned.

"There's more," Caine said. "Although she was dead and zombied, she was also still being used for sex."

Vyk snapped his head toward Caine. "By who?" he shouted.

"DNA evidence was scant, but we don't need much. Among others, was a government official."

"Who?" Vyk turned and pitched his head back from disbelief. "Admin Colsten?"

"Ah, no." Caine knit her brow and pondered for a second if Vyk just threw out a famous name for dramatic effect. "No. It was Chairman Fukuda's secretary--"

"Olong."

"Right," Caine nodded.

"I see." Vyk grasped his chin in his right hand.

"You do? Because this is beyond freakish to me." Caine pitched up her arms and let them slap at her sides.

"It is." Vyk took a breath glanced through the portal and then back at Caine. "So go get Olong. Quietly. But take seal-suits. If this plague is especially virulent, Olong and other sick freaks--" Vyk let Caine finish the thought.

"Understood, sir. I'm on it."

"How did she get out?" Gillen roared. Spit tossed from his sharp lips. His angular face seemed to melt from the redness and heat of his anger. He shouted at three of his thugs in his office of draped, plastic sheets. Two slabs of muscle flanked Loco, the man with moving train tattoos. Gillen's stare threatened to cut the terrified thugs in half.

Loco finally dared to speak. "Olong paid me. He wanted to do her in private and without wearing seals."

"Is he suicidal?" Gillen raved. He paused in thought. "Actually, I hope he is. And dead in an alley. Nice and quiet dead."

"But, uh, it seemed okay." Loco continued. "'Cause, you know, Reedy's dead. But not a zombie. I mean, not a zombie that bites."

Gillen inhaled deeply before he began screaming again. His first words shot out like cannon fire, but he fired the last three as a machinegun burst with spit. "But! Still! A! Zombie! You *soondeadfreak*!"

Gillen fell into a chair behind him. His breathing returned to normal and his features eased. His thugs mistakenly thought they could relax.

"Now, you two." Gillen pointed at the thugs flanking Loco. "Take track for brains out somewhere and kill him."

Loco turned to bolt, but his once loyal colleagues grabbed him and forced him to the ground in an avalanche of testosterone and sweat.

"Kill him horribly," Gillen continued. "I want to see a 'gram of it. Pieces, boys. I mean, not a choo-choo intact." Gillen bolted to standing and shouted. "Small pieces!"

Gillen did not actually wait to see the hologram of Loco's grisly derailment. Instead, he slid snake-like through the zones of Single City. He left the custom living modules of the Upper Sec and slithered into the prefabricated and makeshift huts of Lower Sec. In truth, he felt more at home, here. Modern locks were a joke to experienced criminals, unless they guarded something you had to pay to access. He soon stood inside Christie's small but separated flat. She was behind a good lock as she sat unawares in her rented, personal sanitation unit.

"Christie! Listen!" Gillen called to her beyond the smooth white door with brilliant red *FAST FLUSH* logo.

Christie's reply came after a shocked pause inside. The unit's insulated plastic muffled her yelling. "Nas? What the hell? Get out!"

"There's a complication, but my plan can still work."

"Get the hell out of here!"

"I lost a worker, today. A prostitute. They found her body."

"They're gonna find yours! Get out!"

"They found her body while it was walking." Gillen paused. There was silence from inside the *FAST FLUSH* unit.

"Now, this is bad," Gillen continued. "But my long game is still in play. My sex business is just for leverage. Prostitution is legal, but sex is still naughty. Especially if you like it weird, like the necrophilic crap. The money is good, but leverage is the real profit. Sell sex and buy shame. Shame equals power. I'm banking more of that, Christie." Gillen frowned and stepped back from the *FAST FLUSH* unit. "Geez! What have you been eating?"

"Shut up!" Christie kicked the unit's door.

"Anyway, power gets access. Access to things no one else gets. Like orbiting ships. Ships from apocalypse worlds that may have sleeping zombies."

"So what? You want more dead hookers?" Christie yelled through the wall. "Pop yourself and walk for tricks!"

"I said, sex is the start. The leverage. I'm gunning for the ultimate protection scam. Protection is the oldest racket after sex. To do it, you need to create the threat, but also control the action."

"So the hell what?" Christie yipped. "Get out!"

"Listen. What's a bigger threat than a zombie apocalypse? Nothing. We have old-fashioned zombie plague. We have Docile 12. We can make the threat, a zombie horde on the *Chatham*. We can control the threat. Docile 12. Maybe 13? We cover our sweet asses, of course. But think about it, little, little Christie. How much do you think that scam is worth? Maybe a planet's GDP?"

There was silence. Then a swirling noise. Then the *FAST FLUSH* door opened, slowly. Christie held it partially closed. Her visible face was lost in thought. Gillen pressed his angular face in the gap.

"You can see it will work. It will!" Gillen beamed. "We just need time, and--"

"And Docile 13," Christie finished.

"Oh, yeah. I told you I liked the way you think!"

Christie glared and pushed on the door. Gillen stepped back and smiled with arms open for a hug as Christie stepped out. She ignored his offer.

"Okay. I'll do it," Christie said. "Again."

"Good. Just get it right. Fast." Gillen pressed against Christie and looked down at her.

Christie ducked away. "You just stay back, Nas! Cut the sick threats. You get more flies with honey than acid."

"I don't get what you mean."

"How could you not?" Christie shrugged. "We're from the same planet."

"Same planet, different worlds. I rose from the streets. You fell from ivory towers."

"What the hell is ivory?" Christie added a shaking head to her shrug.

"Synthetic steel, I guess. So, partner, can I stay here for a while?"

Christie sighed. She dropped her head back with a look of genuine pain.

"C'mon, Chris!"

Christie closed her eyes and took a deeper sigh. She was surprised by a rare moment of silence as if her loquacious, criminal intruder respectfully waited for her reply.

"You stay out of sight." Christie finally said.

"That's why I want to stay here. Who would look for a wealthy business man in this crap field?"

Christie stiffened. She glared at her new, conceited roommate. "You know what, Nas? I got some ivory for you right here."

Christie thrust out her left hand in a gesture that remained universal across time, space, and multiple colonial societies. Her middle finger stood erect and alone.

"Maybe later. Right now, how do you use this thing?" Gillen grabbed the closed *FAST FLUSH* unit's handle. It was locked tight.

"You need a slide key." Christie droned.

"You pay?"

"You will." Christie took the only chair in the room. She considered the supposedly respected man she called Nas would then jump on the bed. She got up and sat on that, instead.

"C'mon Christie!" Gillen jerked the handle.

"You stay. You pay." Christie said. "Call it ass rent."

Where the human race settled, they eventually built everywhere. When buildings rose, alleys appeared. Then came bins and large cans for storage and trash. Even in an age of advanced interactive technology, people found themselves sitting and drifting in alleyways. In was an unofficial human niche. It repeated on Opportunity 80-8-18. The alley was a sheet of plazphalt flanked by a row of one-room cubes several meters north and south. In it sat one adult male named Bert. He was annoyed.

"Man this is stupid!" a young boy named Tyne spat.

Tyne and two friends knelt and watched three, brightly colored and fuzzy rocks creeping inside a lane made by a *FIDO'S BIG FUN KIT* box placed near a garbage bin.

"They're too slow to race them!" Tyne stood. "Lame idea, Bert!"

"Worked for me," Bert groaned.

"What? You don't even have a rock!"

"You know why I told you to race your rocks over there?" Bert asked.

"Nuh-uh," was the collective reply.

"To get you the hell away from me over here," Bert gave a mocking smile.

"You're a punk and you smell!" Tyne yelled and received laughing adoration from his pals.

"Man, that stench ain't me!" Bert noticed the foul odor himself. "Now get outta here! Or I'm gonna--!"

Three brightly colored and fuzzy rocks pelted Bert. Bert leapt up. The three kids looked down the alley at something behind Bert. Their eyes all widened.

"I guess that's what smells." Tyne said just before he and his two comrades bolted.

"Oh, sure. Run! That's brave!" Bert shouted. He smelled the stench become stronger. It was from something awful.

Something dead. He turned to the sound of a low growl and shuffling. He screamed.

The zombie Olong looked at him with shock, but still lurched forward and grabbed Bert's shoulders. Bert's struggling triggered a hunger and murderous impulse. Ben's screaming ended as the zombie bit through his throat.

The man now called Peter Gillen had long thought about killing the woman he knew as Christie. He always imagined doing it after she had perfected the Docile program. Taking her notes and then killing her would cut her out of the profits and ensure he had full control of the product. He would have all the profits now, although Docile 13 would never happen. The imperfect Docile 12 would have to do. Its maker lay dead.

Gillen shook his head and smiled. He found what drove him to strangle Christie a bit humorous. It wasn't business related. It was his colon. Christie enjoyed spicy food. He did, too. But not as spicy as the food Christie had. Soon after he ate some, he needed to use the toilet in a very bad way. Christie still insisted he pay. He wanted the slide key. She refused. They fought. She died. Now the swirling sounds from the *FAST FLUSH* ended and he heard a bumping from under the floor. He also saw a small red light flashing on Christie's wrist unit. He reached for it and a 'gram popped into the air at a skewed angle from her wrist.

"I'm Doctor Christie Halstead," Her tilted image said. She had recorded the hologram while standing in a lab coat for effect. "I've patched an ident packet to this transmission I'm sending to authorities and across the local net. I also patched a formula that may help stop zombie outbreaks. Maybe."

"Christie! What did you do?" Gillen screeched as he felt panic begin to vibrate though his body.

"Sorry," Christie's hologram continued, "but for revenge I've cause a small outbreak right here. I timed aerosolized plague to spray over a few cadavers. Sorry I killed those people. But it was in an effort to stop the plague. Honest. But, well, I guess I'm not as good as I thought I was."

Gillen could feel his chest and face tighten.

"Now I'm dead, or my wrist unit is no longer sending my vital signs." Christie's recorded image showed her sway for a moment from that thought. "No vital signs is the signal to spray the plague on the cadavers. I used some specific DNA in the plague to program the zombies. They'll hunt down the bastard who probably killed me. I think that'll work. Sorry if the zombies kill anyone else. I also sent an ident packet on my likely killer. If my zombies don't kill him, just shoot the bastard. You think I'm bad? You got no clue about bad until you deal with this guy. Shoot me, too. At this point, I don't care. I'm dead."

Gillen screamed high, unintelligible syllables trying to find words that would somehow change what just occurred. He saw his image replace Christie in the transmission. It vanished behind a hand erupting through thin flooring. More hands and now heads burst through the plastic flooring. One head had a ball gag in its mouth. Decayed flesh and eyes reached for and glared at Gillen. He didn't need the slide key to thrust the *FAST FLUSH* unit onto the emerging zombies. It crashed into the small chamber under the floor. He didn't hear the sound of crushed bones and growls. He was running through the door as more zombies climbed out. Some still inside the chamber grabbed Christie's body and dragged it to them as her own corpse began to stir.

Limbs flailed on blue sand. A pack of zombies charged. Apocalypse had come to Opportunity 80-8-18. With each squeeze of the trigger, Caine hoped she could kill it. Her rifle rounds blew apart undead heads. Their bodies fell and flailed, but they couldn't bite any civilians. Caine and her officers wore armor and face shields. For them, infection was unlikely. Especially if they kept killing zombies at a distance.

"Clown! A flipping clown!" Cpl. Jerry Synd aimed at the approaching zombie.

The shambling nightmare wore flaking face make up and a flashing red nose. A rifle shot from Caine took off the painted head and bright wig. The body in its polka-dot suit fell backwards. The initial onslaught ended in Lower Sec. Living people still raced toward more police and med-techs guiding them to a secure zone close to the Capitol.

"Seems harsh killing these things," Jerry said. "No joy in cutting down your neighbors."

Suddenly, Caine's face shield collided with Jerry's helmet.

"Your neighbors are the living!" Caine admonished. "These are zombies. Monsters! And they want you dead. Ripped open. Kill them! Or you're off frontline duty!"

"Crap. Okay. Sorry. Sir!" Jerry saluted Caine in earnest respect.

"Incoming!" Another officer yelled.

The officer ran to Caine's unit from a side street. She slid next to Caine as they all spun to meet the charging cluster of zombies making a collective roar. Jerry switched his gun to full auto. Multiple detonations of explosive rounds blew apart the charging zombies. The officers' deafening counter attack ended, but an odd sound left the unit.

"What the hell was that noise?" Jerry asked.

"Um, me. Trying not to burp." Officer Leoung admitted in a low voice.

"You failed." Vyk said as he approached with his rifle but only clad in his typical uniform.

Caine's unit snapped to attention.

"People burp. Zombies gurgle." Vyk said as he stopped beside Caine. "You need to burp, then burp!"

"Ah, sir. Wouldn't that alert them?" Leoung dared ask.

"Why the hell do you think we're here?" Caine barked. "To offer them free Fast Flush credits? We want them coming at us. Get your mind off the skit, Leoung!"

Leoung felt a flash of anger at his superior, but stayed at attention. In colonial culture, *skit* was a four-letter word more insulting than ones describing what you left in a *FAST FLUSH* unit, or sex reduced to a curse. *Skitting* was jumping between frontier colonies for free transit, meals, and housing. People called *skits* were considered less than colonial vagrants because they had useful skills but used them to keep scamming passage instead of bettering one world. Yet, being on a skit, a free ride, almost appealed to Leoung right then.

"Unit, reload and stay alert." Vyk ordered.

"Yes, sir!" Caine and her officers replied.

"I watched Christie Halstead's death note," Vyk said to Caine.

"Bitch in doctor's clothing. Anyway, sir, our population is still small enough. We can scan it almost at once. Our blue Opportunity doesn't have to die in apocalypse. That Docile drug Halstead made, when the med-techs duplicate it, this will end."

"Maybe." Vyk sighed.

"Why Maybe?" Caine asked.

"The prostitute, Reedy, became violent." Vyk replied. "We had to burn her. The Docile drug, whatever it is, doesn't stick."

Caine and her officers sighed.

"But we can still save our world." Vyk said with confidence. "If it slows them down, we can get the edge."

"Sir, we have one part of this outbreak unaccounted for. Gillen. If he's infected--"

"We've tracked his escape path. I'll get him," Vyk said. "You stop the zombies, Artie. Save the world."

"Affirmative, sir. But just watch for spatter. Don't get smeared or sprayed by anything flying off Gillen."

"Not even bad vibes?" Vyk asked and then checked his magazine.

No reply came from Caine.

"An attempt at humor, Lieutenant."

"Oh, now you joke, sir?"

"Affirmative."

"Go get your man, Commander." Caine said. "Our officers are well trained and well placed. We will save the world."

"Just watch for--" Vyk began.

"For spray. Got it, sir." Caine saluted.

Vyk saluted and actually smiled back. He turned and ran south.

"Geez! That guy can move!" Jerry said.

Leoung nodded in agreement. He glanced to his side and snapped up his rifle to fire. "Incoming!"

One man had run what seemed the circumference of the world. He realized the entire planet had no real name. In truth, he didn't either. He slumped against the slope of a blue sand dune.

The grains were more like gravel far out from the edge of town. There was still enough fine dust to inhale and burn his throat. He indulged in a moment of rest and self-hate. He failed in another scheme on another world. He caught himself thinking of his former name, Praylen Naslock. Now he was Peter Gillen. The real Peter Gillen had run up the shuttle ramp just ahead of Naslock as they both escaped Camponon.

The real Peter had government access codes as a supervising social worker. On the shuttle, he met a very social man with a ready smile and secret desperation to remake himself, fast. Bad fate for the old Pete, good fortune for the new Peter Gillen. He recalled later strangling the real Peter and doing an ace job of body stuffing into a contaminated waste pod on a CF relief ship. That vessel with shoddy security and dark passageways took them from the shuttle to await the *Chatham*. Now he laughed to himself. He heard another repetitive noise behind him. Boots were crunching blue gravel.

"Well, look who can move fast over sand!" The former Naslock and current Peter Gillen turned to see Vyk and his rifle approaching. "You must be in some fine shape, Vyk! You enhanced?"

"I'm sure you know the drill," Vyk said aiming at the man slumped on the blue dune. "Hands on head. Turn and stay on your knees."

"The more things change--" Gillen said but only shrugged.

"Do it." Vyk stopped several paces away and kept his weapon aimed at Gillen's head.

"You're really going to arrest me? Seriously?"

"If you're clean, yes." Vyk answered. "If you're infected, I'll shoot you."

"You're going to shoot me anyway. C'mon! It makes sense. I'm a threat to security. Gun me, Vyk. It's what I'd do."

"You'd do a lot of things I wouldn't, Mr. *Naslock*."

"Ya got me. Finally!" Gillen smiled. "At least you got my names for here and Camponon. There's a few more. Not that I was a skit. I worked hard at what I did. I was building an empire. But a few things got in the way. Zombies. Apocalypses. Cops. One revengeful little scientist. But it's locks on toilets that really piss me off."

"So who were you and where?" Vyk asked.

"I'll keep that to myself. That last annoying secret. It's supposed to bug you. Revenge of the dead. The dead-dead. Not the walking kind."

"Not sure there's a difference between you and them." Vyk said.

"Ouch!" Gillen said and then laughed again. "You know, it's pretty complex the way it all plays out. Life's little bends."

"Yeah. Bends. Hands on head."

Gillen looked up and away from Vyk. He squinted. "Light bends. It bends in the atmosphere, then it hits this planet's endless dust. The minerals absorb the blue. The whole damn planet is blue."

"No," Vyk kept his rifle steady and Gillen in its sights. "The sands absorb most of the light except for the blue wavelengths. That's what passes through the sand and makes it to your eyes. That's why you see almost nothing but blue."

"Renaissance man with a gun. Dangerous." Gillen looked straight at the bright white disc of the main sun through the clouds. Its partner was a smaller and dimmer dot. "You know, Vyk, so was I. I had vision. Still do. This can still work for both of us. You can still have your order and I can still have my empire. It's not mutually exclusive. I mean, hell, look at the damn zombies. They're dead, but alive. Duality can exist in one entity."

Gillen heard no answer as he looked away from the sky and blinked. He was both king and subject. One in the same. Alone. The blue sand had already partially filled the boot prints where Vyk had stood. Gillen looked over the expanse of dunes. His empire was all the drifts of alien, blue sand. He grabbed up a handful and stood.

"It's gotta be worth something to someone! Right, Vyk? Hey, Vyk! Come on! I get it. It's justice leaving me here. But, come on! It's inhuman. You want me to feel alone? That's it, right? Okay! I'm alone. Terrified. Crap, I'd kiss a zombie right now for the company. Okay? I get it! Now be the good guy and just arrest me. I mean, you know it's a crime to leave me. It's cruel. It's wrong! It's not you, Vyk! It--"

The former Praylen Naslock and current Peter Gillen heard the rifle shot as a loud, sharp bark. He didn't feel the bullet's impact. His corpse fell across the blue sand with a small tunnel through the skull and brain. Windblown sand would cover it. It would not stay buried. Vyk would return with a burn crew to destroy the infected body. Vyk's scans showed the plague manifesting in the man as they spoke. He made sure he was far away from any spray when he fired.

Vyk would stay plague free. He, his officers, and many more would fight to contain the outbreak so the colony could integrate, grow, and live free. At least live free from the threat of undead plague and apocalypse. He would try to keep it that way. He looked across the dunes of sapphire, azure, and other shades of blue. He considered them beautiful.

UNDERFOOT

The dirt was hard and icy. The cold reached straight to the bone even through thick calluses. Most people gathered around the communal bonfire to warm feet, bones, and hearts. There was a sense of peace in the moment and of strength from the tribe. The gathering carried a sense of human persistence in a hostile world. However, there was unspoken fear that reached deeper than the cold. Unlike the towering trees they lived among, the tribe was always ready to uproot and run in seconds. This was typical life in America, 2027 AD.

Humans survive, but their enemy has greater numbers and rarely rests. The enemy; the smucks. Mostly they're called gumbies. The name 'smuck' came from the annoying sound made from gnawing the stuff that destroyed civilization. 'Gumbie' came from the rubbery gunk itself: chewing gum. The world killer evolved in the discarded globs stuck to the sidewalks of every city on every street on the world. Some dubbed it the Soul Stealer Bacterium. A more direct name was the *Sole* Sticking Germ. It was the unseen horror on the bottom of your shoe. The pathology was simple. Stick to the sole, contact human skin, get in the system and take over the mind. It jumped several steps of punctuated evolution right underfoot. Its survival strategy was perfect. Control the species that controls the world. Now, something a thousand times smaller than a sidewalk stain dominated the planet. Its gumbie hordes always moved. Chewing. Smucking. Spitting. Chewing again. A generation had been born on the run from gumbies. There seemed no end to their supply of gum, or the horror brought by its constant, slow gnaw.

A murmur rose around the bonfire. People turned to the stump called the "soap box" even though now a single bar was a rare and precious commodity. A white-haired man looking like a sage from the past stepped on the stump. People exchanged nods and knowing comments in anticipation of the speech that was to come. It was well known, but tolerated. Besides, no one else wanted to speak and voice was the only form of broadcast entertainment available.

"People!" the white-haired man called Charles began. "My great, barefoot masses! It's time to unite! It's not too late to save our once-great, technical civilization! We can have the internet back. Space travel. We can once again live in cities! We can go back to wearing shoes!"

The crowd murmur grew louder.

"All we need, is this!" Charles reached into a pouch and thrust up a tool as if wielding a weapon of tremendous power. The murmur grew into laughter as Charles brandished a scrub brush.

"He's insane." Toshiro said with little pity.

Kaplan looked at her with surprise. "I'd expect a tone of sympathy from our tribal doctor."

"Well, trust me, he is." Toshiro shrugged.

"He's just old." Kaplan offered.

He glanced back at Charles and then back at Toshiro. She looked him over as if he lay out for an exam. Kaplan looked down across his passed middle-aged body. He sighed.

"Yeah. Okay. So am I. But I also remember life before the end of our cities. Before the fear of just stepping on pavement. And shoes."

"You saw it happen." Toshiro mused.

"I did." Kaplan nodded in reflection. "I tried to fight it."

"But there were too many." Toshiro offered.

"Oh, we might have beaten the parasites before the gumbies became so vast." Kaplan glanced over at several large, wooden vats on carts. "Now, we wait."

"For what?" Toshiro asked with interest.

"It's only a matter of time before their hosts die off completely. The smucks. Gumbies."

"Yeah? Really?"

"Yep. If we survive long enough."

"Will we?" Toshiro asked.

"Hell, I'm still here." Kaplan shrugged. "I didn't know a tree from a utility pole when this crap started. Now?"

Kaplan looked up at the expanse of interlocking evergreen limbs above them. The tree limbs were colored red by the fire light and blocked out the stars. He darted his eyes back to Toshiro who stared at the fire. She was half his age. Young. Attractive. That was no small feat now that make-up was a thing of the past, just as Wi-Fi and mobile phones. Still, there was little chance for romantic success, Kaplan thought. They were both scientists. Yet, Kaplan doubted his memorization of Benfey's and the ADOMAH versions of the periodic table would wow her. She had no doubt memorized at least one alternate table, herself.

Kaplan was born before handheld machines could recall whatever data you needed and wherever you stood. Toshiro was born in the time when all those devices were omnipresent and then suddenly useless. Good memory techniques were important again. Kaplan was glad he could teach them to future Toshiros. However, on most days he wished he had studied podiatry instead of biophysics, just to take care of his own feet in a world without shoes and endless pine needles, rocks, and cones.

"You know, there's no damn reason we can't wear shoes." Kaplan grated. "It's purely a cultural thing. An irrational fear. Some nights I give a million bucks for a pair of socks."

"You work on that. I'll worry about the disease becoming airborne." Toshiro said. "It evolved so fast, before. I wonder if we would recognize such an infection in time."

"Well," Kaplan looked off as his mind scrolled back through history. "The first case was misdiagnosed as a psychotic breakdown. But, soon there were others. Soon the staff treating the first patient became zombie chewing machines. Just chew, spit, chew, spit. All the while seeding the environment with more brain-enslaving bacteria. Lovely."

"No drugs could kill the bacteria? None at all?" Toshiro asked.

"Nothing. It was a super bug. Both a microbe and a complex colonial organism. Mutated from other types of cephalic bacteria." Kaplan shook his head from long-lingered amazement.

"There was no way to stop it once it evolved." Toshiro said.

"Oh, maybe through quarantines and behavioral changes." Kaplan sighed. "But the gum lobby kept filing suits and hired the best ex-congress people and other ace lobbyists. It was a political quagmire. Of gum. Big and sticky. The people demanded action. The gum companies gave them new flavors. The problem grew. And our world got chewed—"

"Yeah, I got it." Toshiro shook her head. "Do you think its rate of mutation has changed?"

"I'm sure it has." Kaplan crossed his arms for warmth. "But so will people. I hope. For the better. In biology and otherwise."

"According to Charles over there, all we need is an ocean of bleach and a billion or so scrub brushes." Toshiro said.

"And gloves." Kaplan added. "But even today there's a black market premium for gum."

Toshiro gave a guilty nod.

"Just be sure to swallow it." Kaplan smiled at her.

The gentle murmur of conversations suddenly ebbed as several people heard shouting from out in the night. The words were indistinct but the urgency was clear. A watch runner from the East entered the far edge of the camp. Most people understood the warning and ran to their jobs before the runner's words were clearly heard.

"They're coming!" The runner drew a breath and nearly collapsed. He exhaled a scream. "Gumbies! They're coming here!"

Kaplan saw Toshiro bolt to her triage tent. He flexed his feet against the cold ground.

The tribe kept moving through the night. Their escape was so successful that they had to take a small group to double back for the nearly mindless horde to catch their trail again. The risk was necessary to enact their plan. Contrary to culture and the successful strategy of flight, the tribe's warriors would take a fixed position and attempt to stop the horde. The action would be similar to a castle stand of millennia ago, but with a huge backdoor to bolt through if it failed. Kaplan wished they had an actual castle. He also wished he could finally quit running.

"How did they find us?" the young Bayner asked.

It was easy for Bayner to run and speak. However, Kaplan wished he'd quit cigarettes while they were still being made.

"Well," Kaplan panted. "Just walk in one direction long enough—"

"This time we want them to follow us!" Marris said as he came up next to both men. "This time we fight and kill them!"

"This wave, anyhow." Kaplan panted on.

Kaplan glanced at Marris, the tribe's de facto military leader. A belly lurched from side to side as he ran. Kaplan wondered how a man whose discipline did not extend to his diet got the job of leading them into zombie combat. Still, he could jog faster than Kaplan could sprint.

Their destination was in sight. A bulwark ascended a hillside formed by a river delta. The dry river channel made a narrow canyon that would funnel the zombie horde in pursuit. The counter assault would come from the high ground ahead. Kaplan vaulted the ditch at the bottom and started to climb. Pride made him ignore Bayner's efforts to help him. He used his hands to help climb the slope in a style similar to a drunken chimpanzee.

"You know--!" Kaplan puffed. He looked across the bulwark while climbing. "Once we built sky scrapers. Out of steel, glass, synthetic compounds. Hell, ancient man built giant temples. Out of granite!" He puffed. "Now, we use plant fiber ropes. And sticks. Sticks!" He stood for a second and inhaled. "If the soul stealer bacterium was a man—" Kaplan puffed. "I would kick the crap out if it. In a pair of shoes—no, boots! With thick wool socks!"

They reached the summit. Marris offered Kaplan a battered plastic bottle filled with water.

"Got anything stronger?" Kaplan wheezed.

Marris smiled and pointed a thumb over his shoulder to the wooden vats. Their contents originated in Kaplan's strong desire for a very strong drink. The result of one experiment proved too potent for cocktails. It did become the tribe's best hope against gumbie hordes.

"Damn. I didn't bring marshmallows." Kaplan smiled and then drew a long pull from the bottle.

"What's a marshmallow?" Bayner asked.

"Worse than gum." Kaplan answered. He enjoyed Bayner's shocked expression. Bayner was child when the outbreak occurred. He had survived carried from civilization, and then made to run to survive. Now he entered adulthood in this weird, new world. Kaplan hoped society could soon enjoy aging in one place.

"You think anyone has tried this?" Marris asked Kaplan. "I mean other than the radiation weapons and flame throwers the military used."

"Yeah, hard to fight a war when the society you're trying to protect has disintegrated."

"I thought you would've stayed with them. Gone to a bunker, or something. Orbit?"

"Nobody sent a helicopter or humvee." Kaplan shrugged.

"Taxi?" Marris asked with a smile.

"Too expensive." Kaplan said.

Marris laughed.

Bayner knew he would get too annoying if he constantly asked about all the things Marris & Kaplan mentioned. He decided it was just a foreign language spoken by the old. And that maybe he shouldn't have skipped so much school.

"Others might've done something similar." Kaplan mused. "Maybe that's why after the global outbreak I heard Houston called the city of flames. Maybe the perpetual fire was from roasting gumbies." Kaplan shrugged.

"Where's Houston?" Bayner risked asking.

Kaplan glanced at the sun and jabbed a finger South.

"If it's still there." Marris said. He looked out across the landscape in the direction of his enemy's inevitable assault.

Sheckly watched for that assault while hidden atop a ridge along the river channel. He became worried. His precious binoculars failed to magnify a distant torch or glimpse someone running towards him. Somehow, the system failed. His friends in the messenger corps were either dead and eaten, or dead and marching with the horde. Now, Sheckly was the last in the line of messengers, but the first chance to warn Marris the gumbies were close. He heard the shuffling mass. He could smell the horde before they came through the dry river bend. The stench rolled into his sinuses as if thick ooze poured into his nose. The odors were a swirl of rotted meat and sickly sweet like flower blossoms and mint. It all wafted from the decomposition and artificial flavors of death. Sicker still was the sounds.

Smuckt! Pop! Smuckt! Skwirsh-skwirsh. Smukt!

The gumbie horde rounded the bend. The sight was worse than the sound. The ones towards the front looked almost alive. The subsequent waves were animate rot. All they needed was teeth and enough muscle to work the gum. Most outer skin, even checks, was optional. For a second, Sheckly wondered how the gum stayed in. Sometimes it didn't. He focused on a corpse in a tattered sundress. The gumbie lost her wad from a cheek-free face. She stooped to reach for it. The smucks behind knocked her over and trampled her into a flattened stain. There was no mercy even among the horde.

Sheckly recalled Kaplan's sickening briefings. When whatever biology remained needed a recharge, the faster ones would turn and eat the slower ones. All the while, they oddly had the presence of mind to save their gum. The eaten gumbie would attempt to scratch itself onward if so much as a finger with some attached muscle still linked to the brain on a thread of nerve. Sheckly became nauseous. He grew angry as all the stories of loss from the elders raced through his mind. He lost his sense of discipline and stood in defiance. It was a mistake. They saw him. Immediately the entire horde moved to ascend the ridge slope and reach him.

The distinct sound and smell also shambled at him from behind. A smaller group had climbed up from the opposite side of the ridge. Sheckly picked up his club. The family heirloom .40-caliber Sig Sauer P226 rested in his belt. It had five shells left in the magazine. He drew and fired. Five gumbie heads exploded in fast succession. The bullet impacts only triggered the spectacular head bursts. Most of the skull explosion came from the internal pressure built up by the bacteria. The bloody eruptions projected spores when a gumbie was finally immobile or head trauma came knocking.

The club never needed a reload, but it was a close-range weapon. Sheckly swung and shattered a gumbie skull. The gory mist of smashed gumbie brains and spores splashed his face. He swung again. He hit another skull with a loud crack and more gore hit his face. Another swing; another crack. He raised the dripping club again before the true enemy did its work inside his own skull. He collapsed against a wall of gumbies. They looked down on his body. In a moment, he would join them. But now he was still. Fresh. And they needed sustenance to carry on. The smucks removed their gum.

"They must've gotten the watch runners. Damn!" Marris shouted as the gumbie horde appeared in the distance.

"Here they come." Bayner said, and suppressed a shudder.

"You still want to be here, doc?" Marris asked Kaplan.

"Yep." Kaplan answered. "It's the only show in town. If there was a town."

"There's a prepared defense. Thanks to you." Marris said. "I'm glad our tribe has your genius."

"The real genius was simplified stills on wheels." Kaplan said. "But the stroke of luck was finding that valley covered in huckleberries."

"I love huckleberries." Bayner added.

Marris turned to his troops of all genders and ages to yell orders. "Get ready, people!"

Those stationed at the vats' valves and levers tensed. Fire crews stood ready to light their torches. A chorus of metal bolts and heavy springs rippled from the rifle teams chambering rounds into well-maintained but aging assault and hunting rifles.

"At least the predicted rate of shuffle is still the same." Kaplan said.

"What's that mean?" Bayner asked.

"The bacteria aren't modifying the hosts to be faster." Kaplan answered. "Good news. Sort of."

"Hey, old man." Toshiro crouched next to Kaplan. She slung a large satchel onto the ground. "You ready?"

"Are you?" Kaplan smiled.

"Yep." Toshiro patted her satchel. "For bruises, burns and most other wounds. Anything short of a plague."

"We got one of those, too." Kaplan pointed towards to advancing horde. "We're about to use one of the most effective antibiotics to treat a very big infection. Fire."

"Hmm. All that meat and no barbeque sauce." Toshiro said

"Ooh, Dr. Toshiro, you're turning me on." Kaplan replied.

"They're over the covered troughs!" Marris bellowed. "Let it pour!"

Kaplan drew a deep breath as the crews up ended the wooden vats. His distilled hope began to flow down channels and into the covered troughs. Within them awaited several cisterns containing a napalm-like goo created from evergreen sap. The months of circuits through the forests and back to the dried river would be either a great victory or nothing more than a waste of time. People on the edge of doom needed hope and a project to focus it. The desire to fight back was a potent fuel for motivating people to scrape channels in hard earth and haul heavy sacks of berries. Kaplan was certain of success. However, he was also willing to take the brunt of the emotional backlash if it failed. He worried such despair would kill the tribe better than a bizarre disease spread by animate corpses.

The fire crews hurled their torches. Flames erupted in the exposed channels. The first eruption of flames didn't look intense enough to stop the gumbies who walked through the fires. Then an inferno exploded beneath the horde. The tribe's warriors cheered. Kaplan held back a smile. He stared intently at the inferno. He nearly jumped back at what stumbled out of the intense blaze. They were still advancing. Flaming gumbies shambled out of the fire holding their heads.

"Ah geez, the heads!" Kaplan shouted.

"Are they in pain?" Toshiro said looking at the gumbies.

"No! They're trying to shield the bacteria. Crap! Spores!" Kaplan bolted up and shouted at Marris. "Shoot! Blow 'em away before they get close."

The rifle teams charged to the edge of the bulwark and opened fire. Gumbie parts blasted off as bursts of automatic fire cut through the advancing, flaming gumbies like invisible chain saws. Gumbie heads began to explode from more precise rifle fire.

"The legs!" Toshiro screamed. "Shoot 'em in the legs!"

The tide of gumbies walking out of the inferno ran into a copper jacketed and lead wave. The tide stop. Flames rolled over the fallen corpses. A few eager rounds still flew into the blaze. The shooting stopped. The only sound was the wind rushing to feed the inferno curling into a searing, orange twister.

"What about the smoke?" Toshiro asked.

"We're safe." Kaplan answered. "The inferno is too wide for the spores to make it out even if they escape the heat." Kaplan bent and placed his hands on his knees.

A renewed cheer drowned the inferno's roar.

The tribe moved again. They would repeat the effort of distillation and excavation at another place. Yet all hoped never to see a gumbie horde ever again. Toshiro, Marris and Bayner accompanied Kaplan to scout the edge of the waning inferno.

"Don't touch that!" Toshiro yelled at Bayner.

Bayner froze, but he kept his eyes locked on the brightly colored box. Across the box's top, a dancing, bright purple hippo held a huge bunch of bright purple grapes across its top. The words 'Delicious! Delightful! Chewlicious!' swirled across all of its visible sides in bulbous lettering.

"Is it a peace offering?" Bayner asked.

"Are you nuts?" Marris barked. "They want us to become like them! Torch it."

"But it's grape chewlicious." Bayner said. He rolled his tongue in his mouth anticipating a sweet, fragrant, artificial flavor.

"It's suicide!" Marris barked.

"Can you test it to see if it's parasite free?" Bayner asked Kaplan.

"Nope." Kaplan said. He stood next to the box, and then kicked it into the remaining flames.

"Hey!" Bayner nearly bolted after the box.

Marris glared at Bayner. He jerked him thumb in the direction of the bulwark. Bayner obeyed and walked up the slope. The hippo burned away.

"Ow!" Kaplan shouted and began stomping his foot burning from a dab of evergreen napalm. He limped up the hill and sat on a flat edge of bulwark.

"You may have just saved us all." Toshiro retrieved her satchel.

"Yep. That's me." Kaplan rubbed cool dirt over his foot. "PhDs and a life of science, and I save humanity with a barefoot kick with my ass covered in dirt. I feel fulfilled. Really."

"Oh, shut up and take the praise." Toshiro said. She gently brushed some of Kaplan's tousled hair from his face.

"All right, I will." Kaplan looked up at her and smiled.

"So, to bring that gum." Marris said. "It took planning."

"Well, only maybe." Kaplan shrugged. "I guess it explains their constant supply. It's probably the one, sure thought of what's left of their brains. Back when this began, we figured the infected brain could still manifest rudimentary intelligence. But—"

"Has it evolved a smarter gumbie?" Toshiro asked.

"I don't think so. These smucks looked like any other horde. Some of them carry junk with them. In photos of the first hordes, I saw gumbies with purses, pack packs, dolls. One even carried a dead cat and a spatula."

"Yeah," Marris added and looked back over the field of ashes and bones. "Some of these smucks held chunks of wood or rocks."

"I think it's a rudimentary impulse to pick up something and carry it." Kaplan said. "This wave probably passed through some abandoned town and some did what comes natural. From our perspective, that case of gum made sense as part of a sinister plan. But it could just be just impulse. P-O-P."

"Pop?" Toshiro asked.

"Point of purchase." Kaplan answered. "In ye olde stores there would be stuff set up at the cash registers to lure you into an impulse buy. Stuff like gum."

Marris shook his head and walked towards his troops loading equipment.

"Impulse. Hmm." Toshiro said as she examined Kaplan's foot. "Well, why don't you come over to my place?"

"Oh, really?" Kaplan suggestively and raised his eyebrows.

"Yes." Toshiro said. "I'm the tribe doctor, and you have an injured foot."

"Well," Kaplan stood. "At least I didn't put it in my mouth."

Toshiro groaned. "Any more of that, and I'm kicking you into the fire trenches."

"Ooh! Hot!" Kaplan laughed.

Toshiro shook her head. She helped Kaplan limp towards the line of the living descending the opposite side of the hill.

OPENED BOX

Somewhere, a world was eating itself. Masses of human dead chased the living not infected by a lethal, corpse-animating plague. Somewhere, a sun shone on a planet and did not threaten cancer from radiation, but only brightened a peaceful, verdant valley. Dr. Nora Everett imagined the two possible days. Where Nora sat, she enjoyed neither peace nor carnage, but did endure the horror of an interim colonial committee meeting.

Nora looked at the floor set with empty chairs for colonists who never attended the meetings. The people of the pioneer world dubbed Culsans had plenty of work to keep them occupied. Nora imagined the seats filled and the citizens suddenly bolting when a horde of zombies ran towards them. She looked at her fellow committee members. In all but one she saw a hideous zombie face looking to bite off her own. Her imagined horrors made her smile. She stifled a snorting laugh. The audible noise was lost among the raised voices of her peers. Human civilization had reached across interstellar space. Yet in this metal dome, civility seemed to draw back and die in a vacuum.

The population of Culsans was a balance of cultural and genetic backgrounds extending from the inner colonies. Their varied heritage reached back to far off Earth. Every colonist's age fell within plus/minus five years of thirty percent of the modern human lifespan. Their age was supposed to grant youthful vigor, experience, plus the capacity to breed. Government and company officials approved a list of potential leaders based on professional accomplishment. Social engineers then arranged the committee members personalities and intellects to run Culsans as a well-designed program. Nora understood programming was like DNA.

In that molecule, glitches form. Mutations rise. Some add benefits. Others create disease. Plagues take unexpected paths, such as animating dead tissue with hunger. Even precise codes fail and systems crash. Nora watched a crash in progress.

The one member other than Nora not shouting was the colony's technical boss. Administrator Ahmbet Koller sat in a chair at the end of the curving table under the domed roof. All walls, furniture, and fixtures held a curve. Nora saw them as mere arcs that never completed a circle. Pressure to make Culsans complete stoked the committee's conflict. The planet's ecological reengineering, mining, and manufacturing status was plotted on a timetable by officials that never set foot on Culsans. The plan crashed. Zombie outbreaks on other worlds accelerated demands. The increased stress was its own type of plague that caused council members to feed on each other. Koller remained calm.

Nora ran the medical sector. She made her argument soon after the meeting dome was erected: fund the medical sector if you want to live. The shepherd corporations, inter-colonial council, and even Culsans' petulant committee agreed. Nora had what she needed and her clinics kept everyone healthy. She looked at her bickering peers and thought of introducing a resolution to pump potent, mood enhancing benzodiazepines into the water supply. Or, maybe just ration coffee to a single cup per meeting.

Koller leaned back in his chair. He never used the administrator's center chair to foster feelings of equality and camaraderie. The act failed. All council members were the sovereigns of their fields and tyrants when asked to share. Nora considered Koller attractive, probably because he wasn't shouting. Her husband was shouting. Louis Quary and Nora had contracted marriage as part of the grand plan to settle Culsans. In a set of psychological profiles, they were well matched. At times, Nora hoped the person who created the set of profiles had been eaten by zombies.

Quary currently pressed for less oversight for building Culsans economy so truly free markets would stimulate more growth in other sectors. His stare was an effective, silent counter point against opposing members. He dared level it at the head of security, the powerfully built and armed Caden Zhul. At least

Quary did not lack testosterone. Lacking that hormone was a charge often brought against the tall, placid Koller. Nora realized he simply let his enemies expend their energy while conserving his own. It was either that, or he had a secret stash of benzodiazepine. As a former frontier pilot, he was likely just good at keeping calm.

Koller sat up straight as he watched the arguing between Zhul and Quary was become heated. Then things became worse. A true emergency came careening from an arc around the sun. The alarm sounded as a holograph projected images from the ceiling apex. A display of Culsans' inner solar system flashed over the empty chairs. An image of a squat, cylindrical ship and its projected path appeared in the display. The ship's course intersected Culsans' orbit. The voice of a female security officer replaced the alarm.

"Commander Zhul, priority." The officer said in a clipped, calm tone.

"Zhul, here. Report."

"Outreach buoys are tracking a cargo craft entering our system along the edge of the solar well. Craft appears to have no q-com or ident broadcast. Sir, inter-col reports an unidentified ship fled the Damalla system." The officer's voice gained pitch with her last words. "That system was quarantined."

She halted her report. A murmur rolled through the committee members.

"Understood," Zhul said. "ETA?"

"Projected rendezvous with planet is less than nine." The officer finished.

"Acknowledged," Zhul replied. "Continue to attempt a link or com. Keep display continuous to this dome."

"Understood." The officer's voice channel cut with an audible click.

"Okay. This is interesting." Nora said and stood up facing the hologram of sun, planets, and unknown ship.

"No supplies were scheduled to arrive." Quary said and copied his wife Nora by standing.

"It's not a supply ship. It's unregistered." Koller said. He stayed seated but leaned forward and stared at the red arc in the hologram representing the ship's course and noted the milliseconds tick off its expected time of arrival.

"You know if it's heading here it's probably manned," Husain Royo, the colony's atmospheric engineer pointed at the hologram but turned his head to Koller. "And that crew was exposed to the cadaver plague!"

"We should ready the nukes," Quary said.

"Yeah!" Royo shouted. "Make it vapor before it makes orbit."

"The missiles only reach the mesosphere," Zhul said. "They go inop before space."

"What?" Royo turned his head to Zhul to question the missiles' range and Zhul's jargon.

Nora glanced over at Koller. He still focused on the holographic ship above them. His lips pursed. Koller inhaled. He broke the rigid silence and reignited the shouting with two words.

"We wait."

Koller stood, still looking at the hologram. He suddenly dropped his stare at the shouting committee members. Even Nora jerked her head slightly back. The typically placid Koller had summoned a glare on the level of Quary's own. The room became silent again.

"We do not even know if it is the same ship that fled Damalla." Koller said in a clear and metered tone.

"Well, how many unregistered ships could there be?" Royo dared to ask.

"Potentially, a lot." Zhul answered and flexed his shoulders.

"Our warheads are for extreme defensive needs," Koller said.

"Like this one?" Quary asked.

"We don't know," Koller answered. "Right now we are only guessing about this ship. The nuclear weapons are a one-shot solution."

"True," Zhul added. "Once they're fired, the colony will be defenseless to another incursion or plague threat."

"More so," Koller looked off as he recalled another tense meeting from his past and spoke as if quoting from it. "Once colony leadership fires its warheads there is a long review by inter-col and corporate over whether or not to keep resupplying that potentially tainted colony."

"That's better than death!" Royo retorted.

Koller turned to look at Royo. "It's a potential slow death."

"Then we may as well initiate apocalypse protocol." Nora said and found herself receiving scowls from Quary and everyone else except Koller.

"We will reconvene when the ship is within an actionable range." Koller said and looked back up at the hologram.

"Then it might be--!" Royo started to say.

"Enough!" Koller actually shouted. "Go home. Our time here is over."

Nora raised her eyebrows at the apocalyptic sound of the comment, but said nothing.

"And keep this quiet," Zhul said firmly. He glanced at Koller who nodded approval. "I don't want my officers overrun by panicked civilians who think a plague is falling from the sky."

Royo opened his mouth, but shut it as quickly.

"Leak this and I will nuke you." Zhul finished.

The committee members except Zhul and Koller moved to the dome hatch. Nora followed the group as they propelled themselves on a vibration of grumbles and low curses. Quary slowed and joined his wife. He glanced at her with a quick smile, but seemed suddenly distracted. Her mind finally lost its hold on tension when seeing the reflection of the hologram on the curved dome wall above the hatch. Her heart raced as she considered the real threat of Armageddon they might soon face. The hatch opened. Although artificially processed atmosphere hit their faces, it was refreshing compared to the dome's now humid and stale air. Royo took a deep breath to sample his gaseous handiwork. Everyone else put on solar lenses to ward against the bright, white sunlight from outside.

"I'll catch up," Quary said to Nora as he turned to the left and away from the group along the walkway circling the dome. The ringing in his ears was not from the committee arguments. It was a sound only he could hear. The sound maker was so well hidden even his wife's medical scans did not reveal it. The sound grew as the quantum entangled connection opened between Quary on Culsans and his real employer far away from the colony. He walked to his private office dome to answer the summons.

Quary's office was cramped, metallic, and sparse. The curved dome wall facing outside had no window. The walls had no art. Most office furniture vanished over time as file keeping and document making became virtual and more natural to people. The one thing still constant in all offices through the centuries: a rolling chair. Quary sat in his.

"Secure room." Quary said as he rocked back. "Verify ident. Open com."

A ball of faint, red light appeared before him as the communication system became active. The person demanding Quary's attention sent only voice through the channel. The hologram stayed as a matrix ball with no image within. The voice was stern and at least designed to sound female. The name assigned to it, but likely an alias, was Madhuri Sharren. Quary assumed Sharren was human. No intelligent aliens had called on humanity at any inhabited worlds. Quary didn't want to think he worked for an intelligence whirling around in a machine. Although, his own brain was grafted to part of one, and one he didn't own.

"About time," Sharren said through the blank projection.

"The test results look favorable," Quary said in a confident tone. "Even with the taint of coming from a plague system, Koller refuses to destroy the incoming ship."

"It will be able to land. You're certain?" Sharren asked.

"Certain enough to tell the captain to continue here." Quary shrugged. "After all, neither you nor I are not on the ship."

"That's a cold and high-risk gamble." Sharren said with a near-pleased ring to her voice.

"It is what we do." Quary nodded while looking at the arc of his dome wall.

"We? So you will cover the loss of the ship and payments made to the crew?"

Quarry cleared his throat. "I assumed that was covered under venture capital."

"I will assume you will meet your contractual obligations, and the name Louis Quary will not be added to the loss column."

"I will." Quary sat up and addressed the ball of red haze. "Culsans will become one of your assets, very soon."

The air was fresher but the tension remained. The committee members stood in front of the curved conference table and looked up at the hologram now showing an actual satellite image of the battered, mystery ship over Culsans' mostly umber surface. A small, flat square rested on the table near Koller. It was the launch key calibrated to Koller's genome. A characteristic red button projected from its top. A crackle of radio static echoed through the dome and rasped the ears and nerves of the committee members.

"The ship has gained a static energy envelope from pushing its radiation screens to maximum and passing near the sun." Koller informed. "It's prevented any accurate surface scans and interfering, we assume, with most of the ship's systems. We are still attempting contact."

"Are you still reluctant to use that?" Quary said and motioned his head toward the launch key with its projected red button.

Koller said nothing but inhaled, deeply. The excited voice of the female officer cut in.

"Sir! Com open! Com open!"

"Patch." Zhul ordered.

"Done, sir."

"Unregistered ship, identify." Zhul said.

There was only static transmitted for a long, taught second. The committee jumped at a sudden voice from the ship.

"This is the *Xolotl*," A male voice broke through loud crackling. "We are an unarmed cargo hauler. We need supp--" a spike in static cut through, but the voice continued unawares. "Medical. We have a--" he cut out, again. "--crew. Request assistance, Culsans. Repeat--" the static cut in. "Assistance. We--" a loud pop sounded. "--no harm."

"This is the Culsans' admin." Koller spoke. "You are not permitted to land. Discharge the radiation so we can get a clear scan of--"

"Negative, admin." The voice from the *Xolotl* said clearly. "We are landing on Culsans."

"You are not granted that right." Koller replied.

"We can't--" static interrupted the man's voice again and continued to break up his signal. "--the engines. We can't divert course. We will land. Request medical--I assure--but we must land."

"You must alter course or risk destruction." Koller said firmly.

"We are destroyed either--" was the incomplete reply. "We must land, Culsans. We mean no harm--but--no choice."

Both the static and the man's voice cut out. The image showed the squat ship rotating to position its aft thermal shields for reentry.

"*Xolotl*, respond." Koller said. "*Xolotl?*"

"Com lost, sir." The female officer's voice informed.

"Well, that settles that." Royo said. He folded his arms and glared at Koller.

"A day's pay says they can still read us," Zhul sneered.

"Are you really going to let them land?" Quary asked Koller.

Koller took a long breath. "We still have no clear picture of who or what is on that ship."

"It doesn't matter!" Royo spat out.

"It does," Nora said in a low voice while watching the hologram of the ship prepare to enter the atmosphere.

"Can we risk our colony for an illegal smuggler?" Quary turned to Nora.

"Maybe they are smuggling people," Nora said to Quary. "Off-book workers."

"If so, there are many more people than just the criminal crew onboard. Possibly as many as one hundred." Koller added. "Families. Children. You want to kill all of them, too?"

"If it means saving ours on Culsans." Zhul said as he watched the hologram overhead. He flexed his cheeks and pitched his eyes at Koller.

"And if there is a better way?" Koller asked. He watched the motion of the ship's image. He knew he had a short time before the plasma of reentry truly prevented the *Xolotl* from radio contact.

"There isn't!" Royo shouted.

He lifted the black launch key with its red button image to Koller. A collective, high moan rose from the others. Koller fixed Royo with a harsh stare. Royo dropped his head and slowly returned the launch key to the table.

"Yes there is," Nora said and almost leapt within the group. "They don't have to land near our population. We have a whole planet! Have them drop into a sterile sector in the transitional zone, southeast!"

"TZ-335." Koller nodded in excitement and then regained his placid expression.

"We keep them off the surface and sealed inside the ship." Nora continued. "There will be no risk of contamination to any life, native or human. They could spit on the ground and the stripers or just the sun's heat will kill anything larger than a quark."

"It's still too risky!" Royo almost screamed. "Don't even let that ship enter the atmosphere!"

"Your protest is noted," Koller said.

Royo's continued protest was lost in the committee's chorus of shouting.

"Enough!" Koller's voice boomed over the others. He looked at the *Xolotl*'s image. Its heat shield was yet to glow.

"How in good conscience can--*hrmph*!" Royo began but Nora's hand clasped over his face until he leaned back in silence.

"If this doesn't work, you get your wish to kill the ship and all onboard." Koller said. "Security, broadcast the coordinates of TZ-335 and this message in a loop to the ship: *Xolotl*, if you do not touchdown at these coordinates you will be destroyed. Land at these coordinates, or die."

"Done, sir." The voice of the female officer replied.

Koller placed his hand over the launch key. Nora stared at his fingers over the red glow. All the others stared up at the brightening image of the *Xolotl* as its heat shield began to flare. Nora looked up and wondered if she would see an even greater flash. The image of the glowing ship over Culsans' hemisphere vanished. Everyone jolted. Koller quickly steadied his hand over the launch key. An image of a fireball cutting through a high sheet of thin clouds in a light-blue sky replaced the satellite images on the holograph's projection.

"Switching to surface cameras," the female officer informed. "Ship descending under control. Projected touchdown at TZ-335."

There was no cry of joy, only a slight smile on Nora and Koller's faces.

"Once it's landed, then what?" Quary asked.

"We give them a few essential supplies and send them off." Koller answered.

"If they won't leave?" Quary pressed.

"They will." Koller said. "They'll take what they need and go. No unregistered ship will want attention for long."

"But if they do leave the ship?" Zhul asked. "How are we to respond?"

"You know anyone or anything trying to cross the sterile zone will die before they reach us." Koller said in a reassuring tone.

"Even if it's already dead," Nora said to preempt any fears of zombies marching from the *Xolotl*.

Koller nodded his approval to Nora. Quary noticed their shared smile. Everyone flinched as Koller reached down and picked up the launch key, but the red button vanished and Koller simply put the key in his shirt's breast pocket.

"So this is what we're doing," Koller said "Prepare some surplus for transit on a terra-hop. I'll take it. No one else will be at risk."

"You'll need help," Zhul said.

"I'll go." Nora spoke quickly. "I'm the head of med sector. I can assess anything we might see and determine the threat level."

The group was silent. On the projection above, the *Xolotl* was now a glowing ship falling quickly toward the barren, umber terrain of TZ-335.

"I understand you are all afraid," Koller stepped in front of the committee members. "I also know you are all capable of overcoming your fear and seeing a humane solution."

"I understand we are all under threat of becoming zombies!" Royo screeched. "Thanks to you!"

"If you act on fear, you are already mindless." Koller sighed.

"Geez!" Royo yipped. "Shove your philosophy rant!"

"All right. You want an act of power?" Koller asked Royo and stepped toward him.

"Yes!" Royo hissed.

"Then shut up or I will have you dragged out and imprisoned as a threat to colonial unity." Koller said and looked down at the shorter Royo.

"What?" Royo said and stepped back. He looked over to Zhul. "Can he do that?"

Zhul simply nodded his head in confirmation.

"Read your info packet before getting on the transit ship, next time." Nora chided.

"Okay. So we have a plan." Koller said and looked back at the holo-feed of the *Xolotl*.

The ship dropped below the camera's field of view. The feed switched to a zooming shot from remote camera. The downward thrust of *Xolotl*'s braking engines kicked up brown dust below it before its landing struts deployed.

"Okay. So now what?" Quary asked.

"We wait for the ship's crew to complete touchdown checks." Koller said.

"And maybe for doom," Quary said as verbal camouflage and forced himself not to smile.

His last comment brought a glare from Nora. Quary glanced down and nodded to himself. He looked back at her. "Look, Nora, be careful."

Nora cocked her head to consider the true concern offered by her contractual husband.

"Well, thanks, Lou-que." Nora looked at Quary. She took a moment to consider her future both with and without him. She smiled. "I will."

Koller brought the terra-hop to a full stop. It sank to the surface as the grav-rails slid into their slots along the hull. Koller had piloted much larger crafts on far longer journeys. He had navigated unknown space on ships bigger than the *Xolotl*. That mystery ship sat dead ahead. Its squat, conic top stood out of view above the upper edge of the cockpit portal. The box-like terra-hop was a utility vehicle that only flew a few meters above the surface.

Still, Koller was glad to be at the controls of something that quickly responded to his commands. His slid the controls against the instrument panel with ancient, digital displays. The instruments were reconditioned and reused over perhaps a few generations of colonies. The Vehicle Exit Suits he and Nora wore were newer, but still reissued equipment. Their stale smell made that obvious. Koller stood and took his helmet from the stowage rack.

"Time to get this done." Nora said and took her helmet.

After a minute outside, Nora threw her helmet off. It hit the sterile, umber soil that stretched beyond the *Xolotl* and to the horizon. There the ground met the light blue sky that harbored the bright white sun overhead. It seemed only twice as large as any star in the night sky of many Earth-like worlds. Yet this sun still sent the heat cooking Nora and Koller in their odorous, oven-like VE suits.

"Piss for water! That's just too damn hot!" Nora yelled and then panted.

"The cooling systems seem faulty." Koller said.

He set the long grav-jack handle vertical. It stopped. The supply boxes lurched on the pallet it held. Nora threw off the suit's bulky arms and torso unit revealing the white uni-shirt clinging to her sweaty frame.

"That ship's crew has balls to set harsh demands for delivering their mercy supplies." Nora took deep breaths and glared at the *Xolotl*.

"Well--" Koller stopped speaking and followed Nora's lead by throwing off the top of his suit. He pulled the wet front of his shirt from his chest and let it sag back against him.

Koller agreed to the *Xolotl* captain's terms to expedite the mission and return, quickly. Koller knew his own rank was at jeopardy and his only ally was the wife of his greatest political foe. Such was colony life.

"What's the time limit for us? From exposure?" Koller panted.

"A few minutes more than before," Nora replied.

"Specifically?"

"Just move your ass." Nora took hold of the grav-jack handle and started walking.

Koller caught up to Nora and grabbed the remaining exposed handle. They both pulled the pallet closer to the *Xolotl*. A cargo bin sat between them and the ship. Somehow, the crew or its automata had placed the bin with no trace of boot prints or tracks. The bin was a dull silver color similar to the ship. It measured a meter wide by two meters long and a meter deep. For Koller the mundane object held ominous potential.

Koller stopped. "This is as far as you go, Dr. Everett."

"Why?" Nora asked. Her sweaty face wrinkled in confusion.

"For all I know this is some form of elaborate assassination." Koller said in a pant.

"Are you serious?"

"It's possible." Koller ran his left thumb across his brow to stop the cascade of sweat into his eyes. "An admin has a lot of trust put in them by the off-world powers, and a colony's population. All through history, people identify with a single leader more than any senate or parliament."

"Or committee." Nora said and panted.

"Right. But we need the balance. In theory it provides choice, even if the admin has final say. That means I stand as final power and open target. So if this is a moment of danger, I am the one who--"

"Wrong." Nora said and took a dry swallow.

"Huh?" Koller blinked away sweat and confusion.

"If this is an attempt to kill you, and it succeeds, then Culsans becomes a world I don't want to live on. I'll go load the supplies, admin."

"But you're the top doc. You have a more important role on colony."

Nora took a quick laugh between pants. "Don't tell my contracted hubby that. He'll try to use me against you."

"Would he succeed?" Koller asked.

"I think you know he wouldn't." Nora smiled and resumed quick breaths.

"Good." Koller returned the smile.

"But I'm still going to load that bin." Nora wiped away the sweat on her brow and down her left cheek with her free right hand. "If you die, our next leader is Quary."

"Not Zhul?" Koller took another dry swallow.

"He has muscles and guns," Nora panted. "But Louis is a better schemer. A better snake. I like a little regulation. But mister economy over all, Louis Quary, sees things in a more food pyramid sort of way, but stacked with people not nutrition."

"I think I get that." Koller nodded. He let go of the grav-jack's handle and placed both hands on his hips.

"So then let me do this." Nora pulled the grav-jack handle towards herself.

"Well, I don't like it." Koller said and reached for the handle.

"It's my choice." Nora pulled the handle rather away and began walking.

Koller took a deep, hot breath. Nora was already several steps ahead of him. He exhaled, and was glad he turned the live-feed cameras off.

"Good luck!" Koller shouted to Nora.

"Yeah," Nora called back. "Let's poke the cat!"

"Cat?"

"Yeah. Is it dead or alive in that box?"

"I'm not getting that."

Nora only waved back across her shoulder. She reached the cargo bin. Its lid retracted automatically. A brief gust of cooler air escaped the empty box. Nora wondered what it had contained before now. It was from a smuggler's ship. Maybe it had contained alien life. Or something exotic, like baked bread. She placed a box from the pallet on the right corner of the bin. The weight tipped the bin, slightly. A narrow shadow hid a strip along its left side.

For other people far away, the day had been even worse. The cameras of a flo-drone recorded the panicked flight of four hydrology workers down water supply tunnels. A fifth member of their crew had shouted for the others to run from the dark. His screams of horror made them heed the warnings. The mass of zombies hunting the tunnels ate him and sought more. The surviving four crewmembers ran frantically in their green, rubbery work suits. But somehow, the dead legs of the zombies were very fast.

A blonde woman slowed just a step behind. Hands of animate bone grabbed hold of her suit. She shrieked to her three coworkers ahead of her and reached out to them. Terror and then cold fingers pulled her long hair and features taught. One man stopped and turned back to her. Living arms in green suits yanked him back as the woman disappeared among grasping, rotted arms pulling her body to bared teeth. Her rubbery suit seemed to explode dark red as the zombies tore her apart. The three ran. More zombies trampled those at the front devouring their victim.

The flo-drone followed the three crewmembers through a hatchway and into a tunnel junction. The two men and one dark-haired woman immediately swung the heavy hatch and thrust themselves against it to slam it closed. The blond woman victim's torn-free arm blocked the hatch from shutting. The man who had turned back for her fell from shock. The dark-haired woman and other man kept pushing against the hatch to seal it. They failed.

A zombie surge forced open the hatch even more. Zombies pressed through the gap like a fleshy paste with erupting bones. The jaw of a nearly complete skull opened and shut in an awkward attempt to bite the closest ankle. The fallen man pushed and kicked himself away from the hatch and the woman's arm that now pulled itself by its fingers towards him. The man still thrusting against the hatch looked in desperation at the dark-haired woman straining next to him. Another zombie surge rocked the hatch. She jerked her head in the direction of an adjoining tunnel. He glanced at the panicked crewmember on the tunnel floor and then looked back at the dark-haired woman. They nodded to each other. They ran from the hatch down the tunnel. The hatch slammed wide open. Zombies flowed in and swarmed the fallen man as he screamed.

Louis Quary shuddered. He adjusted his posture in his office chair. The tunnel images from another colony finished playing in his mind, but they were not memories. The quantum entangled communication halo in his skull transmitted directly to his brain. He could only receive images, not send. Nor could he edit what he received. He was a captive to what data or images his covert employers sent him. For two-way communication, Quary still needed old fashioned, hard technology.

"Things are going well," Quary said to the ball of red haze representing Madhuri Sharren. "The ship has landed."

"And so it sits at a port for all to see?" Sharren asked.

"Well, no." Quary paused. "It sits in an uninhabitable region. But it is on the surface."

"Then things are not going well. The test has failed. Our plan was to cause panic among the population for political gain. Are you now the admin?"

"No. But--"

Sharren cut in. "Then not only has the plan failed, you have failed. This is unfortunate for our syndicate, but mostly for you."

"There is still time." Quary pleaded with upturned palms to the red, hazy ball. "The ship is here. I can leak the information to the public. The panic will still occur as planned. The taint of the plague will mark the colony. The inter-col council and corporate will write us off. The workers will be trapped, and a captive market. Culsans will be a syndicate hub, and I will be admin. Our ships will have a free port for moving all manner of product in this sector. Illicit enterprise is not dead."

Sharren waited a taught second before she replied. "I can see why you were chosen for a political assignment. We have invested a lot of capital on you and this plan."

"It will work." Quary nodded. He looked to the side considering his entreating actions were to a blank hologram.

"It should." Sharren said. "We've given you a powerful lever with that ship. Use it. The plague, its mere suggestion, has created many opportunities for us."

"What would we do without zombies?" Quary smiled.

"Oh, it's not the zombies. It's the fear. So long as people are afraid, we'll be in business. If they want to escape it, we sell them distractions. Sex. Drugs. Tech. If they want to fight it, we'll sell them weapons. All for a profit. And with the promise of plenty more. All right when we've arranged for them to need it the most. But to expand we need a safe haven to fulfill orders. That haven will be Culsans. Once it's marked by fear, no one will go snooping there."

Quary slowly nodded considering Sharren's words. He could foresee a new era and empire dawn, albeit illicit and immoral. "Yes. It's one small step for crime, one important leap for criminal enterprise."

"Make it happen, Quary. Or I'll mark you. I expect a report within an hour."

The channel closed. The ball of red haze vanished. Quary stuck his left hand with extended middle finger where it had floated. He opened his office door. The door's shape now made him uncomfortable because it was similar to the hatches in the tunnel recording. He took a breath and entered the central living space. It was the one room he and Nora still shared. She sat on the plump couch staring down at her hands on her knees.

"Hi," Quary said with surprise but genuine delight. "You're back already. Mission go well?"

"Yep. I guess." Nora said without looking up.

Quary found her manner odd. "Feeling okay?"

"Yep. Um, no." Nora took a long, deep breath. She exhaled with a rattling wheeze. "Something was in the bin they sent out. Bastard smugglers. It bit me. Damn thing bit me."

Quary froze in fear. He inhaled and then spoke, slowly. "Uh, what bit you?"

"Something small." Nora answered. She still kept focused on her hands. "A bug. Or a ship mite. Maybe a tiny rodent. A jimp."

Quary thought Nora's staccato delivery strange, but he was relieved the biter didn't have human teeth set in a corpse's jaw. His tension eased, and then rose again as Nora continued.

"But, you know, it was a vector." Nora said.

"Vector?"

"Yep. Yep. A means, living or otherwise, that transmits a disease. A plague."

"Plague?" Quary said in a high pitch.

"Yep. Yep." Nora nodded. Her nods became quicker. She suddenly stopped and stared straight at Quary. He felt as a mouse seeing a hawk for the first and last time. Nora stood. Quary jumped back. Nora walked to a cabinet and withdrew a syringe from a drawer full of medical devices from past ages. She collected them as a hobby and as potential emergency equipment if supplies ran low.

"Is that for you?" Quary asked.

"Yep. Sort of. The gestation of the disease was a lot quicker than I thought it would be. So far, I have control of my mind. Pretty much. But I do need some of your blood."

"For tests?" Quary backed to his office door. "A cure?"

"No. No. No. No." Nora shook her head violently, and then snapped her now bloodshot eyes back squarely at Quary. "I want to consume it. Of course! It's kind of a drive. Fairly strong, really. Now come here, hubby. Lou-que. It won't hurt. I don't think. Roll up a sleeve. Drop throw. Or just, just lean your neck towards me!"

"I need to go!" Quary backed up, but stumbled and hit his office door. It shut behind him with a slam.

"You can't." Nora said. Her voice and posture were now calm. But her eyes were small, suspended pools of blood that began to drip."Maybe that's why I trapped us in here on a med-emergency. Maybe. I don't know, really."

Quary grabbed his office door handle and jerked it frantically. It was sealed shut. He heard Nora approaching.

"Now I'm really going to need that blood, Louis. And maybe a lot more."

Sharren called back. She was enraged. The *Xolotl* captain sent word the ship was leaving Culsans. The plan for a smuggling hub was a complete debacle. Quary had not answered his summons. Sharren called his home directly and used an arsenal of communication hacks to hide herself and the direct contact. She only wanted to tell him his contract was terminated, and soon, he would be as well. She was too late.

Her hologram displayed the interior of Nora and Quary's living space. The former Nora and now murderous zombie looked back at Sharren with three eyes. The one eye not her own dropped from her mouth. Sharren saw why the implanted com device had failed. Small, filament loops sat lodged in the zombie's teeth. The former doctor had found the hidden receiver in Quary's brain. Sharren realized Culsans was lost to her syndicate and the living. She wondered if her life would become the price of failure. Sharren wished she had not sent a ship from an actual plague system. It was supposed to be sterilized, but fellow criminals sometimes lie. Trusting them was another questionable choice. All choices create paths and potential fates. Life. Death. Undead.

Being undead was similar to a so-called quantum state when one state or another exists together in a single frame of spacetime. Both states coexist until an observation determines one, definite state inside the frame. A physicist named Schrödinger once created a thought problem threatening an imaginary cat with a life/death, sort of zombie fate until an experimental box was opened and the cat was observed. At that moment, the cat was certainly dead or certainly alive. The moment of observation decides the flow of events beyond feline fates. Nora mentioned the living/dead cat to Koller as she walked to the *Xolotl's* cargo bin. Her acts at the opened bin decided the fate of an entire world. Different choices in a single moment create different paths, different fates.

In another set of events, Nora reached the cargo bin. Its lid retracted automatically. A brief gust of cooler air escaped the empty box. She took a moment of curios thought. Then she placed a box from the pallet inside the left corner of the bin. The weight tipped the bin, slightly. Strong sunlight bathed all of the metal box's interior. A small creature leapt out. It landed on the hot, umber ground. The sudden heat caused it to collapse. It was a jimp. They were small, dark grey creatures human ships had spread to several terraformed planets. Its eight, stubby legs and thick, spring tail visibly withered in the heat. Nora's impulse was to save it. It was an innocent, little creature. It was also a creature with teeth from a potentially infected plague ship. She watched it burn between the hot ground and searing sunlight.

"Everything okay?" Koller called from behind her. She nodded affirmation to herself, and then turned and waved to Koller.

Quary took a deep breath. He walked into the living area he still shared with Nora. He saw Nora asleep on the couch in a uni-shirt that had seen better days. He was surprised her mission with Koller was already over. He walked to his bedroom, and then thought he should have draped a blanket over his supposed wife. Then another thought dawned in his partially franchised brain. He returned to Nora. He stood by the couch and watched her sleep with pointed interest. He wondered if she ever wrote down her access codes to the colony servers. If he could find them, he could steal them. The medical network connected to almost everyone. It would be a great venue for leaked zombie files.

Sharren screamed. It was a cry of frustration. Her fists hit her grav-net keeping her auburn hair from losing shape in low gravity. Quary's time was up, and now maybe her time as well. Quary's physician wife caught him stealing her access codes and put him in the hospital. His injuries were not severe. The felony charges would be. Then the *Xolotl* captain sent word he was already off Culsans and heading for deep space. The colony would not be a smuggling hub. Sharren feared she might not be alive for long. Yet the method of her death would not come as she imagined. A tone from her hatch signaled a visitor. The hologram showed her favorite purser and occasional lover on the luxury starship *Mìngyùn*. He hovered by her door in the passageway. She was in no mood for a visit in his official capacity or for after-hours duties.

"What?" Sharren shouted as her cabin door slid open.

"Well, hi." The purser jerked back. "Look, things are falling apart fast. So stay in your cabin. Don't leave if you want a chance to live."

"Why?" Sharren's shout was even louder but tinged with fear.

"Vermin problem in the galley--our kitchen. Jimps." The pursuer explained.

"Vermin? I eat from that kitchen!" Sharren's fists clenched and she floated up slightly in the low gravity.

"Yeah. The problem is now the galley crew. Actually, it's a problem with a lot of the passengers. Plague. Zombies. You've seen the news."

"What--here?" Sharren's rage burned to shock as she began to grasp the magnitude of the pursuer's warning.

"Yup. Stay sealed. I'll come back if I can."

"To hell with that!" Sharren gripped the border of her doorway and set herself on the floor. "I'm getting off this chum ship!"

Screams and hissing echoed down from the passageway.

"I don't think so." The purser said. He hit a panel outside the door and it slid shut with speed.

Sharren screamed at him. She punched her own controls, but they were now locked out. She then repeatedly slammed her fists against the door. Once exhausted, she leaned against it. She suddenly felt someone--something beating against the door from the other side. Even through the thick metal and thumps, she was sure she could hear hissing and bony fingers scratching the door out in the hall. She allowed herself to float away from the door, and hoped it would never open.

"I repeat: we are a plague ship!" The voice of the *Mìngyùn* captain shouted over holographic images of torn corpses. They wore rags of fine clothes and slowly began to stir in a cloud of blood drifting in a passageway. "I am nearing Culsans with no course control. Fire your warheads, Culsans. Do not let us crash!"

"I understand, *Mìngyùn*." Koller said in the meeting dome.

He dropped his head from the hologram overhead. Koller knew the scale of the cruise ship was four times that of the *Xolotl* in size and potential crew and passengers. This time, the plague was confirmed. More live images showed the zombie onslaught throughout the decks. The committee stood beside Koller and stayed silent. Koller looked up and caught the gaze of Zhul who nodded with understanding of the decision to come.

"We will comply with your request, *Mìngyùn*" Koller said. "I only wish--"

Koller stopped talking when he heard only the hum of an open com and distant screaming. He reached over to the launch key projecting the red button. Nora reached out her hand and rested it on top of Koller's hand. Together they pressed down.

LIVE FEED

Off. The view was black. A battery icon flashed for a quarter second. The camera came on with a quick shot of the clear night sky pinched by aging skyscrapers. The audio of distant screaming sounded as the camera slashed down. It stopped to frame a standard urban male holding a fixed smile and cordless microphone. A glint from the streetlamps ran along the reporter's dark-dyed, brushed-back hair. Behind him, empty cabs and cars sat in a static traffic jam of abandoned vehicles. Beyond them flashed neon and scrolling LED signs along the street. The signs lit storefronts and small, seedy theaters with colors brighter than the reporter's light blue blazer and metallic-orange tie. Most signs advertised entertainment not typically seen on a newscast.

"I'm Ramone Ammatie, live in the red light district near the city's heart where red blood and civilian hearts have spattered the already debauched zone as a reported, yes, zombie outbreak has occurred. This one looks real. The body count is said--"

Louder and closer screaming diverted Ammatie's view from the camera to a theater marked in flashing red *All Nude 4 You Revue!*

"We may be close!" Ammatie announced with a well-rehearsed tone blending concern and aplomb. "Too close! It seems Armageddon is right upon us!"

The camera zoomed in on the theater. A stampede of strippers in various tight costumes and many only in glittering makeup charged out the swinging doors, into the street, and ran by Ammatie and the refocusing camera. Bare skin raced by in the restricted, chopping gait of high heels and at the speed of bare feet running on jagged pavement. Fear spurred them all. The charge of screaming and undulating entertainers ended. The camera operator resisted following their flight from the dorsal perspective. The lens stayed focused on Ammatie. His focus was still on the naked mob.

A finger snap sounded from behind the camera. Ammatie straightened and snapped his attention back to the camera lens.

"It seems quiet, here, now. The dangers, and a lot else, has passed. We can only hope our world stays quiet. At peace. And that zombies stay dead. I'm Ramone Ammatie. Butt--back to you in News Base One."

"Clear!" The shouted word came from behind the camera. The image lowered but kept Ammatie in frame. The photographer held the camera to his side, but kept recording.

"News Base One," Ammatie shook his head. "Who comes up with that crap? Was it you, Ronnie?"

"Nope," cameraman Ronnie answered as he jostled the camera.

From its new angle, the lens now fit in more of Ammatie's body but lost the top of his head. His light blue blazer draped over worn and faded jeans. Their ragged cuffs draped across battered, brown leather shoes. Ammatie looked back in the direction of the stripper stampede and laughed.

"I tell you, Ronnie-oh buddy, that was the shot of my life. I can just see the view-toob royalties. I might retire!"

"It's my shot," Ronnie said, still unseen. "I got it."

Ammatie rocked his visible head and tossed the microphone behind the camera. "Oh, yeah. And you're the one everyone will remember. Sorry, Ronnie. It's my face in front of the lens. Besides, my contract says if I appear, I get the internet cut."

"You think the world will last long enough to cash in?" Ronnie asked. A fumbling of fingers against the mic created a loud drum-like noise for a second.

"What, you think some zombies can really bring on an apocalypse?" Ammatie asked in a mocking tone. "Get real."

Suddenly more screams echoed down from beyond the abandoned cars. The sound of chain saws slashed through the shrieking.

"Chain saws! Chain saws!" Ammatie yelled as he stretched to look over the cars and down the street. "Since when do zombies use chain saws?"

The burring roar of the chain saws and shrieking grew close. The camera dropped. Only Ammatie's brown shoes were now in focus.

"Ronnie, are you--?" Ammatie started to say. His shoes turned as he looked for his missing photographer. "Ronnie! Ronnie you chicken-ass prick! Get back here!"

The heels of Ammatie's battered brown shoes backed against a car tire as combat boots topped by ripped cargo pants stomped into the ground-level shot. Ammatie screamed. The loud burring sound cut it off. Ammatie's head fell in a muted *splat* in front of his leather shoes and the camera lens. The expression of a scream twisted his red-flecked face. The burring became a sputter and then quiet.

Ammatie's head left the shot as someone lifted the camera. The focus worked to adjust for a clear image of a man's face painted as a skull depicted with clinging patches of dead flesh. The new camera user stepped back to frame the large man with zombie makeup. He wore ripped clothes, the cargo pants, and brandished a bloody chain saw.

"We are the corps of the undead to come!" The large, ersatz zombie bellowed. "We are the living who bring the prophesized zombie plague to life! Join us in our quest to cleanse this world with gore and begin an afterlife of undead justice on Earth!"

The fake zombie pitched his painted head toward the lens as if to see if anyone might have heard his insane tirade.

"Man! He is the best one of us, yet!" The shouts came from behind the camera. The shot moved to locate the reason for the remarks. "And he's got friends!"

The camera swung and then stopped to show a quickly shambling group of what appeared to be walking cadavers closing on the camera. Their teeth appeared bared, until the focus showed there were no lips over their jaws, and little skin on their faces. Wet, dark red dripped from the bared teeth and bony fingers held like claws.

"Whoa!" The large, fake zombie exclaimed.

The camera turned to back him for an instant before dropping back to the street. The shot then only framed the man's combat boots.

"Lester!" The large man's voice sounded from above the camera. "Lester, do you think--! Lester?"

The end of the chainsaw blade dropped into focus as the sound of its starter chord being pulled frantically hit the mic. A foot kicked the camera. The angle of the shot pointed up and showed the large man as he swung his stalled chain saw at a mass of true zombies. He struck only a few as they swarmed him. He screamed as the undead mob slammed him into the ground with jaws biting his bulky flesh. Kicking boots next to Ammatie's corpse flicked red flecks on the camera. The man's high-pitched shrieks became gurgling and ended as his boots fell still. Zombie hands pulled them out of frame.

A hissing sounded. A zombie face came into close focus. Its eyes threatened to pop free and roll down its skinless cheekbones as they stared into the lens. The zombie's eyes rolled to the right and focused on something. The zombie snatched up Ammatie's head and ran out of frame.

The camera autofocused on the edge of a car roof and the night sky beyond it. The microphone caught distant screaming. The image flashed into a blur of colors as the camera suddenly flipped end over end. There was a sound of breaking glass. Then, no sound. Then, dead black.

ACID TO ASHES

The planet was named Kolibri. It was an ancient Russian word for hummingbird. Ennis Tate had never seen a living hummingbird. He learned of the small, swift birds when researching the name of the world. So far as was known, no flying creatures ever evolved on Kolibri. However, the shimmer of light on the planet's mineral rock reminded one geologist of sunlight glinting off a hummingbird's colorful feathers. To Ennis, the comparison seemed a paradox. Wings versus rocks. Now he found himself digging into the planet's surface instead of flying over it with speed. And speed was as necessary as caution as he dug. He aided a plan that might save the latest humans living on Kolibri. The first colonists were long dead.

Ennis took a second to rest. His stillness allowed him to feel the sweat against his skin inside his thermal suit. Its wick function had failed. Again. He knew his love, Hala Muer, regarded his quick pause with apprehension. He felt her hover at the edge of the excavation. Ennis leaned on his shovel. The digging tool was unchanged since its invention. However, since the first shovel hit soil, humans had built ships to sail oceans and eventually the gulf between planets and then between stars. Some of those swift, massive ships sent humans to distant worlds, such as Kolibri. Along with atmospheric reactors and engineered lifeforms, they brought shovels. Like invention and exploration, backaches seemed a perpetual human experience.

If ships and other machines did much for humankind, it was easing toil. Yet humans always ached first. Kolibri's original colonists had dug out a long chamber nearby with small tools anticipating an easier life when heavy lifting equipment came.

Those machines never arrived. All the first colonists were dead before those machines entered cargo ships. And now Ennis labored while facing similar doom.

Ennis pushed the shovel blade into the cold soil. He dug deeper into a grave. For the people of Kolibri's first, failed colony, the most beautiful site they knew became the spot to bury their dead. It was near the site where the mineral rock first dazzled human eyes. Ice from compressed layers of snow now covered the makeshift cemetery. That snow fell long ago in the reengineered atmosphere. Thankfully, Ennis had a small slash-hoe excavator that tore up the ice and rock from the grave's top layers. Now the articulated arm of the automated digger sat still. The rest was up to Ennis. Nearing the body required a more careful approach.

Ennis dug toward a fellow pioneer. Like Ennis, it might be straining against the packed soil. Unlike Ennis, the pioneer at the bottom was dead. It was a zombie. Ennis knew this, but kept digging. Graves were not an efficient means to dispose of bodies. The first colonists used graves to spare fuel for incinerating moving corpses. The weight of compressed soil immobilized potential zombies, and saved plague samples to make a cure. The cure never came. More zombies rose than people could burn or bury. Kolibri fell to the dead.

The failure of Kolibri's first colony was public knowledge in most systems. The fact a zombie outbreak killed the colonists was kept secret by omitting that important, horrific detail. Quarantines were expensive to enact and maintain. Kolibri orbited an outer-rim star. Distance seemed a good shield from infection and liability. Years and several omissions and deletions later, the horror was forgotten. Then Ennis and a mass of ignorant and eager new settlers landed on the far world. Soon after they arrived, the truth attacked with bared teeth. The second wave of pioneers had fewer resources than the first colonists did. Some of them rose up to kill again. Fighting the plague horde seemed another doomed effort. Ennis knew if they didn't fight, they might as well dig their own graves. He strained his shoulders and back to find a way to live. Still, the aches and fatigue made odd ideas rise in his head.

"Humanity--" Ennis started to speak, but took a deep breath. The cold, dry air felt knife-like in his lungs.

Ennis looked to his left and up at the expectant face of his partner in grave robbing, Hala. She stood by the edge of the grave and held a massive power drill modified with cylinders and tubing. The same wind that tussled her shoulder-length, black hair had reddened her typically pale and delicate face.

"We build interstellar ships," Ennis said as he came back to his thought. "We reengineer whole planets. But with all that technical power, with all my degrees, I'm still doing brute labor with a shovel. People along trillions of miles and generations of inventors are either laughing at me or cursing my fate."

"You'll scream curses if you dig too deep and expose the corpse!" Hala said and looked down into the grave.

"This one was buried deep," Ennis took another breath.

"That's why I chose it," Hala nodded. "The weight of the dirt keeps it down. Oddly enough, the next subject we need, the clean body, is in a much shallower grave."

"Why is that odd?" Ennis asked and stretched.

"It's a later grave when there were more zombies. I guess as the plague spread and survivors were fewer, the graves weren't dug as deep."

"Less enthusiasm for preserving inert and incubating bodies," Ennis added. "I guess people still died from things other than the plague or zombies."

"Eventually, there were no graves," Hala sighed. "Official reports said the first colonists died of starvation. They died as zombie food."

"And then zombies ate zombies until the last of them dried out on a world as cold as deep space." Ennis shuddered. At first it was from a cold gust down his suit's neck opening that chilled his sweaty back. His second shudder was from looking out across the icy plain beyond the cemetery and imagining what might shamble towards them. He calmed his nerves, but looked at the ground under his feet with more caution.

"Desiccated," Hala spoke the specific term for moisture loss. "And we brought them into our domes thinking they were only mummified relics to study."

Neither Hala nor Ennis finished the story of the infection and horror.

"Just get to four meters," Hala said. "We can shoot the probe through the rest of the soil and collected a sample. The corpse will stay locked under the mass of packed dirt, even if it's really hungry."

"Yep," Ennis said and hoisted another shovel full to his right. "And then we inject the acid."

"Yes," Hala looked at her drill-probe. "The acid will dissolve the corpse and the plague."

"I hope it works on a larger scale, with your predator."

"It will." Hala nodded with confidence. "I'm a good engineer."

"And the most beautiful woman on Kolibri," Ennis said and looked back at her and winked.

"You say that because I'm your only woman on Kolibri."

"Forget polyandry. I don't need more than one. So long as it's you." Ennis looked up and down Hala's body and nodded approval, even though she wore a heavy thermal suit.

"Geez. Then for the sake of sparing other women fatigue, I'll keep you. Now, dig my mighty man."

"Your wish--" Ennis said only half the cliché. He smiled and continued digging, carefully. He considered the odd state of being happy during a colonial apocalypse while digging in a zombie's grave. Life on a pioneer colony life was supposed to be hard, but not lethal. If Hala's predator failed, Kolibri would see a second human extinction. No one on the planet had a hope of rescue before being torn apart.

Hala caught a glimpse of Kolibri's sapphire moon through a break in the canopy of pale clouds. The moon's color was a shock among the white layers drifting above an expanse of compacted snow beyond the cemetery. The orbiting world might as well be in another solar system. Unlike most recent colonial endeavors, Kolibri's second immigrants were on their own. Hala, Ennis, and the multitude that now lived on Kolibri were wildcatters. There were no obstacles to their attempts to make the planet habitable. However, they had no off-world help or official sanction. No corporations or governments sent supply ships or offered open lines of credit. A ship sitting on emergency standby was simply too expensive. If they made Kolibri viable, interstellar interests would reach out. However, for once a colony's people would control their planet's destiny.

Success would place their names in history. Failure meant oblivion and death. They would be dead. Hala's predator would stalk the walking corpses to prevent that. Ennis shook his head to rid it of gathered sweat, fallen dirt, and any more absurd paradoxes.

Ennis felt alone. There was a milling, murmuring mass of living people behind him, but Hala was gone. She had taken her assistant to field test her zombie predator. As an atmospheric engineer, Ennis still proved useful in the solid matters of shovel and dirt. Now he served Hala better by attending the live field test viewing with technicians and officials. Ennis could answer questions, and if necessary defend Hala's work. He was better at politics than Hala. She would praise or snipe at him for that in their private life. In public, she knew it served their mutual causes against colonial leaders looking to cut resources.

Ennis sat at a table near a screen dropped from the ceiling of a small, circular mall built from prefabricated sections for interstellar franchises that never came. The failed gallery of shops had the best power supply system of the surviving structures. The spaces never filled with stores quickly became offices for the second colony's bureaucrats. Their departments multiplied faster than the colonists did. Kolibri's head bureaucrat, Certis Ozek, sat to Ennis' right. The colony elected Ozek Chief Administrator when no one else ran for the position. His pioneer zeal seemed to sag lower than the skin beneath his eyes after the other wildcat colonists showed as much awe for his position as they did in wanting to run for it.

Off to the far left was Aja Calford, the self-appointed Chief of Technology Integration and Reused Frustration. Her short, dark red hair shimmered with phosphorescence that mimicked the effect of Kolibri's namesake bird and/or rock. Calford hunched at her own, small screen rolling with data. Behind it sat a small forest of spike antennae for wireless signals and one to impale her rolled sandwich.

The large screen displayed a slope of rough, faint red and near translucent rocks and boulders. Larger rocks sheltered patches of snow. The slope descended to a narrow valley. The view was slightly stretched concave from the camera focused through the clear dome of a Terrestrial Excursion Suit's helmet. Occasionally the view jerked and grunts peppered the audio.

"This screen is only projects two-dimensions?" Ozek asked with a look of abhorrence.

"Yep. To save energy." Calford said with her characteristic flippant tone and without looking at Ozek. She snatched up her sandwich and jabbed it at the screen before biting off and end but still talking over her chewing. "Other than that, we've pulled out all the stops. Best TE suits. Best coms. All top of the line."

"At least top of what we have," the reply came from the screen. Hala's assistant, Shiro Peters, offered the comment as he followed the slope down to the valley with his trek displayed on the screen. Peters stopped at the bottom of the slope. Hala appeared from behind him. Her head and hands were exposed with her suit's gloves and helmet slung in a net on her back. A thin, black band wrapped the top of her head. She dragged a clear body bag containing a partially decomposed human corpse. Ennis recognized the plague-free body he and Hala retrieved from the cemetery. Hala lowered the bagged corpse flat on the ground.

"You let Hala haul the corpse?" Ennis frowned at the screen.

"Yeah, why?" Peters' voice breathed from the speaker.

"Petes! She's like half your size!" Calford snapped.

"Well, she's the boss!" Peters retorted. "I do what she says."

"Most times," Ennis added with a groan.

"Dr. Muer, do you read us?" Ozek spoke to the screen.

"One second," Calford jabbed her bitten sandwich at Ozek as she watched her small screen. "The suit of our resident Hercules, Shiro, will make the connection."

"Okay," Hala's voice said as Peter's camera showed her standing before him in her TE suit. Her headband held a small lens at the center of her forehead that beaded with sweat. "I'm here."

"Are you okay?" Ennis asked. "That body wasn't light."

"No sweat, Enny." Hala said and wiped her forehead while smiling. "Actually, a lot of sweat. But, hey, whatever."

"So your flying monster will eat zombies?" Ozek asked.

"My predator doesn't really eat anything," Hala spoke between taking breaths. "It causes rapid tissue dissolution of its targets. Its prey."

"Just tell them it burns up zombies," Peters said.

"But it actually--" Hala paused. She shrugged. "Yeah, okay. It burns up zombies, and the plague within them."

"At least we hope it will," Peters droned.

His attention and the camera feed drifted to the motionless corpse in the bag. Half of Hala's face stayed in view.

"It will," Hala smiled and leaned to look straight into the camera in Peters' helmet.

In the mall, Ennis smiled back.

"The acid works," Hala continued. "The cloud matrix will hold it stable."

"The predator is an acid cloud?" Ozek asked and cocked his head.

"Yes. A very complex one." Hala answered.

Ozek opened his mouth and paused to form a question.

"It's a sort of gaseous robot," Ennis offered. "The acid is held inside a cloud by nanoscopic field generators that act as the cloud's nuclei."

"The cloud's glue, or--" Calford began.

"That much I get." Ozek held up his hand to Calford and spoke again to the screen. "This technology seems very innovative."

"For this rock, yeah." Peters' voice piped in.

"The field generators are about the only cutting-edge tech we have." Calford said.

"They were originally designed as rescue tech," Ennis added. "The nano-swarm was originally designed to trap and hold gases from a ruptured suit--breathable air. The flying nanos seek and envelop a person with a suit breach. Then they would hold the person in a safe air pocket until rescue."

"So it seeks people." Ozek observed.

"Originally, yes," Hala said, onscreen. "And with a programming tweak, it now seeks zombies."

"Zombies and people?" Ozek asked.

"No," Hala said and brought her hands up to her mouth to blow warm breath on them. She then rubbed her hands together. "I deleted that part. It seeks human forms, but only ones infected with plague markers."

"These nanos can scan tissues that deep, being that small?" Ozek asked.

"I amplified their sensors and uploaded the new programming to its satellite A.I." Hala answered and then rubbed her red nose.

"We have a working satellite?" Ozek's voice rose at the thought.

"For this system, yeah." Calford said

"We made it a priority for Hala's zombie weapon." Ennis said with a reassuring tone.

"Yep. With the undead apocalypse and all." Calford said and bit off more of her sandwich.

"Why wasn't I informed?" Ozek grated and fixed a stare on Calford.

Calford shrugged and chewed. "Oops. But, now you know. Neat, eh?"

"So," Hala cut in. "To properly test it, we need a zombie. Peters is holing a sample of the plague."

Peters' gloved hand lifted a small, metal cylinder in front of his helmet to bring it into camera view.

"We will inject the sample into this cadaver bag." Hala said. "It should infect the clean body. And then we will have our test zombie."

"And then kill it." Peters quickly added.

"Yes, Shiro. We will kill it." Hala's eyes left her straight look into the camera to glance at Peters' eyes. "Rest easy. Now, let's do it. Shiro?"

"Um. Okay." Peters spoke but the cylinder held in his glove and his whole body did not move.

Hala took the sample. "Fine. I have the finer grip, anyway."

Peters at the test site joined Ennis at the mall in taking an audible, deep breath as Hala knelt down and pressed the cylinder against the head of the corpse. A slight *pop* sounded as the contagion injected through the bag and into the body.

90

"Well, I'm surprised" Hala said as she stood up.

"It's not working?" Peters squealed.

"No," Hala looked at Peters. "That you're still standing there."

At Hala's feet, the corpse lurched. Peters yipped. The view spun as he turned and then bolted up the rocky slope with Hala laughing on the speaker.

"Okay. Fun is fun," Ennis said. "But now you have--"

"An active zombie." Hala finished over the speaker as the view still showed Peters swift ascent. "Relax Enny."

"I'll relax when you put you gloves & helmet on." Ennis said. He looked over at Calford.

Calford nodded. "I'll switch feeds, now."

The view jumped to the camera on Hala's headband. Her cold-reddened fingers of her left hand tapping holographic keys projected from a small, black tablet in her right hand. She had taken several steps up the slope. Beyond the edge of her tablet, the new zombie was visible as it thrashed violently to rip itself out of the clear bag.

"I told you I need my fingers and eyes," Hala said. "We haven't upgraded the suits, and my link can't scan my retinas and DNA through them."

"Then turn on the predator and run," Ennis said.

"It's already coming," Hala said. She looked up and the video feed showed Peters at the crest. "Look northeast, Shiro."

A scarlet nimbus rose over the crest, easily visible against the white clouds overhead. It floated down toward the valley and became nearly invisible against the similar red hue of the glassy rocks. Scarlet flashed over the patches of snow as Hala's predator headed towards her.

"It's vector--!" Calford began to shout.

"I see it!" Hala said and began to move. She turned to look at the zombie. It was nearly on top of her.

"Geez!" Ennis yelled over the shouts of everyone at the mall.

Hala sprinted backwards on her heels. Rocks pelted the zombies head. Its dead face and sunken eyes still expressed outrage at the annoying attack thrown by Peters. Its face then began to blister, suddenly colored scarlet. The zombie thrashed at air as it burned.

"It's working!" Hala cheered.

"Oh, geez." Calford said while looking at her own screen.

Ennis glanced at Calford and back to the burning zombie. He looked back at her when he noticed her intense stare at her screen.

"What?" Ennis asked.

"I've had a drone circling," Calford said. "I didn't switch on the feed to save its battery life, but its sensors just detected motion."

"Motion? What motion?" Ennis barked.

Calford's only answer was a look of dread. She kept staring at Ennis as she tapped her screen. The large display switched from the now skeletal zombie as its right arm fell away and it collapsed into a gruesome pile among the rocks. The new view from the drone was more horrifying. A mass of other corpses marched up the narrow valley.

"They're maybe fifty--" Calford started

"Hala!" Ennis screamed at the large screen as he bolted to standing. "There's a horde on your tail! Get out of there! Hala, run!"

"Stay calm Enny," Hala voice still came through the speaker. "We have the--ow."

"Oh, no." Ennis said almost inaudibly as he stood.

"I see a fault," Calford said.

"I'm not getting a ping from the nanos new programming." Hala panted. "They're not showing the new code."

"Hala, put on your gloves and helmet!" Ennis screamed. "The nanos will think you're suit is breeched! Do it Hala!"

"Okay. That's it!" Ozek also stood. "Get back to your transport and leave the area."

"Hala, do what he says!" Ennis yelled.

The drone images showed the zombie horde plodding through the narrow valley and obviously closing on Hala and Peters. Calford switched the view back to Hala's headband camera. She was ripping open the net holding her helmet and gloves.

"Cally--aah! Ow!" Hala spoke as she fumbled with her equipment. A smoke appeared to rise from her exposed hands. "Can you assist?"

"Been trying, Hal!" Calford answered as she tapped her screen. "The new code is active in the satellite, but not operant in the nanos."

"Retrans!" Hala screamed in pain.

"Okay, but run Hal!"

"Just run!" Ennis shouted

"I don't understand!" Hala shouted. "The connection tests worked. We showed a link between the nano system and satellite at base. This can't happen!"

"Something hit the system since then," Calford said with a tone of dread but kept tapping at her screen as columns of code swirled on it.

"What?" Ozek asked

"The satellite got hit with high rad. Something ionized, or just broke." Calford answered.

"Oh, no. Oh, no." Ennis felt his own life drain as he watched Hala's camera feed.

"Aaaaaaaaaaaaaaah!" Hala screamed. Her bloody, pocked hands brought her helmet over her head, but it slid to the side. The view suddenly lurched downward as she fell to the glassy rocks. The helmet bounced from view. Her bleeding right hand reached around as its remaining skin blistered and burned in the scarlet nimbus.

Peters' boots appeared in the image. The boots shifted backwards as suddenly as he stopped.

"Peters! Help her!" Ennis cried out with desperation cracking his voice.

"There's nothing to help!" Peters screeched. "She's gone! Oh, crud! It's on me!"

"Hold on, Petes!" Calford called out.

Calford switched the view back to Peters' camera. The view flew in all direction as Peters panicked on the slope as he realized he was in the predator cloud. In the mall, Ennis turned and bolted into the shocked crowd behind him.

"Ennis! Don't!" Ozek called out. "You can't save her! Stop him!"

The gathered crowd grabbed Ennis as he fought to escape but the grasping arms were too many. His resistance became static thrashing.

"Petes! Don't panic!" Calford called to Peters as the main screen still showed him careening on the slope but only broken static now came over the speaker. "You have a suit on. Petes--oh."

Calford and the mall gathered saw bony, burning hands swarm over the clear dome of Peters' helmet. The zombie horde was at the site. The convex images became clear as Peters' helmet was torn off. The camera fell among body parts being eaten away by the predator's acid nimbus. It worked well to kill the zombies, and everything else within its red cloud.

There was silence as Calford cut the camera feed. The gathered heard the sound of Ennis taking a deep breath into his lungs and then screamed Hala's name for the last time.

"Ennis, I'm sorry Hala's dead." The words came from Kolibri's medical chief, Indra Kris. She sat next to Ennis with a sympathetic expression, but observed Ennis for signs of a complete mental breakdown.

Ennis said nothing. He continued staring across the table. An hour had passed, but Ennis had never left the mall. Now Ozek and a few officials gathered for a briefing with Calford who returned to her screen and bank of antennas.

"Low deuce, it failed." Ozek said.

"Nope," Calford countered. "The predator cloud didn't fail. Those zombies we saw are gone. Burned beyond ashes. Just gone. Bad thing is--yeah." Calford wiped away tears.

"We lost two excellent engineers," Ozek finished. He looked at the seemingly catatonic Ennis. "Good people."

"But if the cloud works, how do we control it?" Kris asked.

"Um. So far, we don't." Calford said with a wavering voice.

"What does that mean?" Ozek shrugged.

"Like I said, we--" Calford began. Ennis cut off her reply.

"It means there are now two threats to the people on Kolibri," Ennis droned. "Zombies, and the cloud."

"And we don't have much in the way of network to tell everyone not clustered here at Base One." Kris said.

"Warn who you can. As fast as you can." Ennis said.

The table was silent. After a second, Ennis gave a hard glance over at Calford.

"Right. On it." Calford began tapping her screen.

"So, why did the zombies still attack Peters?" Ozek asked. "He was in the cloud."

"They burn, but they don't care." Ennis said in low tones.

"They don't realize their being destroyed." Kris added.

"*They* don't." Ennis said.

The table fell silent again, but for the sound of Calford's tapping.

The ancient concept of a radio towers served to link remote colony locations until reliable satellites again served Kolibri. The time-tested system had the same limitations on any world. Especially if the precious receiver was switched off, or dropped inside a slash-hoe bucket and ignored. The radio for a remote geology crew suffered such a fate. Its flashing red light went unnoticed. Not hearing Calford's warning potentially sealed the crew's fate.

The unit of four assigned surface duty wore suits unique to their base. The suits originally protected starship engine crews. They were thicker from interwoven radiation shielding, but had not been tested against ravenous zombies. The entire crew felt safe from a zombie assault. Their base cut into a mesa that filled their northern perimeter. They could easily spot a horde trudging over a vast plain to the southeast or around a stout mountain to the southwest. Once inside, a massive door sculpted from fused rock would seal off an attack.

The g-dar unit rolled ahead of the crew on knobby wheels. Their leader, Deese, waited for the battery to die. Two of his crew, Goya and Whaling, served as lookouts while the g-dar's sensor probed for radiation traces indicating fissionable elements useful for reactors on older classes of starship. The base was part of a speculators consortium that joined the wildcat colonists to seek wealth or just a day's pay. If they found a sealed source of water, that would be fine, too. Clean water was valuable as a plague-free beverage or for cheap muon generation. The crew's fourth member, Lyst, worked off to the side with his back to his fellow crewmembers. He probed the ground in the oldest manner known to humankind. He hit it with a hammer.

Goya spotted something. "That is some weird weather."

A cloud like red gossamer came towards the mesa over the plain.

"Maybe some zombies let go from their colons," Deese said after he glanced up.

"So you're saying zombies make gas?" Goya asked.

"Well, they eat. Why not?" Deese replied.

"They eat us," Whaling offered.

"So you're saying that's our fellow colonists, my aunt Vesta, spewed out a zombie's ass?" Goya asked and watched the red cloud come closer.

"I'd say it in more technical terms," Deese said. "Like reanimate gaseous release to atmosphere, but, essentially, yeah."

"Huh. Zombie farts," Goya said. "Can't be good."

"All part of nature. Or un-nature. Whatever." Deese shrugged looking at the g-dar's screen.

"It's getting here fast," Goya observed. "Coming right at us."

"It'll blow through," Deese said. "We got our suits on, anyway."

The red cloud overtook them.

"What the--!" Whaling stopped and looked up into the cloud. "It's staying and hovering around us!"

"Deese!" Goya yelled while looking at his arms. "The outside of our suits shouldn't be bubbling!"

"Crap!" Deese looked at his own blistering arms. "Damn alien feck! Get inside!"

The three bolted to their base in the mesa. Whaling slowed and turned.

"Lyst! Lyst!" Whaling called to the fourth crewmember. "Come on!"

Lyst stood and turned. His faceplate was slid open. His face was burning away. He dropped his hammer and then fell back to the ground. The three reached the sensors for the massive door sealing the base. The door slowly rolled open. A mass of zombies ran out. The geology crew was safe from an outside horde, but not an internal infection. The plague had spread quickly during their shift outside. The three men slid to a stop and ran away from the monsters who hours before were coworkers.

"The bore unit cab!" Goya shouted over sharp breaths. "Run!"

"This damn cloud is still on us!" Whaling shouted.

"And we're still burning!" Goya also yelled.

"Hey, the cloud fried, Lyst. It's frying the zombies." Deese pitched his head to look behind them. "Slow up!"

"What?" The two men shrieked.

"The freaks have no suits!" Deese yelled, and then slowed his pace. "They'll burn before the cloud burns through our suits! Just stay ahead of the--geez!"

The faceless Lyst zombie tackled Deese. Whaling and Goya pulled and punched him off their crew leader. The other zombies caught up and bit at them savagely. The men fought back. As Deese said, the zombies' skin burned faster than the suits' surface. The men beat off their rapidly disintegrating attackers. Hala's predator finally acted to save lives. Piles of skin, bones, and ruptured organs splattered the ground. Tissue and dead blood bubbled off the second layer of the suits as the men turned to run to the large boring machine. The cloud stayed with the undead as more ran from the mesa door. Deese, Whaling, and Goya panted and ran for the boring machines cab.

"We've got a deep blue moon, but not a deep blue sea." Calford slowly swayed in her chair staring at incoming reports. "But we are stuck between the acid cloud and a zombie sea. I'll take the devil, whatever the hell he was supposed to be."

Ennis looked at Calford. She was oblivious to the paradox of her last statement. Hell was still a swear word, but the place of its origin and its ruler were forgotten to many. Time had worn away some myths, but not the cultural phrases created from them. Ennis recalled the devil was typically portrayed in red. Ennis now hated red.

"We still have no way to shut it down?" Ozek said as he took his seat at the mall table.

"We? Nope. You?" Calford replied with staccato sarcasm.

"What about our large population centers?" Kris asked as she also sat down. "Base Two? Their mostly in tents!"

"The cloud can't be everywhere, but where it hits the survivors are crammed into underground chambers to escape," Calford answered. "But then they're an isolated buffet if found by the zombies."

"You can't run. You can't hide." Kris said and shook her head.

"Yeah. Us too." Calford added. "Cremated alive by acid cloud, or human tartare for the undead."

Ozek slapped his hands on the table. "Still no codes, no shut off signal?"

"Hala had kept the codes in her mind," Ennis breathed.

"And if anything of her exists, it's a shuffling scar. No mind. No hope of helping us." Calford said, and in the same breath she turned to Ennis. "Sorry, En. I get going and get carried away."

"I noticed. I don't care."

"Okay." Calford raised her eyebrows. "Myself and others are hacking as fast as we can. But you need a machine to hack, and links to the satellite are spotty. Odd thing is--other than me--Hala's cloud is reducing zombie numbers."

"And maybe to manageable levels, if we curtail further spread of the plague." Kris added.

"But we can't act on this because anyone outside without a suit is fried!" Ozek snapped.

"And the temperature and atmosphere are stabilized, so few people have a TE suits, just the crappy thermal ones." Ennis droned.

"Yep." Calford said.

"One of the reasons the plague spread as quickly as it did." Kris mused.

"Yep." Ennis said and stared at the now blank screen before the table.

"We'd better do something!" Ozek shouted. "Can't we just blow this cloud monster apart?"

"With what? A fan?" Calford quipped and tossed up her hands.

"A bomb. With you strapped to it!" Ozek said.

"Ouch! fearless leader!" Calford replied. "I'm just pointing out facts. Big, fat fact for you is we have no big, fat bombs with enough force. With or without my wit boosting the yield."

"If we get enough charges from the tunneling crews--!" Ozek began.

"And who in the hell is going to do that in a company issued jumper? Or maybe a pair of shorts and polo shirt? They're still popular with your generation." Calford snapped. Her snide attitude was becoming quickly one of anger.

"Calford--!" Ozek yelled and stood.

"Both of you, shut up!" Ennis barked.

He slowly stood up. Kris stayed silent as a murmur rolled from the flanking offices. Calford and Ozek shared a moment of unity in their shocked stares at Ennis.

"I know how kill it," Ennis said. "It's been killing itself in all the attacks on us and the zombies. We just need to accelerate its death."

"Right. To exhaust the acid," Kris nodded seeing what Ennis planned.

"Yes," Ennis said. He looked at Calford. "I need you to blind the satellite any way can so the predator can only track me from the surface when I'm ready for it."

"Um, so what are you going to do?" Ozek asked in low tones.

"Like I said, kill it," Ennis answered him. "Hala made this cloud her test predator. It was big enough to work, but given only enough acid mist to test the concept."

"How much is enough?" Calford asked. "It seems to have a lot."

"Obviously we were going to test it against a horde after proving it worked on the initial zombie." Ennis paused and thought. "The acid is more effective, more efficient than she realized. But if we exhaust its supply, the predator will be effectively dead."

"Um, but if it's already killed most of the zombies, maybe there isn't a way to exhaust it. Not now." Ozek said.

"There is." Ennis took a deep breath. "In the first colony's cemetery."

"You want turn all those bodies into zombies?" Calford stood and leaned toward Ennis.

"Are you nuts?" Ozek asked with more volume to his voice.

"Yeah, En. Too risky!" Calford threw her hands up. Her prismatic hair tossed and shimmered.

"This will save us." Ennis said. *And redeem Hala's legacy*, he thought. "I'm doing this. Alone. If I fail--well, I won't fail. I can't."

Ennis recalled his last words at the mall. He hoped they wouldn't be remembered as only a grieving idiot's bravado. He stood in a TES at the first colony's cemetery, alone. The slash-hoe was still there, but it would not provide enough help in excavation, and he didn't need to remove dirt with a shovel, carefully. Caution was done. Now he readied for a bold, maybe suicidal act. Against all previous logic and interstellar history, he was going to create a zombie horde. For that, he needed to do some engineering and use a few devices in ways never thought of.

One tool was a seismic wave generator. Ennis borrowed it from a battered geology crew quite eager to help him. The earth shaker would loosen the soil and free the first colonists already zombies. His second tool came from an idea Ozek had given him. A bomb. An airburst would infect clean corpses much faster than direct injection. He just could not be there when it exploded, unless he wanted to join the horde soon to rise from the graves. He set both tools of his apocalypse and ran. He passed the slow, tracked transport he drove here. The cloud would not lock onto to the vehicle's form. He would need to keep running. And fast. A motion detector pieced together by him and Calford began to flash red. He hated red. And he hated and feared the red cloud now coming his way.

The predator moved too fast. Ennis breathed heavily in his suit. The reprocessed atmosphere tasted horrible. He fought through the nausea the air and his recent life caused him. Now fear began to rise. The red cloud sailed over the cemetery swiftly and barely singed the new zombie horde. Now they also trekked across the icy wastes following some innate, almost arcane sense for finding living flesh. The only living flesh for many kilometers was his. The predator closed on him and so did the horde, but the predator seemed locked on him as its first and primary target.

"What damn glitch--!" Ennis yelled to no one.

His thoughts became cutting slashes in his mind. He needed the predator to refocus on the horde. For that, he would have to run into the mass of ravenous zombies. The cloud or the horde might kill him, but then the two nonliving enemies might kill each other in a clash of dead rage and acid. But he had to know the colony was safe. His heart raced and his body vibrated as the red mist billowed close. He had to take the risk and run into the zombies. He turned to face both horrors and tensed to sprint at them.

And then the memory of the first colony's large storage chamber flashed in his mind.

Ennis ran, but away from the monsters.

Again, he had to dig. He wished for a shovel as his gloved hands frantically tore away ice and prismatic gravel from the chamber's large hatch. He cranked the handle, hard. The hatch didn't open so much as fall into the chamber on corroded hinges. Ennis was running inside the darkness before the hatch slammed fully open. A shock hit his eyes. The overhead lights flicked on. Ennis had no time to be amazed at the longevity of the circuits. The whistling noise behind him was not the natural wind blowing in. He ran down the length of the chamber. The gathered soil at the back of his boots hissed as the predator reached Ennis. Almost in paradox, fear of the acid cloud made him take gulps of his suit's foul air. He glanced to his side and then yelled in sudden shock as he hit the rough, far end of the chamber. He yelled again in fear as he turned against the wall. The zombies were right with him. They attacked. All of them.

Ennis pushed, punched, and kicked. The surface of his suit seemed to boil. So did the flesh of the zombies. They didn't burn fast enough. All Ennis could see was dark jaws and exposed teeth, snatching fingers, and glaring eyes threatening to burst from their sockets. The grabbing, biting mass pressed against him. They pushed Ennis to the ground. He could hear his helmet scrape the rough, rock wall behind him. He kept fighting without thought.

Ennis yelled again as his convex faceplate came free. Instantly his face and eyes felt on fire. He thought of Hala's horrific fate. A hand reached toward his face and gripped the rim of the missing faceplate. Ennis could again see light. He shook his head. The hand fell away. He could hear the hiss of the acid against the viscous remains the zombies. Only he survived to be the focus of the acid predator. His face stung from the burns. But the hissing sound ebbed. The acid was exhausted. The predator died against his skin.

Ennis stumbled out of the long chamber, outside. He was unsure how he got there. The sunlight through the clouds reflected off the ice and snow seemed blinding, but Ennis could still see. He felt the cold against his face, and the pain. The pain was a spur. It kept him moving. Although now, he could afford to rest. He slumped down and let the cool dry wind scatter icy dust over him. Now the chill felt good down his back. He stood and began walking again. The dust and ice stung his acid burns. He kept walking. He was alone, but a survivor. Now, Kolibri might survive on its own. That would require a lot more work, and would be a better tribute to Hala than a grave. Ennis walked forward. The pain spurred him on.

CONDUIT

Darkness. Death. They are not the same. Fear may persuade some to exist beyond a righteous end. To stave off death, some may beseech evil powers to grant their dread desire. If the plea is answered, a form of darkness may rise that is not shadow nor night, but the thing feared within both. An evil soul, or worse, may corrupt nature's final demand of the living. Thereafter, a wave of horror may roll out to drown and consume all that stands before it. Such colorless darkness can reach into daylight to hunt with dead eyes and grasp with cold fingers. Its hunger will only grow. To fight such darkness is to stand against the tide. Some may succumb to fear and drown as undead come for their lives and their flesh. Zombies and evil are one in the same.

Evil hunted the woods one young woman raced through. If she could think, she would recall her name was Lily, short for Lilith. However, fear had released adrenaline. That hormone had coursed through her blood for so long, the flight instinct trampled other emotions and higher thoughts. All she could do now was run. Zombies were chasing her. If they caught her, she would die. But not before feeling their fingers and teeth tear away parts of her body. Lily was an intelligent person reduced to running prey.

Evil twisted human corpses into flesh eating monsters. All they understood was that Lily was warm and alive, and that they were ravenously hungry. The trees almost seemed to move aside as she ran, or perhaps they guided her path. The woods she fled through were a park. Parks needed maintenance and drainage. As a child, Lily would impress living friends by defying darkness and entering storm culverts. The memory rose like an instinct. She ran through trees to a culvert near the edge of the park.

Conduit

Now the culvert was badly overgrown. No matter. Sliding through it was the only way she could escape the undead horde closing through the trees on all sides. She pressed through the tangle of branches and thorns. They only cut and didn't bite. Wet branches slid from her path as she pressed deeper towards the culvert opening. These limbs were wood and bark, not bone and weathered flesh. Finally, her feet touched water in the channel entering the conduit. It was cold and dark. Behind her was hissing and unnatural growls.

Lily dropped in and was stunned to sink to her waist. City engineers had replaced the culvert from her childhood. Now a deep and wide conduit channeled more rainwater from greater storms. She could hear branches snapping as a mass forced aside the tangle of branches. Lily waded into the dark. The collected rainwater had become cold. Very cold. Lily forced her way forward through the large metal tube and the numbing chill. Her body was beginning to feel shock.

A mass of zombies collapsed into the channel head. A wave rolled deep into the conduit and struck Lily from behind. She took an instinctive, quick breath. The surge carried her farther into the frigid waters. She completely submerged deeper into the descending pipe. The water stung her eyes. She could see nothing. Lily was farther away from the flesh ripping monsters, but closer to death. She was cold. Very cold. She needed air. There was none. Only rank, cold water with no light. Her hands raced above her along the twists of the wide, corrugated pipe to find a pocket of air. She only felt the metal and the numbing sting of icy water. Her heart hammered. Her lungs felt as airless vacuums. Lily felt a powerful desire to take a breath.

It was cold. Frigid. It was dark. Lily felt only the numbing water. Sensation sank. She could see nothing. Her heart--was it beating? Everything was cold.

Cold. Numb.

Dark.

Lily felt, was nothing.

Time flowed backwards to a point where Lily was alive and the park was free of undead. Thoughts and emotions raced in Lily's mind. The greatest was disappointment. In the back of her mind lurked the concern of imminent death, but not her own. A loved one of Lily neared life's final moment. However, life's responsibilities still demanded time. Lily paid that duty on the job. She saw only a hint of her future terror. At this moment, Lily waited to see magic and politics merge. Or collide. Lily was unsure what would happen, aside from potentially losing her job. She stood in the same park where a future zombie horde would smell her body and blood. Today, another kind of intrusion disturbed it, but in far fewer numbers than Lily wanted.

The park was mostly woods. The trees stood behind a smaller area with an open-air basketball court beside skate ramps and faded, chipped playground sets and swings. The woods were to be a *manifest zone*. A shift in reality allowed ethereal creatures to manifest themselves on Earth, again. Enchanted life called this the era of *Reascension*. It was hoped that magic creatures would crossover and play in the park, or just pose for pictures. But nice magic creatures, like gnomes, fairies, and good-natured elves.

As the assistant to city council president Mary Cryder, Lily had contacted the news media and posted word on social media about the grand reopening of Norhurst Park. Yet, only one reporter from one surviving newspaper bothered to come. The other few attending were city staff, a couple of local bloggers, and a handful of people walking their dogs who stopped to watch when Daisy or Rex squatted and left a handful for sani-scoops and plastic bags.

Most of humanity was still adjusting to the otherworldly in the everyday world, not merely in myths and media. Adjustments did not bar exploitation. A city council majority led by Mary Cryder overrode the mayor's veto to make Norhurst Park a manifest zone. They majority thought the city would benefit from tourists visiting the park to see magic creatures among squirrels and wild birds. That was, after homeless encampments were removed. The tourists would naturally stop at new, stripmall franchises and declining, local-owned stores. Revenues would also manifest. There was even talk of building a mall. The proposed site was where the park stood. Lily wondered if elves and others would stay good natured if asphalt and megastores replaced the moss and forest. The city council had tabled the issue. No need to worry about the future.

Cryder expected magic creatures at the reopening. To her, that seemed only quid pro quo. However, the sorcerer who cast the tax-funded spell decided to be a no-show. At least, the Great Profecta did not appear visibly. His spell was supposed to screen malignant magic creatures. Lily wondered if paying for a spell was akin to buying something at a megastore. If so, getting a refund could be hell. In this case, a failed product just might bring hell. She hoped the city council had kept the receipt. Demons would be worse than no media coverage.

Bunting and banners were tied to trees and the picnic shelter acting as center stage. Not even the lone reporter had a camera. He was a reasonably handsome young man, Lily thought. Mary Cryder would have to make do with whatever mobile phone video was posted. If it was posted. Other than the video taken by Lily, trying not to look like a sycophant with a phone. This was her job. Or so she was told. The city hired Lily straight out of college with her degree in social science and youthful enthusiasm. Originally, she thought her job would help improve public service in her rapidly altering hometown. This was before magic creatures experienced *Reascension*.

Instead the job gave her a inside seat to hustling businesses to open in rezoned school district lands and sidestepping concerns over infrastructure and quality of life. Norhurst was evolving into a magnet for national franchises visible from the highway. Zombies would come in the future. They didn't eat at burger joints or like fried chicken. They devoured the people in them.

The blue-suited Mary Cryder stepped to the podium to start the reopening ceremony now that it was certain no one else was coming.

"I want to thank you all for coming!" Cryder said as if looking out at a massive crowd.

Lily suppressed a snicker at the word *all*.

"Today is a new chapter for our city," Cryder smiled and continued. "Indeed, this is a new era for our world. Today we embrace the entry of enchanted peoples into our city of Norhurst. They will be welcomed into our thriving community, as are you all.

Please extend our welcome across our county, our country, and indeed our world."

Cryder smiled wide and thrust out her arms as if to embrace an adoring throng. Lily's clapping was all that returned the offered embrace.

"Okay. That was crap." Cryder said to Lilly as she walked from the podium.

"We can always--" Lily started.

"Save it." Cryder said and continued her healthy stride towards her SUV parked in the lone handicapped spot.

"Wait!" Lily chirped. "Look!"

Lily pointed to the edge of the woods where she aimed her phone's camera lens. There, a being that resembled a standing bullfrog in gnome's clothing looked out.

"Okay! That's a 'Chant!" Cryder said using the slang for enchanted lifeform. She approached the small creature that had wandered closer and taken a keen interest where dogs had caused their owners to stoop.

"Couldn't we do better than walking lawn art from a dollar store?" Cryder muttered as she walked by Lily.

"Welcome my ethereal friend!" Cryder said to the curious frog-gnome.

"Um, I think it's some form of troll." Lily said with concern. "Maybe we should--"

"Never mind." Cryder quickly snapped with a sideward glance. She leaned over address the possible troll.

The creature smiled at Cryder's legs.

"Yes, I'm so glad you--" Cryder began with a cloying tone.

The troll hugged Cryder's left calf.

"Oh, crap!" Cryder yelled.

The troll engaged in an act on her leg similar to behavior from an unfixed and oversexed cocker spaniel. Cryder shook her leg kick off the amorous creature to no avail. The small troll held fast and moved furiously. Lily ended the creature's affair with Cryder's calf by squirting it with the water in her squeeze bottle.

"Plah!" The troll exclaimed and dropped to the ground. It recovered itself and stood. The troll snatched off its cap and then wrung out the water. It stared at Lily with amphibious eyes and shouted. "Zah-gas!"

"Uh," Lily shrugged at the peeved troll.

The creature stomped back to the woods. A few seconds of clapping echoed off the trees from behind Lily. Cryder grabbed Lily's bottle and squeezed the remaining water on her calf. She looked up and glared at Lily who shrugged again. Cryder kept the bottle as she walked back to her SUV. Water squished out of her blue shoe with each step. Lily began mentally composing a new resume.

"Dale Jordan," a male voice said.

Lily turned to see the lone reporter extending his hand to her. Lily thought for a moment, and then shook it considering the dark haired stranger with a gentle and genuine smile.

"Lily Hughes," she said.

"Quite a show." Jordan said and released his grip to jab a thumb over his shoulder towards Cryder's SUV as it left the park.

"Yeah," Lily said and took a breath she could feel deep in her lungs. Lily looked over at the woods where the troll had entered. "We aim to please. In more ways than one."

"Lily is a nice name. Your parents liked flowers?" Jordan asked.

"It's short for Lilith."

"Oh! Adam's first wife?" Jordan asked.

Lily cocked her eyebrows and looked quizzically at Jordan. She was familiar with the tale of the female demon. "My father's first wife. I'm named after my mother."

"I see," Jordan nodded. He sensed a need to restart the conversation. "A fine tradition. I'm sure."

"Do you need anything for you article, mister--?"

"Dale Jordan. I would like--"

Lily's phone rang. She thrust her hand into her pocket and withdrew it in one quick motion.

"Oh, no!" Lily's face twisted in sadness. She bolted for her own car.

A few miles away, Sam Marion drove his old pick-up truck up a hill and out of Norhurst's city limits. Milt Bukes rode with him. Sam was driving up to his cabin home. He was unsure how Milt was going to get back to his home, and wondered if he had enough food for both of them. Sam did not intend to drive back down the hill for a long time. The road through the alder forest was still unpaved, but now it was even and covered with fine, rolled gravel. The county considered the road an easement, so Sam's protests over the improvements went ignored. The original rough and bumpy road kept most drivers from risking the drive. Sam had known the stretch of hills since birth. The leveled, improved road felt like a cut across his person. The city and county paid that no heed, and paid for the road so a big business could haul in equipment and build on a chunk of land Sam's father always regretted selling.

The deed was done. All Sam could do was drive on. He still owned the majority of what he saw through the windshield and past Milt's bobbing head. Most of the world around Sam was becoming a city. The only way he could jump start the frontier-style life he knew in his youth would be to sell everything and move to Alaska. But if he did that, land kept in his family for generations would become dense housing and stripmalls. Sam thought he should stay, if only to preserve a wide island of nature among jammed traffic and houses stacked so close you could not drive a luxury SUV between them.

Sam was concerned by officials and contractors bulldozing and paving over a way of life. Milt's attitude was from anger looking for a cause. Still, Sam had few friends. He was likely Milt's only friend. Sam only hoped Milt didn't eat a lot. The reason to improve the road and target for Milt's anger came into view as they rounded a turn and the road split. At the end of a new, short lane stood a chain-link gate. Beyond it were two massive, white water towers. The huge *H2U* logo stretched over a white background in contrasting blue hues on the tower sides. Both logos faced the city under an arc of lights kept on even in midday.

"H-2-U? *Eff* to us is more like it." Milt said as they drove by the towers. He turned his neck to keep staring at them as they drove on. "Maybe we should blow 'em. Knock those towers to the ground."

"Nope," Sam answered. "They would love it. Nothing like a terrorist act to get people to rally around anything. Including a water company hijacking our local waters and pumping who knows what into our taps. No. We already fought the good fight for everyone. Now we protect ourselves. People will come to the cause after they realize the water they're drinking is corporate piss."

"But they open their throats for it. They want it!" Milt yelled and was shook in his seat as the improved road ended past the water tower access.

"Yep. Still, don't give the enemy a break." Sam said and tightened his grip on the steering wheel as he turned to avoid washed out holes in the now completely dirt road. "Wrecking their towers would make them stronger. It would make us the enemy. The town will find their mistake. But we don't have to drown with them."

"Now there's all this other weird crap." Milt huffed. "I mean, you don't what's in the woods when you're hunting, anymore. Maybe something is hunting you."

"The local woods are going to be closed for hunting." Sam said.

"Serious?" Milt hoped in his seat even without the truck hitting a bump.

"Yep. One more reason this place is not where I grew up." Sam droned.

"When you grew up? Hell!" Milt spouted. "You're older than me. I don't recognize the same streets through the town I've driven since I sat shotgun in my Dad's truck."

"Gentrification." Sam grunted.

"Corporate fornication. With our town." Milt sneered and stared out the windshield as if drawing a bead on a target.

"With the town council, for sure." Sam said as the truck rocked.

"So, what are we going to do?" Milt asked and looked at Sam. "We can't let it slide."

"I know what I've done, Milt. What I can do. Best thing now is for others to realize things on their own. I can only read up on magic and odd things. But I can speak out about the water. That's simple and natural. The natural we know. And there is no reason for the city to sell off a good, natural water supply to a big company that sells back water that's not even from the local watershed."

"Whole world has gone wrong." Milt growled.

"Maybe not all of it. Just some things. So, speaking on where things are going, there Milt. How were you looking to get back to town?"

Milt raised his eyebrows. His head pitched as they took another road bend farther up the hill.

Lily had been crying. She gripped a sodden mass of tissues and squeezed tears from them. Her face was red and wet from wiping them away. She followed the gurney and two morgue attendants as they wheeled out the body of the woman she called Aunt Joan. The attendants had been waiting. They usually transported bodies in the familiar, long, black bag. Clothing changes were done later at a funeral home. However, Lily insisted Aunt Joan be dressed in her favorite, bright orange and pink floral pattern suit before her body was moved. A thin gown would not do. The nursing staff had grown fond of both Joan and Lily, so they did as Lily wished as a last act of care for both of them.

They took the elevator to the main lobby. Laundry and food delivery trucks blocked the assisted living facility's service entrance. Joan's exit from the building was well noticed, just as she had been during her lifetime. The gurney continued through the automatic, double doors and to the waiting hearse. Lily would follow, but needed a moment before returning to her car. She sat in the sunny lobby with bright floor tiles and ornate but stiff couches.

Lily felt a presence behind her. "Okay. Step up or get lost."

"Honestly, I'm sorry to intrude." Dale Jordan said and stepped beside the couch.

"But you're doing it anyway," Lily said without looking at him.

"Sorry. Really. At the park, I thought you got called to another 'Chant event. Maybe one better than the last. So I followed you."

"Nope. It's my personal life." Lily slapped her hands into her lap. "Or the end of it."

Jordan said nothing as he cursed himself for being a writer, yet now searched for the right words.

"My aunt--my friend died," Lily said. "She was like another mom to me. Especially after my own died."

"I am sorry for your loss." Jordan said in a low but sincere tone.

"Thanks," Lily sniffled.

"I know how it is when you start out in a new town with no friends other than work buddies. Being alone is hard."

"I've always lived here," Lily looked up at Jordan with red eyes.

"And your friends?" Jordan gave a slight shrug.

"They moved away."

"So can I stay?" Jordan asked. "As a friend?"

"Yeah." Lily sighed.

Jordan sat next to Lily. He stayed silent. A long moment of quiet seemed to stretch time as Lily looked out blankly as her mind raced. Then, she spoke again.

"She wasn't old. Just sick. Damn cancer."

"I hate it, too." Jordan said.

There was another long moment of silence. Lily took a deep breath that verged on a sob.

"I called her Aunt Joan," Lily said and cleared her throat. "When I became an adult, she wanted me to call her Joanie."

"I guess she wanted you to be equals." Jordan said. He felt his phone vibrate, but ignored it.

"She was my mother's friend, not her sister. But she was a real aunt to me." Lily tried to smile but fought to suppress more tears.

"Sounds like a good person," Jordan smiled.

"She was. Very good. She gave me--" Lily stopped speaking. She pulled her lips tight and they lost color as her eyes welled.

"It will be okay," Jordan said quietly.

"How can anyone say that?" Lily said with a cracking voice.

"Because it's what we say we when need to go on."

112

"Yeah. I guess." Lily dried her eyes with her sodden tissues.

"You will get through this," Jordan said.

"I know. But it just doesn't feel like things will be okay. The whole world is different."

"Yeah. It is." Jordan slowly nodded his head. "But we'll get through that, too."

"You're sure?" Lily said as her voice became stronger.

"Always."

It had been a long trek, and Milt had not brought his heavy coat. At least the effort of the hike through the brush kept him warm after the sunset. The moon was still bright, but the visible stars were far fewer than just a few years ago. Too many city lights, Milt thought. Too many people. Maybe wrecking the new H2U site would stop more from coming as well as save those who would drink the water piped in from who knew where. He crept from the road up to the fence and then over it. He slipped the concertina wire just as he and his brothers did in their questionable youth. Now he used those skills for a cause.

Milt figured if Sam was not willing to take direct action, then he would. But he expected a fight. This place had no dogs. That wasn't too weird. However, not dodging security at all made him nervous. Still, there was a job to do. He had no hammers or bombs. So Milt hoped to sabotage the intake valves and cause a catastrophic rupture that would take weeks to repair. By then, he figured he'd have followers, and hammers and bombs.

It wasn't just the lax security that Milt found odd. The world was weirder because of new creatures from places unseen. Yet, that was the least of his current worries. He had a good understanding of how machines worked. He worked as a mechanic and in maintenance. Valves were a very simple system. Open. Close. Even ones controlled by computers held that basic function. Meters displayed rate of flow and pressure. Milt looked at the simple meters on the big but basic valves he tried to close. The meters showed no changes. He cranked the handwheel harder. Nothing. The system was bogus.

"What bull," Milt whispered to himself. At least he thought only he could hear his voice. He was wrong.

"Is there a problem, stranger?"

The voice caused an icy spike of shock to shoot through Milt. The TASER darts sent electricity followed immediately by convulsions. Oddly, Milt thought *that's more like it* before a large wrench followed the electric shock and knocked him out.

When Milt awoke, his head throbbed. It seemed the throbs should echo off the cylindrical wall. Its metallic sheen came in focus. It appeared he was inside a gigantic tube of aluminum foil. The high wall surrounded him. A huge dome capped it overhead. Milt realized he lay centered inside one of the water towers. He could feel his limbs stretched into an 'X' and chained. He flexed against his bonds. His head throbbed. He though it did echo this time, but the sound was footfall as someone approached.

"I know. I'm disappointed, too."

Milt heard the same voice as before his capture. It echoed in the tower from a tall, thin man with glasses and grey hair beneath a yellow hard hat. He wore a clean, white, impossibly pressed H2U uniform. He smiled down at Milt as if they shared a joke. His nametag read *Death Priest* in handwritten black marker. Milt flexed against his chains again.

"Yeah." The man nodded and looked around. "You might expect robes torches and chanting. A stone alter, not a giant can."

"Chanting?" Milt asked while trying to look around.

"Yeah. That stuff is for the followers." The man explained.

He dropped his head low enough when looking down that Milt saw the name 'Williams' in faded letters on his yellow, safety helmet.

"It's a psychological fix that makes them more susceptible because it re-enforces that they're part of a group." Williams continued. "And we humans, the mortal ones, love our group dynamic. We do a lot of insane things if we do them together. Take war, for example. Bad idea as a lone sapien, a thinker."

"You'd better think twice about keeping me here!" Milt shouted and the loud echo made his head throb again.

Williams continued as if not hearing Milt. "But, insane minds don't count. Can you image having a defective mind only to be liberated from your body and then your soul realizes it was the flawed, physical brain that made you a serial killer?"

Williams nodded his head fast. His helmet stayed locked in place, but his glasses slid down his nose. He instinctively pushed them back up.

"And there you are able to think free of the defects. Man!" Williams threw his hands from his sides as his voice bounced around the metal wall. "The guilt! I guess that's hell. Let me know how it all feels."

"What? The chains?" Milt asked with a sneer.

"No. The death."

"Man! *You* are insane!" Milt shouted.

"Yeah. Well, that's the evil." Williams looked up. He shook his head at the thought, and then shrugged to himself. Then he looked back at Milt with an expression of mock pain. "See, I have full control of what I'm doing. But, pretty much, I am a serial killer."

"*Whaaat?*" Milt screeched.

"Just kidding about that part." Williams blinked and laughed. "I mean, well, I have no compulsions other than to gain power from odd methods. I read an article once about how the Pentagon is drawing up plans for water wars, and, well--"

Williams looked up and raised his hands to gesture at the water tower around them. "H2U was born. Of course, fate throws curves. Round wall joke, there."

Milt grunted.

"So now these are going to be repositories for human offal." Williams looked at Milt. He arched his eyebrows as his cheeks flexed. He then nodded at Milt if they shared the same, odd idea. "Yeah. Sick. But it's what ghouls like. Dead human flesh."

"Ghouls?" Milt asked. He rested his head against the cold, metal floor. The cold helped ease the throbbing.

"Yeah," Williams said. He then jerked back and thrust out his palms as if to stop the chained and silent Milt. "Now, don't you go confusing them with zombies. We're going to make those, but they only serve a temporary purpose for her plan."

"What?" Milt snipped. "But--wait. Who is *we?*"

"She's called a Dark Avatar. She wants to summon the mega ghoul. A sort of god of dead, flesh eating things. I forget the name. Well, if I didn't have mine on a name tag--!" Williams jerked his *Death Priest* tag and opened his mouth in comic exaggeration.

"You are a serious loose screw!" Milt ranted. His voice and clank of jerked chains echoed through the tower. "Let me go and maybe I won't kick your nuts through your skull!"

Williams held his chin in his right hand and looked off as if to consider Milt's demand. "Hmm. Yeah. Ah, no."

"Dude, if you don't--!"

"If I do then we both die. Horribly." Williams nodded again. "So I'll leave that fate for you. Look at it this way. You are just the first in a *waaaay* huge sacrifice. I could say it's an honor to die and serve her. This dark avatar is an old, old soul. Like me, she sees an opportunity in the days ahead. And because I'm basically a nice guy--okay, I'm lying. Because my basic nature is to be corrupt and exploit others, I'm compelled to help her. I'm evil. So is she. But more powerful. Again, sorry about no ceremony, but apparently magic rites are all about the intent and truth of the act. That's what pleases the evil-spirit, dark-god side of things. It's what in your heart. What's in your heart is warm blood to sacrifice. Mine just has a dark, dark spot craving money and power."

Williams again made his exaggerated, comic look with opened mouth. Milt only sneered.

"Last words?" Williams asked.

"Hard to get one in edge wise." Milt growled.

"Point taken," Williams nodded. "Now take this. Straight into the aorta."

Williams reached behind his back and withdrew a stout hunting knife. Milt recognized it as the one he kept strapped to his hip. Williams had taken it when he was unconscious. Milt thrashed as Williams knelt beside him and raised the knife. Its blade sunk deep. Milt's screaming was loud and the echoes were deafening. They became a ringing in Williams' ears. He grunted at the spray of Milt's blood across his impossibly pressed uniform. That would need bleach. He could rinse off the blood that hit his face, helmet, and glasses with water. Too bad there was none of it around.

In the morning, two friends in different departments walked through outside doors and into a long hallway in

116

Norhurst's newest municipal building. The hall still smelled of fresh paint and tile glue. Their lab coats smelled of chemicals and the unmistakable odor of dead tissue despite frequent washings. The scent of tissue hung on plump assistant coroner Rolly Pines. Chemical smells clung to lean toxicology technician Max Bushlund.

"Welcome to Norhurst's mega-morgue!" Rolly said imitating a showman's flair.

"It was that or another stripmall." Max said with deadpan tone.

"This is practically retail space for death and necrology. Municipal autopsies. Rented space for mortuaries. This is one stop shopping for the dead." Rolly observed.

"They need to shop for more techs. Tox is backlogged," Max said.

"Nowadays, so is the fridge." Rolly added.

"You have to hand it to them," Max said with a laughing tone. "Who would have thought to make money from renting body lockers to mortuaries and other, underfunded cities? I guess some people's budget cuts are another's budget bump."

"Who'd have thought all the money from the extra bodies would *not* support the coroner's office." Rolly groaned.

"What? You mean you're not getting your kickback from the refrigeration companies?" Max said and dropped his jaw in mock shock.

"Oh, funny!" Rolly looked up to the ceiling with a head roll. "Talk like that will get you suspended."

"No. Fired." Max said as he smiled. "And then I can run for a plush seat on the city council."

"You'll be in the fridge before that happens."

"Hey, in today's world, anything is possible." Max tossed up his hands and laughed.

"No kidding!" Rolly's eyes opened wide at a thought. "I heard of one town attacked by ghouls."

"I heard it was goblins." Max said.

"Pray for goblins. They don't eat the dead."

"I'm more worried about something that eats me. Alive." Max pulled his mouth into an exaggerated frown.

"You?" Rolly shook his head quickly. "Nothing would want you. No meat."

"Ha!" Max flexed his left arm.

Rolly waved. He turned and pushed through the morgue's swinging metal doors. Max walked on with a smile. Suddenly he heard screaming from behind the swinging doors.

"Oh! Funny, Rolly!" Max stopped and turned.

Rolly bursts back through doors. He wacked a corpse with a clipboard that griped him from behind and bit his shoulder. Max screamed, but ran towards Rolly. The metal doors struck him as more zombies burst into the hallway. Rolly kept whacking the zombie biting him, but looked in greater horror at the horde shredding Max. Zombie teeth sank deeper into Rolly's shoulder as he spun, whacked, and screamed. Another body entered the hall, but in a deliberated pace. It observed the carnage befalling Max. The body was of a woman dressed in a bright floral suit. This calm zombie walked past the feeding horde and through the dark slick on the new floors. She paid no attention to Rolly's screams as she continued with purpose and down the hall.

A live camera feed showed a shambling mass of zombies. Most wore matted and clinging hospital gowns. The levels of decomposition ranged from freshly dead to long overdue for burial. All their mouths were open. Oddly, they all drifted across a street intersection as a crosswalk light flashed a green walking man. Most of the zombies had splashes and streaks of blood. A few cars drove around the zombies as they walked over the painted asphalt. The cars sped up and wheels squealed as drivers saw the shuffling crowd were not typical pedestrians. The camera panned to include a dark-haired reporter up the street from the zombies with her back facing them as she addressed viewers.

"What are these creatures?" The reporter asked as the small horde began to walk toward her. "They look and hiss like zombies. Officials have yet to name them within the lexicon of enchanted beings. However, recent reports from Alderville indicate ghouls have moved into the area. Are these monsters ghouls? Are they zombies? Are they dangerous?"

The horde moved with surprising quick for a shuffling mass. A few zombies moved faster and ahead of the undead mob.

"When we hear from civil or ethereal authorities, we'll let you know live, online, and through our newsbeat app available from our app store. This is Sabra Chen, reporting live for--"

A quick zombie bumped into Sabra Chen's back.

"Okay you sicko, 'Chant! Back off!" Sabra yelled.

The zombie growled and swiped at Sabra who stepped back as the others continued to advance in the background.

Sabra pushed back the zombie and then looked past the lens at the cameraman. "Hey, some help Larry?"

"This is good feed, Sabs." A male voice came from behind the camera. "Go with it!"

"Hey!" Sabra ducked the hand swipe of another quick zombie.

Sabra's first attacker renewed its advance. It grabbed her shoulder. The other zombie grabbed her hair.

"HEY!" Sabra screamed and struggled to break free. "*HEYAAAAAAAAAAH!*"

The images of the zombie biting off pieces of Sabra Chen reporting live became shaky and finally cut out as her cameraman suffered a similar if unseen fate. The broadcast switched to a studio shot where a man with immobile hair wore a neutral suit and bright tie. He offered viewers a grave expression beneath pancake makeup.

"We have lost connection with Sabra Chen." The news anchor began to speak.

Lily watched him on her tablet screen inside her apartment. A knock on her door interrupted her attention. She left her couch in a daze trying to process the televised bloodshed. She opened her door to the width allowed by her security latch and peered through the narrow slot between the door and its frame. Dale Jordan stood in the hall and smiled back at her.

"Hi, Lily. I hope I'm not bugging you. Again."

Lily snapped her attention to Jordan. "Geez have you seen the--I don't know, the zombies killing people?"

"I've heard." Jordan answered.

"And what the hell are you doing here?" Lily squinted at Jordan.

"I'm in town. Still." Jordan said. "Just wondered if you're okay."

"Yeah. Why wouldn't I be?" Lily realized what she just said and then spoke before Jordan could answer. "Okay, dumb question."

Lily sighed. She unlatched her door and let Jordan enter. She took her phone and called Mary Cryder as Jordan closed the door.

"Typical!" Lily shouted and glared at her phone's screen.

"What?" Jordan asked.

"My boss. She's not answering."

"She's probably miles away." Jordan offered.

"Right. Typical." Lily said.

"We need to get miles away," Jordan pointed to the door.

"We?" Lily gave Jordan a hard look as she considered the man she was attracted to, yet had really just met.

"Strength in numbers." Jordan gave an entreating smile.

"Numbers need plans," Lily said as her newsbeat app chimed on her phone. She clicked the icon, but the images of Sabra Chen's death began to play. She clicked it off.

"I think I have one," Jordan said. "There was a guy I interviewed--colorful, local guy. Sam Marion. He--"

"He hates H2U." Lily finished.

"Yeah! You know him?"

"He was at a lot of city meetings," Lily said. "He actually made a lot of sense. Don't tell my boss I said that."

"I thought so, too. If I lived in Norhurst, I'd buy bottled water once those water towers go live." Jordan raised his eyebrows at Lily.

"They're supposed to be safer--anyway. You don't live here?"

"Got an apartment in Alderville."

"Why aren't you there?" Lily asked and again gave Jordan a hard look.

"Blocked roads." Jordan jerked his shoulders. "The government is treating this zombie outbreak like a disease. People are getting checked at road blocks before getting on the highway."

"Sounds more like a quarantine." Lily said and looked at her phone again to see if she was somehow included in city decision making. There were no messages.

"That's coming, I'm sure. And probably by the time we'd get to the city limits. But we should probably get somewhere safer if the numbers of zombies keep growing."

"Yeah," Lily sighed.

More screaming from live feeds sounded from the screen near her couch.

"So, what about Sam Marion?" Lily asked.

A few miles from Lily's apartment house, two men engaged in conversation in a place important to their respective careers, the local sheriff's office. One man was Deputy Lon Barret. The other was career criminal Joel Kolquick. Joel sat on his cell bunk. Barret leaned against the bars while holding a paper cup trapping cold coffee. Joel's taste in vices ran hotter and much stronger. The holding cell was actually a large zoo cage bought and tossed inside a storage room off the wide office space of desks, screens, piles of paper, and droning noise.

"So you have someone close, just not someone who can post bail?" Barret asked and then took a sip.

"Yeah," Joel said. "She's real pale."

"You mean pretty?"

"No. Pale. Trouble is, she wears this Goth make-up that makes her look worse."

"You should tell her." Barret sipped again.

"No. It might hurt her feelings."

"So, you'll rob other people and cause them grief, but you don't want to tell your girlfriend her makeup sucks." Barret shook his head.

"Yeah. Well," Joel shrugged, "they're other people and she's my girlfriend."

"You're a real prince." Barret went to sip while looking at Joel but hit his chin instead of his lips.

"Oh, yeah." Joel smiled. "Just looking to keep the right people pleased."

"Like maybe the law?" Barret asked and then looked at his cup to make sure he got the last pull.

"Funny thing is, I don't have much to do with the law." Joel leaned back against the bars. "Usually I'm moving on before anyone files a report. I don't like to stay in one place too long."

"You'll be here for a while." Barret smiled and crushed the cup.

"Maybe. But when I do get out, I know my pale, Goth girl will have a hit waiting for me." Joel smiled.

"What's her name?" Barret asked.

"Nope." Joel smiled wider.

"Well, she's sounds like a real keeper, Joel. You should marry and have little felons, together."

"Nah," Joel frowned. "I don't like to stay in one place too long."

"Good luck with that."

"Thanks." Joel nodded and ignored Barret's intended irony.

Barret heard rising noise from the lobby beyond the desks. He left Joel. Joel stretched out on his dank cot. His cell smelled like a gorilla. He recalled how he knew what a gorilla smelled like and smiled. He jolted as the muffled but certain sound of gunfire echoed through the walls. Barret lunged back in the storage room. He held his standard issue .40cal Glock with the slide locked back. Joel knew that meant Barret had fired all shots in the magazine. Barret was breathing fast.

"Dude! Calm down." Joel said. "What's it? Terrorists?"

Barret only shook his head *no*. More shots and now screams sounded outside the door. Barret slid out the empty magazine from his handgun and replaced it with one from his belt. He released the catch and the slide jerked forward. Barret took a deep breath and grabbed the door handle.

"Dude, wait!" Joel yelled and jumped up toward Barret. "Don't leave me here. I can't run if you cops all die!"

Barret stared at Joel. More shots echoed. He withdrew a key from his belt and unlocked the cell door.

"That's all I can do." Barret said.

Barret charged out the storeroom door. Joel jumped as the loud report of handguns and shotguns assaulted his ears. He pushed the cell door open and crept to the storeroom door.

"Good luck with this, yeah!" Joel said to himself as he reached for the doorknob. He crept low between the wall and the desks. He knew there should be more deputies. Only Barret and another few were firing on a crush of dead meat pushing closer as bullets and solid shot made bloody puree fly out their backs.

In most things Joel had bothered to watch, a zombie brain was its weak point. Pop the brain and the zombie drops. Joel saw three zombies heads blasted right off better than a chainsaw ripping through their necks. But the ballistic decapitations only made the zombies spin and fall. The headless undead clawed back to standing. They kept coming as smaller bits flew off from bullets ripping through at close range. These zombies were weird.

Weird zombies? Joel wondered about that phrase. He then wondered why he was watching the cops waste their ammo and ran to the back of the station.

Joel made it out. He was sure the deputies would come back out, but as undead. They wouldn't be arresting anyone, just trying to eat them. Joel planned to be long gone before anyone or anything could snatch him. He looked for his girlfriend he refused to name to Barret. He found her, Marlie. She was easy to spot on the deserted street with the makeup that made her look worse.

Marlie had been waiting as Joel said she would. Marlie could wait forever. Her body was as cold as the pavement where she died after taking that one last hit she saved for Joel but stole in boredom. Her body was now a zombie. Joel realized that too late after getting close for a hug while thinking about things to say about her pale appearance. Marlie's zombie changed Joel's appearance by biting away his nose and right cheek.

Joel screamed as well as we could. Marlie's new friends came shambling up to help. They helped her bite away more of Joel's face and ripped away other parts. There wasn't much of Joel left to stand and follow as Marlie's zombie shuffled off with the others filled with parts of Joel and washed red by his arterial spray. But he did stand. His zombie's ragged and ripped body no desire to stay in one place for long.

Jordan felt the gravel road was an improvement over the pocked dirt channel he drove when he first interviewed Sam Marion. It was still a challenge for his often resurrected, sub-compact hybrid. The road was not his only concern. Lily was beginning to act strange. Jordan knew she would still be mourning her Aunt Joan's loss. Yet her face was strained by dread, not sadness, despite moving away from the zombie outbreak.

"Geez, I don't know!" Lily shouted and pressed her hands against the dashboard. "The closer we get the worse this feels!"

"I'm pretty sure we'll be safe." Jordan reassured her. "Safer than weaving through zombies in the city."

"But there is something awful up here. I can feel it. It's growing."

"Growing?" Jordan glanced at Lily. Dread began to grow in him.

They rounded the turn and drove closer to the illuminated H2U water towers. A figure pressed against the chain-link gates in a bright, floral suit.

"Something, something bad is--!" Lily halted with her mouth open. Her eyes became wider than the water tower domes. She saw the standing body of her Aunt Joan.

"No way!" Lily shrieked. "No way!"

"What?" Jordan yelled while gripping the wheel. "Lily what is going on?"

Jordan tried to look at Lily and keep his small car on the gravel with only the small headlights to show the road from the trees beyond the H2U site.

"Aunt Joan! Aunt Joan! I just saw her!" Lily screamed her words.

"Lily, there's no way!" Jordan countered as he stared ahead.

"Stop the car!" Lily nearly pounced on Jordan next to her. "Stop this damn car right now!"

Jordan feared a manic Lily would cause a crash. He braked and stopped the car while he was still in control. Road dust rolled from the darkness around them into the headlight beams. He turned to the wide-eyed Lily.

124

Jordan took a breath. "Look, I know you were close to-- hey!"

Lily bolted from the car. Jordan caught a glimpse of her in his rearview mirror cast red by the brake lights. She was running back to the H2U towers.

Jordan ran. He nearly collided with Lily who stood frozen on the gravel road as she stared ahead. Trees blocked most of the water tower light where they stood. Beams shone through gaps in bare alders. Lily stared at the well-lit ground at the H2U gates. The body of her Aunt Joan stared back.

"Lily?" Jordan said quietly. He looked at the floral suited zombie. He was sure it wasn't even a dead employee in that suit. "I think we should leave. Come on."

"Yeah. Uhhh," Lily sounded as if she was about to vomit. "I know. It's not her. Uhhh--!"

"Okay." Jordan raised his voice. "Let's go. Like, right the hell now!"

Lily stayed frozen and locked into staring at the abomination of her loved one.

"Lily!" Jordan grabbed her arm.

"Okay! Let go of me!" Lily jerked away. "Geez! Look out!"

The universe became blinding light and a deafening screech of metal.

At the gates, Williams approached his new employer, the dark avatar possessing Aunt Joan's body.

"Say, oh dark queen," Williams bowed. "Great avatar who can eat me. I am humble and all, but is this public display wise?"

The reply was a low gurgle.

"I mean, that young woman seemed to recognize you." Williams pressed his point. "Or, rather, who that was that you are now in. Nice suit, though."

The dark avatar zombie slowly turned and looked up at Williams. He felt a building sensation of mixed dread and excitement. First, he saw only dead, waxy eyes staring into his own. Then his mind saw a black cloud rolling over an ominous horizon. The cloud was a storm of small grains. Each grain was a screaming zombie. They inundated Williams and filled every aperture of his being. His physical body convulsed. He fell onto his back. The ground knocked off his helmet. It flipped backwards and spun beside his head.

Williams saw his own world again. He looked up at a view of the stars filtered by a haze of light from the water towers' constant lamps. Williams felt worse than if he'd shot himself with his TASER.

"So," he spoke aloud to no one. "That was the dark avatar-zombie-ghoul-monster-priestess thing's way of saying *shut up*. Okay. I'm closing the word valve. Okay. I can't really do that. So, okay. This evil magic accomplice thing is complicated. I may need a new job. Damn."

Williams attempted to move. His arms and legs were numb. His neck felt heavy and he rested his head back against the ground.

"I've been bad. I'll be good!" Williams said to the dark avatar who had wondered off.

A boot kicked his helmet. Williams looked up and saw Milt's body now a zombie. His chest bore the rough-cut cavity cut where his heart had beat beneath hewn ribs. Williams assumed Milt would stay dead as a sacrifice. He was wrong. It was not his only error. Milt looked down. Williams wondered if his dead expression held a slight smile. The dark avatar zombie stepped at Williams' side across from its latest scion. It raised Milt's hunting knife over Williams' chest. Together, the undead monsters grasped the knife's handle.

"Oh, come on!" Williams shouted.

The blade nicked his *Death Priest* nametag before puncturing his impossibly pressed uniform shirt and then his chest.

Moments before outside the gates, the screech of brake pad on metal disk finally ended. The grill of Sam Marion's truck halted a finger width in front of Lily and Jordan. The headlights blinded them.

"What in the hell are you two doing here?" Sam shouted as he flew from the cab.

"Looking for you." Jordan said.

He and Lily walked to the side of the truck. They coughed road dust and blinked away their blindness.

"What the hell for?" Sam demanded.

"The zombies." Jordan answered.

"Yeah, so?" Sam shrugged. "They're why I'm leaving!"

"I think there's at least one here." Lily said and pointed to the H2U site.

Sam's eyes flashed with terror. "Get in!"

The rear of Sam's truck pitched violently as he drove in reverse at high speed back to Jordan's car. Sam looked over his shoulder out the rear window and steered. The cab bounced hard and so did the squeezed-together Sam, Lily, and Jordan.

"I wondered who's car that was." Sam said over creaking metal.

"You ever heard of a vehicle with a suspension--shocks?" Jordan asked.

"Why were you two on this road?" Sam asked, still piloting his truck backwards. "You need to get to safety. A place you can defend!"

"Don't you have a place in the woods?" Jordan asked.

Sam slowed and stopped his truck with Jordan's car now behind them.

"Yes," Sam answered Jordan. "And we sure as hell aren't going up there!"

"Why?" Jordan and Lily asked.

"Because it's in the woods!" Sam threw up his hands. "The zombies could use the trees as cover and get close to us before we could get a clear shot and any of them."

"Shooting them hasn't done much good." Jordan flipped his hands.

"It's better than running up and giving them a big, wet kiss!" Sam countered.

"Maybe you have to shoot them a lot." Lily droned.

"Then we need more guns--big guns!" Sam leaned at Lily. "With lots of ammo. And a place with a clear kill zone. A nice open field where they come straight at us." Sam looked out at Jordan's car. "You think running to your car is safe?"

"Yeah. We'll be quick." Jordan said. He opened his passenger door.

"The old school," Lily said. "Your kill zone. Norhurst elementary. It's by the park."

"They were tearing it down," Jordan said.

"There are still some buildings," Lily said, "and a big field down a hill. We'll see them coming."

"Sounds good. Mount up." Sam motioned with his thumb at Jordan's car.

"Mount up?" Jordan asked with a curious smile.

"You, shut up." Sam said to Jordan. "Stay here if you want."

"Okay, *pardner.*" Jordan said as he climbed from the cab. "I'll mount up."

"Let's just get the hell out of here!" Lily snapped.

After driving miles of smooth asphalt and well-lit streets, Jordan glanced in his rearview mirror. Sam had been following them to the old school. Now his truck was missing.

"Sam's gone," Jordan said. "We lost him or he ditched us."

"Call him." Lily said.

"He never owned any type of phone." Jordan replied.

"Maybe he just took another road." Lily turned her neck to look behind them.

"What road?" Jordan asked.

"Maybe he left the roads. His truck looked pretty tough. Just keep driving to the school."

"Affirma--oh, hell!" Jordan swerved to miss a group of zombies in the road. "We are so close!"

Lily looked at the dead and rotting faces. They seemed to glare straight at her as Jordan's car sped by them.

"Maybe that's why they're here." Lily said in a low voice.

"What?" Jordan said as he swerved through more undead. One hip struck his driver's side and shattered the headlamp.

"Maybe this is part of a plan." Lily continued.

"Seriously?" Jordan yipped. "Look at them!"

"It's not their plan." Lily said with dread.

Jordan's car flew through the intersection near Sabra Chen's televised death.

"I don't think--" A loud pop cut off Jordan's words. He gripped the steering wheel and kept in control as his tires shredded and his rims threw sparks when they struck asphalt. His car stopped with a lurch.

"Spike strips?" Jordan said. "Since when do zombies use spike strips?"

"Be glad they're not using their guns!" Lily said.

Jordan looked at Lily and then at what she saw shambling towards them. Two former sheriff deputies advanced as fresh zombies.

"I guess I can drive on the rims." Jordan said and shifted into a lower gear. "Hold tight!"

"No. We're close!" Lily pointed at a bank of trees rising as a black curtain behind a brightly lit strip mall. "We can run through the park faster."

"No we can't--Lily!" Jordan yelled after Lily as she bolted from his car and sprinted towards the woods.

Lily ran to the back of the stripmall and into the forest. She assumed it would be a quick sprint through trees and paved trails with lighting. She didn't think zombies would also be prowling the woods. Or that they could bite through cable and kill lights. They did both. Now Lily didn't merely run to a destination, she ran to stay alive. The fear of being eaten, of being ripped apart was an intense terror. Adrenaline surged. Lily became another form of mindless creature. At last, a thought pushed through the terror of the zombies always at her back. The culvert.

Soon, Lily was inside the metal conduit. Submerged. It was frigid. Dark. All Lily felt was the numbing water. She could see nothing. Her heart--was it beating? Everything was cold.

Cold. Numb.

Dark.

All Lily felt, was nothing.

It felt as though Lily opened her eyes. Yet, she was not seeing. She felt a ray of white light. The ray was a seam in creation that opened as pages of a book. The pages were luminous sheets that enveloped her. She floated in a place that was all white. She could sense a border of curved walls that was close and yet far away. It was hard to make sense of distance and proportion. Lily thought that here, all physical senses were useless. This was not planet Earth. She remembered drowning. Suddenly she felt herself spewing out water and coughing.

"You really don't have to do that, Lil." The voice was familiar and comforting.

"Aunt Joan!" Lily beamed and felt joy. Suddenly she was sitting in the white beside her adopted Aunt Joan.

"Hello, sweetheart." Joan said and smiled. "It's good to see you. Although, feel you is more accurate. I think so, anyway."

"Where are we?" Lily asked.

"Well, I'm dead. I guess you are, too. For now, anyway." Joan ended with a shrug.

"Dead? For now?" Lily became even more confused.

"Somehow I know this is not your moment, or spot, or something." Joan said and looked off as if hearing a distant voice and looking for its source. "Some other force outside normal life has forced this."

"The zombies!" Lily recoiled from Joan on instinct.

"Oh, my dear. Now you know I'm not one of them." Joan stroked Lily's hand.

"But one is using you--your body!" Lily shouted and then became calm.

"I sort of feel that, too. A little bitch spirit possessed my body. I guess it liked my floral suit."

Lily took the astral equivalent of a deep breath and tried to perceive her surroundings.

"I tied that, too, Lil. It's tough. Just don't worry. Well, don't worry much. You'll be kicked back, soon."

"I am glad to see you Aunt Joan." Lily focused on Joan and smiled. She felt at peace.

"You were never going to call me Joanie, were you?"

"No. I needed an aunt more than a friend."

"Well, it's sweet you always thought of me that way."

"So this is heaven?" Lily looked up. It was the same white view to the sides and below.

"Nope. I'm pretty sure it's not. Not hell either. And that's a relief." Joan raised her eyebrows.

"There is no heaven and no hell?" Lily asked.

"I don't know, yet."

Lily felt a jolt as she suddenly realized a massive presence was with them.

"That strong sensation is awe," Joan explained. "Awe of something greater."

"It's big." Lily now felt afraid to look around and kept her eyes on Joan.

"Right. Bigger than our world."

"And a part of it?" Lily asked.

"Um, that I don't know. I'd guess this is where all dead people go. The souls. But don't quote me."

"Is this where the zombies come from?" Lily dreaded the answer.

"Ya got me," Joan shrugged. "But I doubt it."

"The one that has you, it's--!"

"I know," Joan patted Lily's hand. "It's an evil thing doing evil things. Crappy. I'm not doing those things. My body is not mine, now. It's shell possessed by a demon spirit."

"A demon?" Lily began to fear her return to Earth.

"Something like that. A nasty sort of soul. Dark and foul."

"Can you come back?" Lily asked and leaned toward Joan. "Can you, or this something awesome, help us?"

"The awe I think stays here. I think it is the *here*." Joan glanced to her side, and then shrugged.

"It's this place? And, uh, a spirit?"

"A sort of living capsule or chamber, maybe." Joan offered. "A soul that encapsulates others until we can merge with something even more awesome."

"What is that? God?" Lily asked. She became excited by the thought.

"I don't know. Maybe just a great stomach digesting the energy of this universe."

"Yuck!"

"Maybe." Joan rolled her eyes. "Or maybe it is heaven. Hard to know what comes next even when you're dead."

"Dead. Yeah. The zombies." Lily felt ill with those thoughts. "They're killing more people. They're eating them. Can you help? Can anything help us? I mean, doesn't someone here even care?"

"I do, sweetheart." Joan said with a compassionate tone. "But I'm dead."

"Can you be, well--" Lily halted in hesitation. "Undead?"

"Well, I guess if you can die and go back, there must be somehow we here could return." Joan considered how to fulfill Lily's request.

"Just long enough to kick out the zombies. If your body is possessed, then maybe that's how all the zombies are made. Possession."

"Well, I don't know if we go back to your plane with no living form--we may get stuck."

Lily was silent for a moment as she considered what that would mean. "Like a ghost."

"A ghost forever. No ascension. Or digestion. Or whatever the hell happens next to us. Maybe that's how ghouls and zombies got started. They went back and had no bodies, so they took others and became corrupt."

Lily paused again, but decided to ask her Aunt and anyone around them to take the risk of becoming ghosts marooned on Earth.

"I don't know what will happen," Lily said. "I just know I want to save people like us and at least my town. I can't do it alone, alive or dead."

"I know, sweetheart. Don't worry. Me and my new friends will try to help you. I think we can follow you."

"Okay," Lily felt great relief. "And the awe is okay with this?"

"We'll see." Joan smiled and shrugged. "We'll give it a try. If we can come back, we'll try to kick the demons out of our bodies. Just remember, not all of us are good people. Some of us were like zombies when we were alive. Who knows what those souls will be like as ghosts."

"Creepy," Lily shuddered.

"Yes."

"But what else can we do?" Lily asked and dared to glance up.

"I don't know," Joan shook her head and sighed. Then she smiled again. "We'll try your plan. First, you have to get back to your body. I'm pretty sure it's cold, but kicking."

"Okay. So, um, I just float back?"

"Float? Yeah, maybe." Joan nodded. "Try this: although you really don't have eyes right now, close them. Relax. Drift. I'll be right behind you."

Kalingosangrikatagarah. Selah!

Lily heard sounds. She was cold, but the darkness and white light had both ebbed. She awoke with a start. This time she did need to vomit water. She turned and saw the water splash over dirt and fallen leaves. She coughed violently.

Yah. Groogh. Groogh-gah.

Lily heard what could be a voice or a frog croaking. She was outside of the culvert. There was faint dawn light above the trees. The zombies were gone. But she wasn't alone. She rolled and saw the toad-troll who loved Cryder's leg. His eyes were both mischievous and kind so close. And he was very close. Other amphibian eyes under caps rose up behind him. A small troupe of toad-trolls stood by her. Like her, they were all wet. The sodden appearance looked better on them. Lily realized they had saved her.

"Thank you," Lily croaked.

"Yah," The lead troll said. Thin white membranes slid across his eyes for a second. "Now, the hard work."

Lily raised her eyelids at the troll's use of English. He walked from the culvert site and into deeper woods. His troupe followed him. *Groogh. Groogh-gah. Groogh. Groogh-gah.* The troll murmur and light footfalls echoed low on the forest floor. Lily heard heavier, fast footsteps. She turned to see Jordan charge to her through the trees.

"I've--" Jordan panted. "I've been trying to find you all night!"

The area was appropriately apocalyptic. Jordan helped Lily across a field of shattered cinder block and aluminum framing recently crushed by a backhoe. The huge machine sat ready for its driver to raze the remaining classrooms. Today they would serve as a bunker for the last battle in this ethereal invasion of Earth. Loud pops of distant gunfire sounded in the distance. Police and civilians fought bands of zombies hunting the living. Lily knew they would regroup and come for her now she was alive again.

Lily and Jordan stopped when they heard a door open. Sam came out of a classroom with a shotgun. Behind him emerged two armed and living deputies.

"I thought you two were zombie chow," Sam said.

"Same here," Jordan replied.

"This is Barret." Sam motioned his head at the deputy next to him. "He's a cousin. I got him and some friends with guns." Sam lifted his shotgun. "Big guns. Solid slugs."

"Big enough, I hope." Lily added.

Inside the classroom, the deputy's coat was like a tent on Lily. She felt like a giant sitting in a child's chair the school district didn't take for another school, along with most other desks and fixtures. Unfortunately, the water had been shut off. The men used the bathroom anyway. Lily was getting tired of rank odors. Nevertheless, she took a deep breath to explain her plan.

"All the zombies are going to be drawn to me," Lily said. "My aunt--Joanie, we shared a bond. The demon bitch possessing her sensed that."

Lily paused. Thoughts not her own entered her mind. She absorbed them and continued. "Now that I'm back from death, the dark avatar wants to use me as a link, a conduit, in summoning something even worse than her."

"Then we need to get you out of here." Barret said.

"No. We need to use me to lure her and the zombies out."

"Then what?" Sam asked.

"I think the cavalry is here," Lily looked around the classroom. All she could see was dated maps and a few dusty books still on shelves. However, she did feel a confidence she didn't think would exist just from the men there to support her. "We just need to mass them here so we can defeat them all."

"And if that fails?" Barret asked.

"Then whatever evil plan the dark avatar has is going to work," Lily said. "So we fight so it won't."

"I don't know," Barret shook his head. "It seems getting you someplace safe is a better bet."

"That won't work, either." Lily countered. "She, this dark spirit, is just going to keep coming. We need to fight it now when we have some help from beyond."

"I agree. We fight." Jordan said.

"Easy for you to say." Barret looked at the unarmed Jordan.

"Yeah. It is." Jordan replied. "And it should be for you, too."

"Come on, cousin. It will be fun." Sam said and slapped Barret's shoulder.

"No it won't." Barret sighed.

"No. True." Sam said. "But a man's got to do--" Sam stopped as all deputies, Jordan, and Lily looked at him with arched eyebrows and quizzical looks. "Yeah, okay. Even I hate that one."

"Any rate, leaving is a moot point." Lily said and stood up to look out a scratched, Plexiglas window.

"Why?" Jordan asked.

"They're close. Coming fast." Lily answered.

"Zombies?" Barret asked and jerked up his shotgun.

"Everyone," Lily said while staring out. "Good. Bad. This is going down right now."

Lily walked out and stood in front of the rubble, unarmed. Jordan, Sam, Barret, and the deputies flanked her. All the men held shotguns and wore ammo belts. Lily stood in her still-wet clothes and watched the Zombies come. They walked and stumbled across the grassy playfield between the school grounds and the park. It was as Lily foresaw. Now she waited for her cavalry of spirits to come and repossess the zombies. She knew Aunt Joan--Joanie would lead that astral charge.

"Hold off shooting." Lily said.

"What?" Sam questioned. "The plan was--"

"The plan is to defeat the dark spirit behind this. We have help. Trust me and let this happen."

"If they get too close, I'm shooting!" Barret snapped.

Lily said nothing. Barret glanced at Sam who looked at Lily and nodded an approval. Barret grunted and took aim, but eased his tension on the trigger.

The hiss of the undead horde grew louder. Growls rose over the awkward trampling.

There. There she is!" Lily pointed.

At the opposite end of the field, the zombie of Aunt Joan emerged in her bright, floral suit.

She looked straight at Lily.

The sounds from the zombies stopped. The horde suddenly halted it advance.

The zombies shuffled together to form an arc. They began to merge.

"Joanie!" Lily screamed with all her lungpower. "Do it now! Now!"

Lily had imagined the spirits would look like the traditional gossamer sheets or misty human shapes. Instead, entities like white dust white devils appeared and swirled through the fusing corpses. Many zombies fell away like tumbling dominoes and shedding scales as the tempests whirled through their former corpses and forced out the possessing evil. The undead mass was greatly reduced, but not destroyed. Bodies and limbs of remaining zombies wove into a set of shoulders. A massive head slowly rose above them. A skeletal, ghoulish face looked down with burning red eyes. Everyone with a shotgun opened fire.

Lily ducked and covered her ears. She focused on the standing body of her adopted aunt. It convulsed. Lily could see the earthly echoes of an astral battle. A white tempest curled into a whip that lashed a dark cloud over the body in the bright, floral suit. Lily smiled. She knew Joan was overmatched in ethereal power, yet was tenacious enough to annoy the evil possessing her body. The literally heartless Williams shambled from the woods. Blood soaked almost every inch of his impossibly pressed uniform. The dark avatar fled Joan's body as a black corkscrew that bored into Williams' zombie.

Joan's body fell. Lily instinctively ran to it. Jordan stopped firing and chased after her. They ran down into the field and by the merged zombies that continued to mold into a torso of a gigantic ghoul. Huge, corpse arms erupted from the ground as Lily and Jordan ran around the growing abomination.

The dark avatar now occupied Williams' corpse. She once lived as a queen of a Caribbean island. Her current, dark avatar had worked summoned a demon ghoul whose name was forgotten before humans had language. The dark queen had sacrificed her own body millennia ago for the sinister power that now threatened modern Earth. She knew the hideous ancient would demand greater sacrifice to quell its wrath. At this moment and place, she provided enough perished flesh to manifest the demon of corpses and corruption. The valiant souls led by Joan had culled the zombies. However, the dark avatar's spell was still at work. The massive ghoul took shape.

The divots shot away from its writhing surface by the shotgun fire rippled closed. The men had not staggered their fire. Now they all rushed to reload as the monster continued its rise.

"I wish we could call in an airstrike!" Sam yelled. He pumped his reloaded shotgun and began firing again.

An airstrike could not bring greater carnage than what occurred. The monster ghoul was now a half body that towered above the field. It reached down and sunk its skeletal fingers into its sternum. Its arms thrust out and split its chest open as a massive, gateway of ribcage halves.

Lily and Jordan reached Joan's body. Lily knelt beside her. Across the field, Sam, Barret, and the deputies ceased their futile gunfire. Jordan turned and observed the horror.

"Ah, geez!" Jordan shouted. "This is Hieronymus Bosch in IMAX!"

It was more a portal to hell. Within the monster's chest, an eye stared from a socket in a huge, dark heart that beat slowly. It looked out to the earthly field from across a stygian landscape. Below the heart, demons and zombies ran towards the opened gate of rib bones. The Williams' zombie approached the hideous gateway and threw out its arms. Chants unheard for centuries rattled out of the zombie's dry throat. The prayers became cracking cries of shock. The monster ghoul reached down and snatched up the zombie and the dark queen within it. Giant jaws opened. Massive black fingers dropped Williams' kicking remains inside them.

"What is that noise?" Jordan asked as a muffled yet piercing scream assaulted their ears.

"A scream across dimensions. From inside that monster's throat!" Lily shouted as he held her ears.

The demons and zombies charging from the hellish world were nearing the grassy field. Jordan ignored the pain from the scream and leveled his shotgun at them. Within the giant ghoul, a body fell from its throat. It was not Williams' body. It was the form of a young island queen not seen for centuries. She continued screaming as she fell past the eye in the heart and struck the hellish ground. The demons and zombies turned and ran towards her. The dark queen began screaming again as they fell upon her body and began to rend her in a feeding frenzy.

A booming voice from the giant head drowned the queen's shrieking. "Sacrifice has been made."

Within the hellscape, the heart's glaring eye began to close. The ribcage slid closed and sealed with a deafening slam of two mountains colliding. The giant ghoul vanished. All the fallen zombies lay arranged as if with respect. Their ashen faces held a final expression of peace. The echo of the closing gates ebbed. Then, there was no sound. Lily sensed a vibration that slowly eased. When it ended, a breeze buffeted the grassy field.

Lily stood. She had witnessed the unbelievable but focused on the memories of Joanie, her friend and adopted aunt and maybe savior of humanity. Lily hoped Joan was somewhere, at peace, and smiling. Here, she smiled for them both.

Jordan saw Sam and the deputies walking toward them and waved.

"Hey, Lily, you did good." Jordan said and put his shotgun on the ground.

"Yeah," Lily agreed. She drew in a deep breath. It felt good.

"I'm glad it did it, but why did the giant, hell-monster thing eat that zombie that was really a woman thing?" Jordan asked.

"Well," Lily took another deep breath. "I guess after you've been locked up or asleep or whatever for a long, long time, then you might be really hungry when you get woke up. So if you eat souls, you'd eat the biggest one around. That was the zombie bitch queen. Bye-bye."

"And maybe it ate evil, not just souls." Jordan rolled his shoulders. "Maybe she misunderstood what she summoned."

"Maybe a little. Not a lot. I think we and all our allies made a stand that forced the demon ghoul to rethink things." Lily breathed. "I'm also thinking once we take care of Joanie and all the others, I want you to steal a truck with GPS."

"Oh?" Jordan cocked his head to one side.

"So you can drive me to my apartment. Through whatever."

"Oh, okay!" Jordan lit up with a huge smile. "I remember how to get to there."

"Fine. Then later you can take me home. And then go home, yourself. Because I want to take a very long nap."

"I'd like to join you." Jordan said and then threw up his hands. "On the couch! You got a couch?"

"Yeah," Lily sighed. "I got a couch."

THE TOWER AND THE PIT

"Is he dead?"

I heard a familiar, deep voice from several steps away through the constant city drone. The detective who spoke stood across the street with a young woman. The ambient glow of aged lights gave weak illumination. It was night on clocks, but without some form of lamp it's always dark. Modern Earth lost its views of blue skies and stars to permanent black clouds, long ago. That was after a city ate the planet's surface and weird things emerged that ate people. Fire had recently tried to consume me. I was little more than a ball of burned, cracking skin. It had been a bad day.

Buildings towered around us, but one lay in ruins behind me. It was what I guarded. Occasionally, flashlight beams swept over me. Light glinted off my last sidearm. My charred hand still gripped it hard. I knew the detective was John Slate. He's as close to a friend as a person like me can have. For a time the woman seemed to be like a friend. But now I knelt on the street, burned, bleeding, and alone.

"Did you try and help Grail?" Slate asked the woman with the tone of accusation as he put on a protective suit. Smart guy, Slate.

"That's his name?" she asked.

"Yeah. Did you?"

"Yeah," The woman replied. "A bunch of us did. But after a while, they left. They got scared. I got kind of scared, too. But I stayed over here to watch him."

"Nothing on the screens or at home?" Slate asked as he sealed his suit up to his face.

I couldn't see them well, but I'm sure the woman gave Slate a look worse than an expletive.

"Look, I stayed!" she barked. "But he said to get away from the ruins. So I did."

"Smart lady," Slate said, now with an assuring tone. "I'll go talk to him."

"You're not scared?" The woman asked.

"Of him? Maybe." Slate answered. "But I know him. Of what he's guarding, for sure."

"What is it?" she asked.

"No clue, yet. But Ice--the stoic Mr. Grail, there. He likes to keep moving. So if he's ready to drop but still on a job site, you should probably start moving away from here. And don't stop."

Slate came towards me. I tried to stand. My wounds had already started healing, but not enough. I just kept my bulk in a crouch and waited for him. I thought of the last, few hours. I hoped I hadn't waited too long.

Before I waited for Slate, I was healthy. My day started with a death. Normal for me. But this one didn't involve me and was broadcast to the world. The man might have been famous. A politician or a media star. Or just someone rich. The man's image was ten times life size. The building screen projected a holographic colossus of a person of ambiguous magnitude. I didn't catch his name beamed in bright letters high above a busy street. Distraction could get me killed. And not by the lousy drivers of hover cars and surface cans. Maybe that's how the notable death occurred. Distraction and a misstep.

The death was the news more than who died. Death is close to being an option for many in the floors risen above street level. The towers encasing their lives are hardened, geometric designs that carve the sky below the dark clouds into slots and straight channels. Earth is now a world of right angles and rigid layers.

The ground-level streets of the global city are my world. The dead man on the news knew another. He knew safety and medical technology that can extend life to however long you can afford to mortgage your cells. Yet, somehow, death got him. So that's the news. Not the person's life history, bad habits, and grand accomplishments. It's the fact he had it all and still died.

Information is broadcast to the streets as a public service, but the effect might be different from mere news. The culture down here likes to know what goes on up there if it shows a similar reality reached up the secured elevator shafts. Equality doesn't exist. So the unexpected death granted a small sense of justice, or projected vengeance. The brightly flashed obituary ended. Then a commercial began. For a health service no one on the street could afford. Smiles aimed at the bright screen sagged. The collective moment of spiteful joy died. Existence went on.

I never stopped walking. Being on foot is the best approach when I'm close to my target. It's quieter. I'm surprisingly stealthy for a large, human male. The skill is well learned and the tuition was painful. The weapons under my coat are not quiet when I use them. They are loud and flash like guns from past ages. But mine are used for real public service. I try to stop unexpected death on the streets by killing what preys on human life. You need a license to walk around and kill things, legally. My license carries the name Joshua Grail. My professional description is Biological Aberration Eradication. On the street, I'm simply a Monster Killer.

No one would broadcast or even write my obituary. Some people still read. The people who still appreciate a well-crafted sentence may be in the multiple billions. That's a big number, but a small percentage of Earth's population. The high mortality rate of us Killers is also why no one would read my obituary. Too typical. And that's fine. All my history would be lies, anyway. My present is focused on having enough skill to survive stalking horrors. It's my niche in the current cycle of life.

Electrical power is cycled sideways in some zones. I walked through one. Here, power radiates from a commercial hub. Transmission is controlled in areas where people can afford to look down and don't want to see anyone looking up. Although my services benefit everyone. I turned down a deserted street. The large building screen's light reflected off an ancient, masonry facade with steel plates in place of windows. Old, ground level storefronts defied the darkness with archaic lights and signs. None had holographic signage. Pocked pixel screens displayed a typical stream of ads. Food. Or its substitute. Sex. Drugs. Their media substitutes. Hens teeth. And fish.

Fish?

Downstream the lights were weaker and the people far fewer. Life looked threatened by the shadows stretching from dark spots and alleys. The shadows had their own problems. Flashed images on battered neode and LEQ signs beat them back. But on the next block it got even darker. There was little power for commerce and comfort in this zone. Pirate lines stole power, even for the street lamps. Greater power rose away from the pavement. Now, I looked up.

Once, the building across from me was a major skyscraper. Now it sat dwarfed by what dominated the region. Straight ahead stood a titanic monolith of artificial diamond and sky-beams fused into a seamless brick shape so vast it created a hemispheric wall of the global maze. The structure was not truly a hemisphere wide, but big enough to swallow all epic structures from past ages and a several recent ones. Its foundation lay deep in the planet's crust. Its smooth body pierced the dark clouds overhead. Other towers at perpendicular angles also cut into the cloud deck, but the massive super-tower was a greater triumph of the ascent of mass pushed beyond the sky. Better than ever, humanity could build huge.

So, of course, that great place was not where I headed. I was privileged to push into the ruins littering the super-tower's eastern zone. It stunk. The target location had a strong odor like offal. Fallen facade and debris lay piled against the front wall. The reports noted screams came from inside. No monster ever just walks out into the street for convenience. I'd have to dig. An old, city schematic displayed across my retina by a few off-the-book enhancements. The schematic showed where the main entrance once existed. I put my large, right hand to work. Quietly. At least as quiet as possible. My left hand gripped my weapon.

The excavation went slowly. Someone or something had shifted the debris. So far, all indications were human. Some fresh. They were probably fresh food, by now. I was supposed to meet with municipal engineers, but I ditched their calls. Some rule probably stated that firearm discharge near a super-tower's foundation required an engineering inspection. The damage would likely be mine from the ricochet. How about the engineer inspect the jaws of the thing I'm going to shoot? If she or he met the beast, I'd have to detail how a well-paid city employee became ripped chunks and a stain. Better the thing become the stain. Fewer forms to sign.

The ruin was an apartment or a hotel. I pushed aside a slab of collapsed entryway roof and found the front door in a hole. This place had died and been partially buried sometime before yesterday. I drew my shotgun from beneath my coat. The term *shotgun* describes the weapon's appearance. No actual shot flew from the muzzle or spent casings from the side. The propellant and projectile is one caseless round. Each round is a small, spin-stabilized, depth-sensing warhead with an armor-piercing core around sections of sequentially detonated explosives. The weapon's designer probably asked a Killer what he or she needed in the field. Something that kills anything was the likely answer. I have large handguns that fire the same rounds. They kick a little more.

I dropped down and push through debris in front of the gilded, double doorframes. Their glass lay shattered into clear, jagged pebbles. I could hear them crush under my boots as I forced my way in, muzzle first. Optical graphics supplemented my vision. It replaced the total darkness. The imaging relayed shapes, information, and more data from my gun's scanners. I entered a wide lobby with a curving reception counter, office doors, and other rooms along the curving walls. No motion. I placed my first *breadcrumb*. That's my term for the small, square packet that will emit light if my scanners failed and kept another, nastier surprise.

I found a different hint of nasty on the floor: blood and tissues traces. Human. The pattern led me to crushed elevator doors. There were scales and secretions that were not human. The scaly fragments were similar in structure to lengths split off from massive hairs. The elevator car had jagged sides at the bottom and no floor. I took the stairs. I placed another breadcrumb at the stairwell entrance. The stair flights seemed to ripple the stench rolling up from below. If life above the streets was a sort of heaven, then existence below the streets was near certain hell. But that would suggest it's a place worse than the streets. I didn't think it was. It just smelled worse. And if you smell what I do in a typical day, that's saying a lot.

I placed breadcrumbs along the stair flights and landings. I put on a respirator to cut the wafting funk. Maybe the world is dead below the scab of the city and this is the stink from its corpse. In the streets, I used a respirator mostly for show. I also have biological alterations to make the job survivable and keep me immune to most pathogens on this cloud-sealed world. I advertise my services, but not my personal improvements. I'd hate to be tagged as something like what I hunt. The effect would go beyond me. A human-shaped monster would crush humanity's psychological prop of being Earth's master. Truthfully, that's now only a joke.

Today's jokes have a sharp edge. Be a clown and the world will love you. Kill a clown and they'll love you more. Luckily for people who used white and colorful makeup, or just had extreme tattoos, I don't kill clowns. Not that often. If I found one hiding down here, no one will know. Oh, I joked with myself. I would not shoot a clown in cold blood. They are brightly colored, and more useful as bait.

I would not need one. At the next landing, the stairwell door was missing. So was most of the wall around the area of the doorframe. The jagged pattern was the same as the elevator car's ripped away bottom. Inside the hall, several talon points had punctured the walls and ceiling as if a huge-caliber machine gun had opened fire. The talons had ripped old fixtures and decor from the walls. The ripper was just a sprint down the hallway.

Bingo.

A mass of spines pulsed in waves as the creature turned. The best comparison to extinct life was a porcupine. A giant, red porcupine. But the monstrous, turning mass had no legs. It used enormous quills for locomotion. The puncture and pull of each spike on the wall and ceiling sounded as if a small avalanche had broken free. As it rolled around to face me, the undulating spikes looked more like giant centipede legs crushed into a ball while still writhing. I'd have preferred a centipede's head. Instead, a thick, bear-like skull with a centered, heat-sensing pit in place of any eyes faced me. It opened its wide jaws. More red quills flexed inside them. All the better for pulling in and ripping apart the prey, or the person. There were still pieces of a victim wedged between the flexing spikes. The beast needed to floss. It would need steel cable for the job. But it thought I was another meal. The thing charged. It was a bulky, spiky freak that was still very fast. I hated that.

My shotgun was already aimed. I squeezed the trigger. To avoid sensory overload, the scans switched off in the fraction of a second before the blast. The fired round hit the monster's skull, dead center. Its heat pit and upper-head shattered from the round's impact. The light from the gun blast vanished. I only saw the diming after-imaged before the sensors flicked back on. That occurred in the same fraction of a second when the round penetrated and then detonated inside the beast. The explosion lit its frontal quills like an inner strobe pulse. Most of its organs were shredded. The thing convulsed and fell dead. I waited for the rest of the second to tick off before I lowered my gun.

Somewhere under the spines was a muscular body that sagged as a deflated balloon. Just looking at the thing caused me to feel slashed. I was glad no one would face it again. Then the thing rolled back to standing. The blood flowed over the remaining bottom of its head and through the tooth spines. Scans showed the spatter across the pocked walls and my coat was its brain tissue. Yet its quills quivered as if shaking off the lethal gunshot. Even for a monster, that was impossible. All monsters were tough. Unique. Nevertheless, they were animals like all predators before. Albeit it twisted mutations and sewer-spawned nightmares. They were still living things. Blow apart enough living tissue and it dies. This thing was dead. Its corpse was a traumatized sack. Yet was moving.

The quivering was something else animating its shattered corpse. Something was already inside it, infecting it. Death had unleashed another kind of monster. Even after what I've seen, that was horrific news. I backed up with gun leveled. An amplified scan revealed some viscous protein spreading rapidly through the body. It acted like a separate, invading blood plasma. It reproduced rapidly in the creature's tissues and kept spreading. I'd tap my science knowledge and figure out the infection, later. Right then the thing tensed for a charge. I opened fire.

The blast concussions hammered and cracked the damaged halls. I would shoot the legs to stop it charging--if it had legs. In place of targeted carnage, I fired on the charging mass of spikes. And kept shooting. Each round hit, detonated, and blasted off chunks of meat, bone, and spikes. I reached for a handgun as the shotgun magazine emptied. The beast's exposed hips and vestigial leg bones blew apart with the final round. The moving pieces now were small enough to call myself safe from the reanimated beast.

I could feel my augmented immune system fight off the strange, viscous protein that had spread through the beast and spattered me. This inner battle made me feel sick. Near my wet boot, a chunk of muscle flexed a fractured quill in a circular arc in blood. I looked over the twitching chunks and realized the bigger, darker, and apocalyptic picture.

A switch to full analyzing mode narrowed the scanner pulses to microscopic. The reanimating plasma was the altered structure of a viral plasmid. The infecting agent was a new, advanced virus. In science classes of yore, a virus, however complex, was not considered alive. One reason was a lack of motility. A virus in any form could not move. Nor was it dead. They held a zombie-like state. Viruses used living cells as reprogrammed factories to reproduce. The new infectors, called virions burst out, went forth and multiplied. If not for a host's immune system adapting to fight and destroy the virus, some might have wiped out whole species.

Here, a virus adapted to using the dead. No defense. Just tissue to rewrite. The virus reanimates the corpse. It becomes a large virion spewer to shamble into other dead things. Soon a mass of moving, dead flesh would attack and kill the living so more could join the party. And the disease itself could kill. No normal human could fight off this infection.

The way a species can endure a disease is to make new, resistant generations. To do that, modern humanity would need to undo an earlier fix to the rampant population. We can fornicate forever with no children to show for it. Unless you pay a fee. Reproduction is like the electricity bill. Pay and get power. Otherwise, it's a switch controlled and owned by others. A natural function is now reduced to a regulated utility. Water is free. It's what delivers the reproduction inhibitor. There would be no way to shut off the valve on the inhibitors before the zombie disease had infected Earth.

I hoped this viral mutation and outbreak was local. If it spread, it would infect the people on the street, and not stop. In a world of billions stacked on billions and many billions upon billions more unseen, the plague will cause a scale of carnage more vast than any global apocalypse ever experienced or imagined.

I thought: I'm one person.

I thought: I need to act.

Joshua Grail's obit would never reveal that once I was a physician. Of sorts. Now, the world was my patient. Right. I knew thoughts like that would make me need a psychiatrist. Or a clown. No. I just needed to act. Period. My com-system should have penetrated the ruin, but a jamming frequency blocked all signals. No doubt the super-tower broadcast the jam to discourage squatters. Now the towers residents might be discouraging their own future. I needed to stay here. If I left to get help, I might lose the trail. I needed to find the source that infected the monster. I had only a vague idea of how big and deep this buried ruin could be. I placed another breadcrumb, and pressed deeper into the stench and blackness. If I couldn't get data to stop this zombie plague, Earth would become a planet-sized monster. And dead.

No pressure.

I was glad I had ditched the engineer crew and could do this alone. I was mad when I heard human voices before I saw the beams of their headlamps slashing the darkness of a lower hallway. Another distraction. I didn't need three lives to protect. All male. Each the standard mix of global ancestry. All of standard size and likely terrified inside standard-issue gray coveralls with equipment packs. One held an assault rifle, but the way he aimed it showed he was as afraid of it as what could be stalking them. And stalking them was easy with high-pitched, frightened speech and lamps. They all literally took one step forward and three steps back.

The city engineers decided to come anyway. They came before me and found another entrance. I wondered how they got passed the big, red porcupine. Then I saw one of them carrying another person's torn pack. DNA traces on it were the same as the scraps in the monster's mouth. So at least one of them didn't.

"Stop." I said as I slid off my respirator.

The one with the assault rifle spun towards me. His heart pounded faster than his weapon could fire. I snatched the rifle away to be sure. They all had nametags fused to each coverall's right breast. The former rifleman was Anzahl. The second engineer beside him was Stoller. Nieder was a cringing third.

"Who the hell are you?" Stoller asked.

"I work here," I said. "You idiots work for the city. Find a way up and out."

"You're the Killer!" Stoller said.

"Yep. Now, get lost."

"Hey, we work for the city!" Anzahl spat. "You can't order us--"

Anzahl quit speaking as their lamps lit my face and the harsh stare looking down at them.

"I think we should leave," Anzahl said.

"But that thing--!" Nieder finally spoke. "It ate Fritz!"

"I killed it."

"Did you recover any remains?" Stoller asked me.

I only cocked an eyebrow, and reached down to lower his lamp aimed at my face.

"I mean, we could at least have a service with something." Stoller continued.

"Get tweezers," I said. "Actually, don't touch anything up there. You all scan clean. So get to the top and call the cops. Call John Slate. Tell him Grail is here and needs gamma ray projectors, ASAP."

"Gamma projectors?" Stoller jerked back.

Obviously he understood using all-penetrating radiation was an extreme measure. The projectors could fry anything from whales to microbes. My immune system had cleared out the virus, but I wanted to fry everything in the zone infected with the zombie plague. Maybe even the whole zone.

"What the hell for?" Nieder asked.

"Get up and out and do it." I ordered and turned back to the stairs.

"Team fifty to muni-central--" Anzahl stopped his com attempt when he saw me turn.

"You think maybe I tried that?" I rasped, and then tossed Anzahl his rifle.

"So have we. A lot." Stoller said. "We all need to get out of here. Come with us."

"I have something I need to do," I said. "I need you to call Detective John Slate when you're clear. Move."

"Hey, no one's job is worth their life." Stoller stepped toward me with his hands out.

"So, you killed that spiky thing." Anzahl glanced at me and then his rifle. "I, um, I didn't even see it take Fritz."

I guessed Anzahl wanted absolution, but I took the rifle from him again and handed it to Stoller.

"Maybe you won't freeze," I said to Stoller. "But you all need to get up and out."

"But if that thing is dead, we're safe." Nieder chirped. "I mean, what could be worse?"

"Another one." I said and raised my gun level with his head. I was aiming behind him.

"What?" Nieder screeched.

I didn't need augmented senses to smell him piss his overalls even through the existing stench. Another second began to unfurl, and more slaughter. I yelled: "get down!"

His muscles twitched to do that, but the monster's jaws snapped shut over his head and shoulders. This beast had a simple form. Something like an eyeless lion with a massive head and a mane of pulsing tentacles that enveloped the rest of Nieder once the blunt jaws clamped down. So maybe it wasn't that simple. It was also dead. The zombie virus had taken it long before it killed Nieder. It wasn't hungry. It was spreading the disease. Whatever remained of Nieder would join it. I fired.

The bodies blew apart. Anzahl collapsed into a ball at the deafening blasts. The braver Stoller came next to me to spray the hall and twitching chunks of monster with the assault rifle's comparatively small bullets. The rifle's sharp staccato ended. Stoller vomited when he saw parts of Nieder's coveralls among the spread of carnage. He stood and wiped his mouth. He never uttered a word of accusation or guilt.

"What I need to stop here isn't just the monsters," I said. "They carry a disease. It must infect them at a lower level. I need to find that. I need to destroy it."

"We're engineers," Stoller said in low, strained tones as he stared at the remains of his friend and the monster. "We can help."

"You could get killed."

"You need a source of energy to cook the disease," Stoller continued. "That's why you want the gamma ray projectors. We might be able to make this ruin a kiln and do the same thing."

"Okay. How?" I asked.

"Eventually the angle of the nearby super-tower has to cut through the lower levels of this ruin." Stoller finally looked up at me from Nieder's remains. "The foundation has to go deep to support the tower. Very deep. The foundation complex is sheathed by a massive, reactive slab. It's a geothermal conductor that moves heat rising from the mantle up through the tower. Like a thermal circuit that helps warm and cool the tower's environment. Without it, even its foundation would melt."

"So how do we tap that heat?" I asked.

"If I can lay a com-node on the foundation slab, any part of it, I can link and tell it to channel heat across this region of its outer surface."

"Then we just need to run." Anzahl spoke as he stood up.

"Yeah," Stoller added. "I can create a timeframe, but it will get hot, fast."

"Won't the foundation slab be hot, anyway?" I asked.

"We have thermal suits in our packs." Stoller answered. "It's part of the job."

"Usually we don't get killed doing it." Anzahl added.

"Nice job, then." I said. I liked the plan. Even if I couldn't find the exact virus source, Stoller's plan would kill all of it and anything infected for quite a wide area. I only hoped it was contained in the ruin. It was worth the attempt, and risking their lives. Mine was always in danger, anyway. "Okay. Let's go."

"Um, I have no bullets." Stoller said. He pulled off his rifle's empty magazine and held it up to me.

I handed him one of my backup handguns, an Aquila *Tyranus*, mark four. It was a heavy mass of advanced alloys. Stoller dropped his magazine and rifle and took my sidearm as if receiving an anvil.

"Proximity sensor acts as the safety. Use both hands," I said. "It's got kick."

Stoller took a moment to consider the gun as boon or burden.

"I'll walk ahead," Anzahl said. He picked up the rifle and inserted a new magazine from his pack. He obviously was summoning his courage to atone for failing to save Fritz or at least shoot his attacker. The rifle would not have done much to stop the red beast. I had another reason to let Anzahl take point.

"You'll be safe," I said in assuring tones. "I'm right behind you."

I pocketed my respirator. Maybe they had intra-nasal versions, but I kept mine off for camaraderie. I lifted my shotgun and pointed down the hall. Anzahl nodded and walked to the stairwell.

As a Killer, I make choices that seem harsh and uncompromising. But most are complete compromises. A Killer endangers personal safety for a job. You can see it as serving the greater good, or serving your bank account for the bounties. You faced death, either way. The engineers found themselves faced with death, unexpectedly. All were ill suited for it. Now only one of them was still alive. Stoller still breathed. His breaths were labored because of the heavy air and stench. Anzahl shambled ahead of us. Dead.

I had to make a choice in the hall about telling him he was dying from the zombie infection, or play my hunch the virus would draw his freshly infected corpse to its source if we were close. A sort of undead nesting instinct. As long as he faced forward and didn't notice Stoller and me, my plan might work. It would make finding the virus' origin source more direct. The infection drew him home.

The stairwells became more sparse, walled with unpainted concrete. The flights were narrower with a greater gap in the open shaft in the center. And the stink got worse. It seemed many of the zombie plague victims never left its source. Their bodies might be making a reservoir of virions. The reek grew thicker the deeper we went. My scans could analyze the chemical makeup. The strong stench was rotting humanity. Stoller wretched.

"How can you two stand this air?" Stoller wheezed.

"It will smell worse when we cook the place," I replied.

"Is the stench from monster crap?" Stoller asked

"No. It's death. Decomp." I said and watched Anzahl. "The mass of plague victims. Monsters. Squatters and explorers. Mostly people. There down at the source."

"Hey, Anzahl." Stoller called out. "You have water, right?"

There was only silence and shuffling.

"Anzahl!" Stoller yelled.

"Watch your volume, Stoller." I said. "Something hungry could hear us."

"What's with Anzahl?" Stoller asked.

I paused, and took an unfortunate deep breath. "He's a walking corpse."

"What?" Stoller froze.

"Keep it tight," I tried to sound calming and in control. "I didn't tell you because I didn't want you to freak out. Your friend is dead. But he's leading us to the source."

Stoller stumbled like a zombie. But his broken gait was from exhaustion and shock. I grabbed his shoulder and propped him up.

"We're going to find it," I said. "And then your friends and the victims here will be the only humans lost."

Stoller said nothing but stared at the shambling Anzahl in fear. I pulled him in line behind me and kept walking. Stoller clutched the big handgun I gave him tightly but followed.

Anzahl turned.

"Crap," I muttered.

Anzahl lowered his bottom jaw and waved the rifle as if it was a hook, not a gun as he came at us. My shotgun barrel clipped his skull. Anzahl's zombie fell against the inner railing. The rifle fell and banged against a lower landing. My second swing knocked Anzahl straight down the shaft. The awful splat sound came soon after. We were near the bottom.

I slapped another breadcrumb at the last landing. Rubble buried the next flight of stairs. There was a smear on the ground left by Anzahl's corpse before it got up and stumbled through the skewed doorway.

"I don't know why you do that," Stoller shook his head with a weary neck. "They don't give off much light."

"They're not just for light," I said.

We went through the skewed door. It was suddenly much hotter. An odd, faint luminescence allowed unaided sight. The ground was disturbed, natural dirt inside a chamber cut by the excavation for the super-tower's base. It felt strange to enter a large space after trekking through cramped and rotting halls and down slick, stinking stairs. Behind us, part of the hotel's outer wall was exposed and crossed with wide cracks. It looked ready to collapse and fill the hole. The chamber ceiling was a patchwork of exposed pipes, cables and undersides of buildings and ancient streets somehow still intact and mocking gravity. What loomed across from us proved Stoller right. A black expanse of the tower foundation lay exposed. The black field extended down to the ground at an angle. It appeared as a slab cut from night itself and then thrown through the Earth's crust.

"That's a foundation section." Stoller pointed to the black field.

A slope of rock and debris rested below the naked section of ebony. The foundation cut deep with no respect to anything already there. I assumed the people were warned to leave before the epic excavation. Maybe. We stood on the opposite side on a narrow ledge of rough ground. Beyond its edge, the dirt and rubble fell into a mirrored slope of the one beneath the ebony field. The opposing slopes created a wedge shaped pit. At the distant bottom was the Holy Grail. Or hell. We had found the viral source. This chamber next to the foundation created a perfect incubator for whatever might evolve in the current, twisted ecology. In the pit, a rippling mass of goo formed tendrils reaching up to touch and infect anything that moved.

Anzahl's corpse had stumbled and fallen down the slope. It was not alone. Along the slope sides near the bottom was a horde of animate corpses. Most were human. Some were hideous beasts.

The bodies suffered various stages of rot, from first infected to last. It looked almost as a horrific example of sediment layers in an exposed hillside. All zombies swayed with the moving tendrils. There was finally a unity between humanity and its bastard children predators. And it needed to burn. But the zombies didn't only donate virions to the pool as they rotted. They were also its defenders.

"There are too many," I said.

"I made that same calc." Stoller replied. "Even if you attacked and distracted them, there are more of them than bullets in a hundred guns. They'd overpower you and then get me before I turned up the heat."

"We need to move out," I said.

"All this was for nothing?" Stoller wheezed.

"No. Now we have a location. We can return to the surface and get help to incinerate this on a molecular level, either by your method or by radiation. The plague goo will become fried goo. The virus will be destroyed."

I said all that and hoped it was true. I felt defeated, but I needed to lift Stoller's spirits so he could haul himself out. One of us needed to survive now that our plan was busted.

"Um, maybe we'll be destroyed." Stoller pointed down.

The horde had noticed us. The mass of monsters and humans gazed up with vacant stares and some with empty eye sockets. The pool's tendrils waved frantically. A cascade of dirt rolled down the slope from Stoller's boot. Rocks struck the staring Anzahl. Stoller stepped back. I pushed him toward the tilted doorway and aimed downward to cover our exit. The zombies were beginning to climb.

We raced up the stairs. At a safe distance, I touched off the last breadcrumb I had stuck at the stairwell bottom. A wonderful bloom of heat and orange light flashed with the sharp boom of the small, plasma mine going off. The blast shook the stairwell. We fell against the stairs. I hoped the violence took out a mass of zombies, not just Stoller's front teeth.

We heard more feet, claws, and other appendages clank against the metal steps as the surviving horde came for us. After a few more flights, I set off another breadcrumb. This time I grabbed and held Stoller so the shockwave didn't knock him back into the edge of the steps.

The noise behind us stopped. I allowed myself a sense of satisfaction. But a wave of zombies crashed down the flight above us. They must have crawled up the exposed side of the hotel and forced their way through the cracked, outer wall.

Damn.

Another second ticked off. I raised my shotgun and fired though the steps above us. My rounds blasted through the mass of zombies and thinned the numbers that closed on us. Stoller screamed, but lifted the big handgun at the oncoming horde of rotting humans and beasts. As I feared, the gun's recoil was too strong for him. Stoller fired one shot. I was surprised he managed to fire a second. His shots had good effect in blunting the attack, but pain forced him to drop the gun from his sprained hands. I reached for him. The zombies got him first.

I grabbed only a ripping sleeve as the storm of tearing, thrusting arms and oversized jaws pulled in Stoller. His short scream was muffled by the zombie mass that tore and bit him apart. The arm from the ripped sleeve tumbled back out of the flexing horde. A brief, wet sound splashed my ears as Stoller's blood and pieces flowed across the horde. My gun blasts cut it off. The shells struck and blew the horde of dead people and monsters into more shredded parts. The attack on Stoller had concentrated the zombies. Several shots blew a crease through the grasping, biting wall. I forced my way through the reeling mass of rotted bodies. Limbs swiped at me. Some severed arms locked onto my legs. They fell away as I charged up the steps.

I spun to shoot stragglers in my way. The human zombies exploded from gunfire made to kill much larger bodies. For the first time on this job, I felt like vomiting. I kept running. Zombies and some of their parts kept up the chase. I set off more breadcrumbs to thin the herd close behind me. The heat scorched my exposed skin. But there seemed to be as many zombies as steps. I set off another breadcrumb. The super-hot plasma incinerated the zombies near the explosion and set ablaze those not crushed in the blast. I heard a loud, collective hiss. The sound was from protesting zombies and steam from venting fluids still in their bodies.

I finally fell onto the floor of the lobby, winded. Of course, I wasn't alone. Street people had found the hole I dug to the old lobby entrance. They used it to explore and scavenge. That same impulse had fed the zombie virus. Now these people were going to feed the zombie horde.

Damn.

The noise of my breadcrumb explosions brought people out from the side rooms and offices with pilfered fragments of no value other than proof of their bravery. They would never get to boast. I fired on the burning zombies emerging from the stairwell and climbing up the elevator shaft. They were still hell bent on ripping me apart. The slower fools from the street satisfied the horde's urge. Burning fingers and jaws tore into the flesh of their shocked, screaming victims.

I fired the last few rounds in my shotgun's magazine. A sizzling mass of dead flesh and newly torn skin and muscle covered the rear lobby. And there were more flaming zombies. The people ahead of me fled. I could see their butts shooting through my excavated hole in quick succession to the street. I set off the last breadcrumb in the lobby. Someone had knocked it free. It was in the wrong place.

Damn.

On the street above, people could see the flash of light and heat through the hole as my breadcrumb mine exploded. In the cavern below, my exposed skin burned. The blastwave knocked me far enough away to suffer but not completely sear. The final wave of zombies was fragments and ash. Like the red monster, I rolled back up. I pushed my body up onto my hands and knees as flames flickered out on my coat. Slowly I pawed like a zombie up to the street. But, I was still alive.

I was colored black by the smoke. So was the inside of my lungs. I coughed, gasped, and wheezed as I crawled onto the surface and lay flat. Of course, I could see the super-tower rising high above. People gathered and watched me. That was all they did. No applause for saving them. They didn't know I was trying to save the world. They did know my face was a gasping crisp.

Through my pain, I considered the only difference between them and zombies was that this horde just stared. They might as well be a bunch of clowns. One could have at least juggled.

Finally, a few people approached. One young woman offered help.

"I'd call a quick-med," she said. "But we can't call anyone around here."

"Tss-okay," I rasped. "I guess--*cough!* "I guess you're not a clown."

"I don't get it," she said.

"Don't wh-orry," I wheezed.

"You need a pump," she said staring at my accidentally altered complexion with wide eyes. "Meds!"

"Really, I just need a shower." I groaned. "Maybe some water."

"We can get that. But you really should watch drinking the stuff. Water is dangerous."

I look up at her with eyes staring out from a face burned and blackened. She realized the irony and smiled. I would have, too. But right then, it hurt.

"Cops." I said. "Slate."

"What's a slate?" She asked.

"A cop." I rolled into a crouch. "Get to a clear link and call the cops."

In the time that passed, my introspection made me quiet and the brave woman decided to listen to my warnings and step back across the street. Slate now stood where she had been. For once, he looked down at me.

"So, big man. What can I do for you, today?"

Cough! "Save the world."

"Oh, no worries, Ice." Slate chimed. "Did that by lunch hour. How can I repeat step A?"

"Drop the smarm. Listen."

"Okay."

I grunted as I handed Slate an encapsulated infomere I had created while waiting. It contained data sequences on the events, the zombie virus, and how to kill it.

"And we need gamma ray projectors here, and an engineer crew--*cough*!--at the super-tower." I said with the assumption he would load the infomere right then. He did, and then turned his head to com with subordinates at his precinct. It would all get done. The virus, not humankind, was doomed.

But tomorrow, there would be another monster. Problem was, I might take the day off.

AT PEACE

Craig Miller entered the old building. The whole place smelled like formaldehyde. Craig thought the reek fit the old community college labs. The college had grown, moved, and locked up this place years ago. Now, renewed funding allowed the school district to rent it for a high school advanced placement program. Craig was one of its students. He volunteered to help his science teacher, Mr. Alvarez, reopen the place. He just wished it didn't smell like one, giant specimen jar. Every surface reeked. Even the dust. Craig hoped it wasn't all toxic. Formaldehyde's formula popped into Craig's mind. CH2O. Systematic name 'methanal.' These were only a few of his many memorized facts and formulas. Mr. Alvarez went to find the fuse box. Craig took the case of CFL light bulbs and wandered the dusty, tiled halls.

Horror movie scenes played in Craig's mind as he slowly walked through the darkened halls and into a shrouded lab. Then he saw it looking at him. Craig's pulse increased. It stared out from a glass dome capped with dust on a counter. The dome's sides were clear. The eyes behind the glass stared right at Craig. Beady eyes. A rat's eyes. Luckily, it was dead. Craig took a deep breath of relief and wished he hadn't after the smell and kicked up dust hit his sinuses. Craig peered closely at the specimen rat. It seemed to have a glint of life within the eyes, visible even in the shadowed lab. Craig put his case down and nervously moved even closer. The world seemed to explode into light.

Craig yipped like a poodle. Mr. Alvarez laughed as he flipped on the last light switches.

"Man, Craig! That was priceless."

"Thanks, Mr. A. I like heart attacks."

"Too young, too soon, my friend." Alvarez smiled. He pointed to the old light fixtures. "Replace as many bulbs with CFLs as you can. Do the reopened labs, first."

"Okay," Craig looked at the lights. Instead of a glass cap, each unit had a circular wire frame as if to trap the old incandescent bulbs inside. "Weird."

"This place is old." Alvarez said. "But we'll make it work. Can I trust you?"

Alvarez held up a set of keys to Craig. His honestly was why Alvarez had chosen him to help reopen the labs. Craig knew it and smiled. He took the keys. He would get to know these old labs and their secrets. He looked back at the rat. Even dead, it seemed to be studying him. Craig wondered what other weird stuff the cabinets held. Probably more dust. And bad smells. Maybe even some living rats.

The smell was still in the old labs the next day. Craig wondered if it would ever leave. Formaldehyde was a popular disinfectant and preservative, before its toxic effects were fully understood. Craig liked to think that science was always moving forward, but it sometimes seemed to make itself take a step backward. For the better, he knew. He peered down at the specimen rat. It still seemed to stare back at him with flat but knowing eyes. Craig wondered why someone would leave it sealed in this old place. He thought it might look cool in his own room. He shelved the thought and went to work. Mr. A. told Craig that he would only need some antihistamines to work in the reopened labs. However, Craig's mother insisted he wear a respirator and gloves after he had described the place to her. Craig tucked the gloves under his belt and the respirator hung around his neck. Technically, he was wearing them. He pushed a wide mop along the floors. He thought this was hardly a good use for his advanced placement intellect.

To make matters worse, Craig had loaned his earbuds to Janet Brooks in math class. The only noise to entertain him was the occasional squeak of the mop handle. After a circuit of the hall, Craig found himself back in the lab with the rat. He stopped. He wiped the dust from the glass dome with his gloves. He put them on, and lifted the dome from over the rat. It still stared back at him. Craig found it odd that the wire frame was outside the rat's body, as if it held the rat captive rather than support it. Craig flipped the tail. It moved easily, unlike a body part for a dried corpse. The lab was eerily silent. This rat was weird. Really weird. Craig fell deeper into his curiosity as if lost in a daze. A sudden voice knocked him awake. He hit the mop handle. It struck the tiled floor with a hard rap. Craig spun. A smiling man stood behind him.

"I say again, hello, young man!"

"Uh, hi." Craig squeaked over his pounding heart.

"You seem startled." The man said.

"Uh, yeah." Craig recovered the mop handle. He wondered if he would need it as a weapon.

"I'm Peter Dorral. Mr. Alvarez didn't tell you I was coming?"

"Uh, I guess it slipped his mind." Craig answered. "A lot of stuff does."

"Well, now. Ask him if he takes a statin." Dorral smiled. "He asked me to check out the place. I used to run this lab for the instructors. When it was a college." Dorral looked across the lab. His mind filled its emptiness with memories of students and colleagues.

Craig calmed down. He studied Dorral. There was an odd, flatness to his eyes. They seemed to be missing that sheen of tears that reflected light. Dorral's eyes appeared more like gray marbles set inside a wax sculpture. Craig guessed that was just another fact of being old. Really old. But Dorral seemed nice. Craig figured that when this guy worked here, he must have been at least as old as Mr. Alvarez is now. Mr. A. must be close to forty. And that's old, Craig thought. By now, this guy must be close to death. Craig hoped he didn't keel over while he was here. Craig had taken CPR certification as extra credit. But he didn't really want to use it on anything other than a rubbery dummy. Certainly not a man. A very old, old man.

"You've been busy!" Dorral broke both their reveries.

"Yeah, Mr. A, uh, Mr. Alvarez has a big list." Craig said. "Other kids were supposed to show up. But they bailed."

"But not you. Good work. Nice to see some work ethic out of the young. I'm not sure I had that when I was your age." Dorral looked at Craig with a grin and cocked his head. "That was about a thousand, ten-thousand years ago."

Craig smiled. He began to feel at ease with the stranger. After all, he hadn't blown up over the rat. Yet.

"Did they have the wheel back then?" Craig ventured a joke.

"Ha! Good one, kid. It was just out." Dorral chuckled. "I see you found Rex."

"Rex?"

"Yes." Dorral pointed at the rat. "Rex, as in king. Sort suggested by King Rat." Dorral looked at Craig but saw only a curious but lost expression on his young face. "The book. James Clavell?"

Craig gave a meek shrug.

"Kids. No sense of the classics. Even modern ones."

Dorral smiled. "That was true even when the wheel was new. Anyway, just be careful. Rex is about as old as this place. And you can guess that's old."

Craig thought of saying 'but not as old as you,' but in a moment of deference, he refrained.

"You, uh, worked here?" Craig asked. "As a teacher?"

"I only filled in for chem labs. I did all the work behind the scenes and graded lab reports. The instructors got all the glory."

"Old Rex there became our biology mascot. He originally belonged to a fascinating man. Dr. Leonard Carsters." Dorral looked to see any hint of name recognition in Craig, but he only shrugged again.

"Yep. Carsters." Dorral continued looking over the lab. "Controversial. Misunderstood. He had a career in academia, but like other forward thinkers, he hit barriers. But you would've liked him. He was a rebel. Kids still like to rebel, right?"

Craig nodded affirmation.

"He quit the ivory halls to teach in ones like these. He figured influencing young minds was as important as fighting entrenched thought."

"Is he still around?" Craig asked. He wondered if any other ancient ones would be joining them.

"Sorry to say, no. Heart attack. Kind of ironic." Dorral frowned and fell silent.

"Why?" Craig asked.

"Oh," Dorral paused. His ashen face flexed as he thought of his answer. "No reason. Today we know so much more about hearts, brains, and even rats." Dorral nodded towards the rat. "Don't let him bite you."

Craig did a half-spin to face Rex. He glanced back at Dorral who was smiling.

"I'll go see if I can kick on the air circulation." Dorral walked to the exit. "You'd like to filter some of this dust, right?"

"Yeah!" Craig nodded. That might mean less mopping.

Dorral left. Craig was alone again with Rex, the rat. He almost thought its eyes went from watching Dorral leave and focus back on him. Craig removed his gloves. He'd need his fingertips to start removing the wire frame.

"Uh, when are you going to be here, Mr. D?" Craig asked.

They both entered the parking lot. There was only one, old sedan. It was obviously Dorral's car. The bicycle was Craig's ride.

"You have the keys, Craig. I guess I'll get here only after you do." Dorral smiled. He turned and walked to his car.

Having the keys gave Craig a sense of security. He thought this old guy, Mr. D, was okay. Craig freed his bike and watched Dorral get in his car. He wondered if he should tell Mr. D about the rat. After Dorral had left the lab, Craig had carefully removed its wire frame. He had turned away from Rex to put the frame aside. When he turned back, the rat was gone. Rex had vanished like dust beneath a mop, but without even a fallen hair from its preserved body. It freaked out Craig even now. He felt bad over losing the lab's old mascot. He hoped Mr. D. wouldn't have some nostalgic crying jag over it. Rex was just a rat. A dead rat. A dead rat that disappeared as if it was still alive. Craig wondered if its limbs somehow had that same, weird animate quality in its eyes. To be dead, but move. A zombie. Craig began to think about Mr. D's flat, tearless eyes and ashen face. He pumped his bike pedals hard to get home fast.

The next day, Craig hurried to get the light bulb swap done while he still had some time alone. He had no way of explaining Rex's disappearance. He hid the wire frame and glass dome inside an empty file cabinet. Before Mr. D arrived, he hoped to unlock more doors, peer into old labs and offices, and maybe find Rex, the dead rat, partially chewed by a live one. And that rat would be dead from Rex's formaldehyde toxin. Maybe he could use it to replace Rex. That might work.

Craig now had a box full of old, incandescent bulbs to shove away. He tapped a cabinet door. It sounded empty. After fishing for the right key, he unlocked it. There was something inside. Old notebooks sat on the bottom shelf. He took them out. Rusting, binder rings had stained the pages. But the words were still legible. There was even a photo series on Rex when he was alive. In one photo, Rex clung to someone's arm who wore a lab coat. In the next photo, Rex was dead. In the following photo, Rex was alive again. Someone had made Rex a rat zombie. A typed note stuck to the last photo. Craig read that the subjects—he shivered that there was more than one—experienced a catatonic period similar to rigor mortis before mobility returned. A handwritten note read 'A coma for the dead?' Craig wondered if the immobility ever reoccurred. Maybe someone had later put Rex in that wire frame thinking it only a specimen. How many years had Rex stared out from under the glass until Craig freed him?

No way!

Craig thought he couldn't be reading this. But the penned and typed words confirmed that Carsters had made Rex a zombie rat. Now, that little zombie was now running free. Craig froze. He felt he was being watched.

"Hey, Craig!" Dorral's voice made Craig yip like a poodle.

Craig stood. His heart pounded again.

"Wow! That was some note you just hit. Must be scary reading. Can't be me, right?" Dorral smiled. "What did you find, there?"

Dorral looked at the notebooks. His smile ebbed. He seemed to know what Craig had been reading. Craig could see questions, concerns, and even fear light up Dorral's flat, grey eyes. A long, silent moment passed. Dorral broke the quiet.

"Wow. I didn't think any copies of Dr. Carsters' work survived."

"You know about this?" Craig asked.

"I was his lab rat. Um, assistant." Dorral said. "I helped him."

"Then you, you knew about Rex?"

"Well, it wasn't right, of course. But yes, we used animals back then. Now you can probably just write a computer model for tests. In the day, we were more direct. I'm sorry you had to see that, Craig. Obviously, things are better now. You okay?"

"Yeah." Craig drew a deep breath. "Yeah. I'm fine."

"Okay then." Dorral patted Craig on the shoulder. "Say, maybe we should put those notebooks back. We still have a lot of work to do. Right?"

"Right." Craig closed the notebook. "Yeah. Right."

The following day, Craig went right to the notebooks. They were gone. He wondered if Mr. D. still had an old set of keys. Maybe he had left an outer door open. Either way, Craig was glad he had snuck back and photographed all the pages with his mobile phone last night. Every bit of their data was now digital. No one could prevent it from going viral. The key to making zombies was only a few megabytes deep. And Craig owned it all. He hoped Mr. D would understand. Maybe now people didn't need to die or stay dead, not just rats. Craig remembered the horror film versions of zombies. He wondered if eating the living was something Carsters' test subjects ever did. He thought of Mr. D. and his ashen skin. How old would you be if you were older than forty when this lab was open, and you were still alive now? Craig thought the answer was: you'd be dead by now. And Mr. D. was not dead. Or maybe he was, just reanimated. Sort of like his Dad after a morning coffee. Craig wondered how far Carsters went in his experiments. Was Mr. D. a zombie? Would he eat Craig's brain? But he never tried, and he had plenty of opportunities. Maybe he just wasn't hungry. Craig wondered where his mop handle was. It was too late to find it.

"Hi, Craig!" Dorral said as he entered the lab. "You're early today."

"Uh, yeah." Craig closed the open cabinet.

Hours went by. Craig and Dorral waved when they crossed paths on individual jobs. Afterwards, they worked well together as a team restoring water and gas lines to the labs. Dorral was a kind and understanding teacher. Craig's concerns drifted from his mind. Then, as they were preparing to lock up, Dorral stunned Craig with a comment.

"I guess you're wondering why I took Carsters' notebooks."

Craig dropped his jaw but stayed quiet.

"I think you know." Dorral nodded slowly. "Just like you realize why Rex took off after you freed him."

Craig's heart began to beat hard, again.

"I was surprised to see Rex." Dorral said. "I guess he showed after I retired, had a coma fit, and someone wired him up. Weird, huh?"

Craig nodded.

"Don't worry, kid." Dorral gave Craig a gentle, understanding smile. "I am your friend. Really. I'd never let anything happen to you. It may sound a cliché, but young people like you are the future. You're smart. And you seem well raised."

Craig nodded.

"Do you, uh, do—" Craig felt his cracking voice lose volume, and then he lost the ability to form words.

"I don't eat brains, if you're curious." Dorral said. "I'm dead, so I don't need to eat anything. Just pump in some lubricants to keep everything moving, and I'm set for the day." Dorral flexed his arms. "You can't believe how much I save not buying groceries." Dorral gave Craig a wide smile.

Craig nodded. He swallowed and regained his voice.

"How did you die?"

"Heart attack. Right here." Dorral pointed at the floor. "It was after class. Only Carsters and I were here. It was a doozy. I was done for before you could dial nine, not all of nine-one-one. Don't smoke, by the way."

Craig's eyes locked on the floor. He nodded.

"I guess it was an act of curiosity as much as compassion when Carsters injected me with his formula." Dorral continued. "It worked. He was amazed. I was a bit perplexed."

"Did you see anything? When you died?" Craig asked. He and his own heart started to relax.

"I don't remember anything other than opening my eyes to see Carsters looking at me like I was either his newborn son or his means to stick it to his former colleagues."

"Did he?"

"He never got the chance." Dorral inhaled as if drawing a sigh of relief. "That's why it's ironic Carsters died of a heart attack. So did I. But no one was around to inject Carsters with his own formula. There was none of it left. He'd used it all on me, and he hadn't yet synthesized any more. I guess he waited too long to do both things." Dorral paused and lowered his head. "I blame myself for his death."

"Why?"

"I had asked him for time." Dorral looked plaintively at Craig. "I needed time to think. To adjust. And then, he was gone."

"But his notes!" Craig shouted, but stopped himself from revealing his digital copies.

"They can give clues as to how to recreate the formula. But Carsters was canny. He never fully revealed all his secrets. Not even to me." Dorral drew another deep breath. "I thought I had all the copies, until you found the early draft. I destroyed those, too. I don't think humanity is mature enough for everything it can do now. I don't know what would happen if death was less certain than taxes."

Craig paused. He drew his own deep breath. "I made copies."

Dorral paused. He sat against a lab table and massaged his forehead. "I see. Digital, no doubt."

"Yeah."

"What are you going to do with them?"

"I don't know."

"I'd like you to delete them. Destroy the drive they're on, too. I'll repay you."

"That's okay."

Dorral took a long look at Craig. "So, here you are. You have to make a huge decision without much life experience. I guess I have to appeal to your intellect, and any innate sense of ethics. I can't stop you from publishing Carsters' notes. But I would like you to think about the consequences if you do. Mostly, please think of me. I'm the only living example of his work. People will come looking for me."

"They don't have to know." Craig said. "I won't tell them!"

Dorral face took on that knowing smile. "People are smart. Even the evil and greedy ones. I don't know how the world keeps a balance between good and evil. Maybe we really don't. But they'll figure out who and what I am. I don't know if I even qualify for civil rights, anymore. No laws have ever dealt with the rights of the animate dead. And I'm too old to start protesting with signs again. Of course, it would be a demonstration of one."

Craig stared off in thought.

"I see you need a little more civics classes as well as the advanced math and science."

"No. I get it." Craig said.

"I'm glad." Dorral paused. He looked around the room, and slowly stood up from the lab table. "Well, there really isn't much for me to do. All the labs are up and running. Mr. Alvarez is going to come by and hook up the new computers and Wi-Fi."

Craig was confused, but nodded.

"I hope to see you again, Craig. As a friend."

Dorral extended his hand. Craig shook it. He felt Dorral's grip was firm but cold.

"Please consider what I said." Dorral said. He turned and left the lab.

A day passed. Craig and Mr. Alvarez took the Wi-Fi routers to the lab. Craig was hardly helpful. His mind was distracted by more than Alvarez understood. Alvarez sent Craig home believing his young mind and body were overworked. Yet there was a lot more for Craig to consider. He could change the world. He could destroy a friend. He wondered if one act would do both.

A day passed. Craig mounted his bike outside his high school and waited for the kids with cars to rocket out of the parking lot. He turned and was surprised to see Mr. Dorral approach him.

"Hi, Craig."

"Hi."

"I was curious." Dorral said. "Have you made a decision?"

"No." Craig dismounted his bike. He felt more adult with both feet on the ground. "It could help a lot. A lot of people, I think."

"Maybe." Dorral nodded. He looked to check that no one was within earshot. "It might change the world as we know it. Maybe into something good. Maybe not. Even the Earth consumes the land and renews it. Death is a part of ecology for a reason. I know that sounds odd, coming from me."

Craig nodded. He drew a deep breath. He looked at Dorral. He seemed more alive outside in natural light.

"Okay, Craig." Dorral looked to the side and slowly nodded. "I know it's probably too much to ask you not to publish those notes. They can set you up for your life even before your old enough to vote. Just get a good price."

Dorral turned to leave. Craig watched him take a few steps.

"I haven't decided!" Craig shouted.

Dorral walked back to Craig. "I know. And I trust you. But maybe it's time I went and found and ice floe, anyway."

"Ice floe?" Craig asked.

Dorral smiled. "Kids. No sense of the classics. Even the older ones. Take care, Craig."

Craig watched Dorral leave. He rode back home, slowly.

The coed screamed. Her blonde hair and other assets bounced as she ran. The zombies followed her into the warehouse. They shambled through every entrance and surrounded her. Grey and rotting hands grabbed at her limbs and clothes. She screamed and feebly attempted to push back the horde surrounding her. She fell at the center of the moving, dead mass. A sudden boom halted the coming carnage. Several shot gun blasts made the zombies flying puree. The hero continued to fire. He shot so many rounds that he paused to reload and restore an iota of plausibility. The zombies turned towards him with no sense of self preservation. They advanced and the shotgun fired again, and again. Bits of gore and black blood flew liberally into the air as if pitched from buckets. The final zombie head exploded from a buckshot decapitation. The hero helped the coed to her feet. She was miraculously uninjured, other than the zombie teeth left in her scalp. She bit the hand that saved her. The hero screamed.

Craig ejected the old DVD from his laptop. He flipped the disk across his room. It hit a game cartridge that also promised "Guns Against The Dead!" His own encounter with a zombie was different. Mr. Dorral--Mr. D, had never tried to eat is brain, or infect him, or do anything else other than be nice and trust him. It was the trust that ate at Craig. He had a means to change the world. The photos of Carsters' notes could bring fame. They could bring fortune. They could also destroy an old man. Actually, a living dead man. A zombie. But a nice one. If Mr. D. survived the release of the notes, he could be like a strange uncle to Craig. However, this uncle's strangeness came from his odd existence, rather than how he behaved after too much holiday booze.

Craig sat and wondered about the future. Right now, he had homework. He had IMs and texts to answer. Maybe there were naked pictures of a young, female celebrity currently enjoying a scandal. None of it appealed to him. For the first time, he would neglect his homework and the other things that occupy a young man's mind. He simply sat in a dark room, and thought. The person he felt most comfortable talking with about this was the same person it could harm the most. Craig knew what Mr. D's answer would be. He didn't know his own. He sat and thought. Dawn and another day would come too soon.

The next day, Craig was stunned. He was getting tired of the sensation.

"I'm sorry Craig." Mr. Alvarez said. "I guess you two got close."

"Yeah. Sort of." Craig answered. He sat in the chair next to Mr. A's desk and tried to absorb what he'd just been told. Mr. D-- Mr. Dorral was dead.

"He died in his sleep." Alvarez said. "Peacefully."

Craig knew that was impossible, or so he thought.

"The body—?" Craig began.

"It's at the funeral home. Why?"

"How long?" Craig quivered.

"A while. So, why?" Alvarez eyed Craig with interest.

"Uh, I don't know." Craig slumped deeper into the chair. "It's just, just weird." And then probably not some coma fit like Rex suffered, he thought.

"I know. I'm still not used to death, myself." Alvarez offered. "I don't know if a person ever is. Would you like to go to the funeral? If you're folks think that's okay."

"Yeah." Craig said. "They will."

Craig's mother took him to the funeral. He wanted to see it all. The chapel service and the burial. Craig still didn't get how a zombie could die, not a zombie like Mr. D. Still, if anyone understood and could undo Carsters' formula, it would be Mr. D. The service had an open casket. Craig almost expected Mr. D. to open his eyes and wink at him. He suppressed a giddy laugh. At the graveside, Craig watched the same, closed casket lower into the ground. He suppressed a tear.

Another attendee was unseen by Craig. Rex felt an odd compulsion to travel to the cemetery. A rat was motivated by hunger, the urge to breed, and to fight or flee whatever tried to prevent either act. But those were the impulses of a living rat. Rex had been dead for a long time. He crouched beneath a car and wedged himself against a tire. The driver got into the car. Rex felt an impulse to run and escape, and a strangely equal sensation to stay and be crushed. He was uncertain which one to follow as the car started.

Craig read Mr. D's granite grave marker. It held the date of Peter Dorral's birth and the lie of his death. The dates spanned over seven decades. The phrase "Be at Peace" sat cut into the stone above them. It was meant as a wish for the dead. Craig realized it could also be a note for the living. And perhaps those in between. He made his decision. To be at peace with himself he would let another be left untouched. Quietly he withdrew his mobile phone and deleted all the photos of Carsters' notebook. If he ever saw Mr. D. again, it would be as his friend.

AMID THE DEEP

Don felt the aft deck roll. It was a stronger pitch than when the ship was docked. The waves would get bigger. They were moving out to deep water. He looked back at the harbor with remorse and anger. His ship left it for the final time. It was also the final moments of the city, Nomos, and anyone still alive near it. He hoped to stop the end of human life, but that could happen if the ship sank. Humanity had claimed this world, renamed it Emerald, and then remade it for themselves. Then a plague came that twisted humanity. Corpses rose to rend the flesh of the living. Soon after, cities burned as they had on Earth and other worlds. The night sky and banks of drifting smoke were flat black. Don looked back at the burning chaos that had been an industrial harbor. It all burned. He felt an urge to run from the smoke and screams drifting out to sea, even though the ship could move faster than any human could swim. The ship turned and the edge of the last standing city came into view. It glowed like a massive ember.

They had to launch their self-contained rescue mission before the next wave of refugees arrived and also demanded passage on a ship already overcrowded and short on supplies. It ate at Don. He couldn't save them. Some people started a riot when they saw their hope moving into deeper waters. The riot spread like an instant plague and rolled back through the city. And then the wave of flesh ripping monsters flooded the streets. Don's homeworld called the monsters chomps, greeze, or the far older and more traditional tag: zombies. On his new planet, Emerald, they called them rippers. All worlds knew the scenario too well. The animate dead attacked and ate living people. If enough of a victim's flesh clung to its bones, the plague that spawned them added one more to the collective horror and the apocalypse got worse.

Live images illustrated the distant screams Don heard. Cam-drones still broadcast video. They still flew like dutiful, mindless things showing pictures of living people ripped apart by wretched, dead, and mindless things. Don saw the video played directly across his eyes. He watched a walking horror with vacant sockets wander and snatch at any moving thing. It collided with a fellow ripper that was once a human female and began biting its shoulder with impossible savagery. The victim ripper thrashed violently and tore itself free as most of its remaining deltoid muscle came off in its attacker's teeth. The victim became the attacker and bit at bare cheekbone and a partially fleshed neck. The fighting corpses folded in on each other and fell. Don hoped they wouldn't serve as a visual omen of life on his ship, with or without a reanimating pathogen. He pressed his subdural sphenoid switch and cut the video.

Don looked with unaided eyes at the destruction that became more distant. His former life as a colony administrator burned among the cinders on shore. The ship was Don's grand project. She ran silent while under power and dark while still near the shore. Both steps were defensive. A horde was still a threat while close to land. If zombies came aboard, the crew and every living thing would fight them off, but the risk of infection meant one bite or splash of putrid blood could annihilate all hope. With contact lost with Earth and the other worlds, survival here could be survival of the human species. Don heard sharp noises between the ship's side and the shore. He stepped over and gripped the deck rail. He had to take a moment and steel himself to look down at the dark waters. He could see nothing in the low light from the distant inferno. The sound was almost as if masses of limbs slapped against the water just as one would expect from a large group of people trying to swim out to a passing ship. Those people might be living, or otherwise. There were no voices, no cries. Don told himself it was the wash of the thrusters as the captain maneuvered the ship.

The weight they carried to sea was heavier than intended. Far worse, there was even more pressure to find a cure. News of a big boat under construction spread faster than a virus. Survivors followed. Some brought skills suited for the mission. Others brought vacant eyes focused to desperate stares when they saw the prospect of escaping a horrific death and wretched afterlife. Although everyone screened plague-free, more people meant a greater chance of spreading other infections and causing total failure. Some of Don's lieutenants wanted to bar any human overflow. They argued that fighting a mass of living, hungry mouths was no different to facing a zombie horde. Don pointed out that in today's environment, crowd control needed to be passive. You couldn't truly kill an onslaught of people, just slow it down. The plague would reanimate the dead, and they would become an even worse threat. And harder to kill. Don knew that if the ship didn't take extra people, they could destroy the project. A violent horde wasn't always made of zombies. Living people would riot just for food for one more day. The city inferno was that fear realized, but he felt no vindication. The ship was completed and loaded with the scientists' equipment. But even with extreme rationing, the additional mouths would suck up supplies and mean less time at sea away from zombie jaws on land.

Don called his scheme Project Emerald Tide. He hoped that sounded hopeful and uplifting. Even if it didn't, he just wanted it to work. The plan was to build on existing data and find a vaccine to stop the plague. If they could stem the outbreak and turn the tide of death, civilized life could return. In the very least, a vaccine would create the chance to fight the hordes without fear of becoming zombies. There were stockpiles of guns and bigger weapons on land. All they needed was willing, living trigger fingers. People would face death with more enthusiasm if dying meant you wouldn't try to eat your mother or son. Don didn't have anyone to fear losing or eating. He just didn't want to be eaten. And he wanted to be able to sleep soundly without fear on solid land. It surprised him that his plan was the best and now only chance at having that simple future. All others had failed. The deck pitched again. The burning shore was now farther away.

"Beautiful night for a sail." Dr. Narren said as he left the superstructure and walked out on deck towards Don.

"Beautiful? Right." Don said still watching the city ember become more distant.

Don looked over to Narren who grabbed the rail. The scientist and physician's narrow features stretched between his sharp chin and wide forehead. He made himself look weirder by wearing eyeglasses with thick, black frames. Such accessories were odd for Don's interplanetary culture. Discreet ocular caps adjusted vision or shielded eyes from intense light when necessary. Narren took to using age-old spectacles when ophthalmology became a lost art on Emerald. Don and others found Narren's reactions more odd than his appearance. Don never knew if Narren's smiles while looking away during a conversation were from a strange sense of humor, or mocking fatalism. Narren smiled a lot. It unnerved Don, who hardly ever smiled. Unknown to Don, his own demeanor got him dubbed 'the Glare' behind his back. Yet before the plague he was thought of as very amiable. Narren was considered weird even then.

"Well, we might as well take pleasure while we can." Narren said.

Don looked at him with a raised eyebrow, and glare.

"With all these extra people," Narren continued, "we are already doomed."

"You think these people will stop you from completing the vaccine?" Don said as a compressed hiss as old aggravations instantly hardened his mood.

"Oh, no! Don't get me wrong, Admin Keenan—or should that be admiral now?"

"Answer me." Don demanded.

"Sorry. I will do my best." Narren took in a deep breath. "So will Dr. Sast and all our colleagues we could save. We won't stop trying. It's just that with all the—"

"All these decisions were debated already, Doctor." Don cut in.

"That they were." Narren nodded and looked out across the ocean.

"If you thought we would simply fail, why did you come on board?"

"I had a pass." Narren said blankly. "A valid pass. It's a good plan. Or was." Narren paused. He made his characteristic smile and stretched out each syllable of his sentence as he spoke again. "But the al-ter-na-tive? Yee-ah!"

"Just do the work." Don said over the sound of waves rolling against the hull. "We need this to come together. And fast. You have the resources. Just work faster."

"Well, I shall get hard at it tonight, sir." Narren nodded. "But right now I'll take some soon to be vanished personal time and have a smoke."

"A smoke?" Don asked. Narren's comment baffled him.

"Yes," Narren withdrew a small, paper cylinder filled with dried foliage from his pants pocket. "Of the indigenous *Ardens pulmone*. I like the older traditions we humans have put aside. Space travel impacted our culture. But we aren't in space, now." Narren grinned and looked toward the red glow of the city.

"No. But we still have rules to follow." Don glared.

Narren smiled at Don, and then pulled a small surgical laser from his pocket and lit his makeshift cigarette. A puff of white smoke curled from his mouth and blew across the deck.

"Isn't that harmful?" Don asked.

"Well—" Narren paused as the ship gently swayed. He smiled again. "Yee-ah."

Don looked at Narren with narrowed eyes and a tightening brow. He left Narren and entered the superstructure. His brow was still knit when he entered his cabin and went to sleep.

Morning found Don on the bridge with Captain Ruiz. Several screens swept along a crescent against the forward bulkhead. Most were blank. A small column supporting a panel of levers stood in front of them.

"I really wanted a wheel." Ruiz said as he stared at the lever panel. "She was built from scrap and hope, but you'd think finding or making a small ship's wheel would be easy. How long has humanity known the wheel?" Ruiz shrugged and looked at Don.

Don wondered how long humanity would last. The captain's mild rant over an esthetic control surface was not of interest.

"You said something was important. What?" Don asked.

"Yep. We have no nav aid from above." Ruiz answered and pointed skyward. "Contact was lost with the commercial and colonial satellites just after we launched."

"Why didn't you tell me then?" Don almost shouted.

"She's a new boat, and she's had no shake down." Ruiz answered with calm. "If I called you up here for everything, you might as well never leave."

"This is something big!" Don grated.

"This is a big ship, Don. It's my job to see she stays afloat. Now that we're at sea, I need to focus on doing that. I run the ship. You run the people. But without my boat, there are no people. No hope."

Don considered Ruiz's words. He wondered if this was a coup, or just a formal division of labor. Either way, Don had to make this relationship work. Without Ruiz, there was no mission. He was possibly the last captain with true ocean sailing experience. He was as necessary to the mission as the scientists. Don resolved to keep him happy, or at least shown respect.

"Okay," Don took a deep breath. "So, both the commercial and civilian signals are gone?"

"Aye," Ruiz nodded. "It's not my hardware, it's the birds. Do you have an admin code to switch Emerald's own satellites back on?"

"No. They shouldn't have stopped. The commercial sats probably stopped when the lease on their feeds ended." Don paused and shook his head. "But the feeds should be permanent, now. We activated our colonial distress beacon at the first outbreak. All planetary networks should be in emergency support mode."

"Someone forgot to tell that to the satellites' OS." Ruiz frowned. "I don't think we really controlled any of them. They all ran the same software."

Both men paused in irritation over the rented infrastructure of their planet, and contemplation of what to do without it.

"Even if they've become electronic zombies," Ruiz said. "We are navigating by stars, charts, math, and hope. We'll still get wherever we need to go." Ruiz ended with a confident smile.

Don thought he liked Ruiz's smile better than Narren's version.

"We never formerly named the ship," Don glanced around the bridge.

"The Iris," Ruiz said. "That's her name. After the flowers that bloomed in springtime on Earth. It's a sign of renewal. I ordered a plank with her name hung on either side. That's the best we can do until we come across a floating can of paint."

"I like it," Don said. "It's better than 'the ark.'"

"What does than name mean, anyway?" Ruiz asked.

"It was some big ship." Don answered. "Or part of a circle. Part of a sextant maybe?"

"Good enough for me." Ruiz said.

"Ru, we need to keep the satellite failure, quiet." Don nodded as he sought his Captain's agreement. "I don't know if anyone among the extra people has a gadget that can tell them the satellites have quit, but I know there is a belief among them that we have a secret system that will save us. It's becoming this community's lore."

"Stories get told if you make them or not, but they can also be hard to control." Ruiz cautioned.

"This story can help us. It's based on hope. Right now that's a more limited resource than food." Don breathed deeply. "We launched already in emergency mode. I don't want us to fall into desperation mode. People will become restless and doubtful of both me and you if too much goes wrong too fast. Doubt becomes despair. That will be a threat to the mission, and perhaps humanity."

"I understand." Ruiz nodded. He then smiled. "Our government just made its first official secret."

"We need to keep the people orderly." Don steadied himself against the edge of the blank screens as the ship swayed. "For now, we need to keep them curious about where we're going, not that we're fighting just to stay afloat."

"We'll stay above water." Ruiz nodded, but his eyelids widened. "Just understand there is a lot ahead of us that's unknown. They mapped out shipping lanes that were never sailed. Outside those lanes, my charts might as well say 'here be monsters.' Honestly, I don't know if there aren't any. This is still an alien world."

"I thought the prospect drones scanned Emerald's entire surface!" Don rocked from surprise, not the roll of the ocean.

"Land, maybe." Ruiz said. "But not all its oceans. They were too deep for the initial probes, and deeper scans weren't done before colonists arrived."

"I wasn't told that." Don sighed.

"No one was told everything." Ruiz slowly shrugged. "There was a push to get people on livable worlds. Almost like someone knew a plague might spread on some of them."

"I doubt that." Don took a deep breath and wasn't sure he believed his own last sentence.

"Well, I never thought the last bits of humanity would see apocalypse on a cruise—on an alien ocean! But here we are."

"Yeah." Don's eyes opened wide at Ruiz. "And you just made me leery of even using a life raft."

"I'm pretty confident. Cure or not, we are going to save these people, Don. No worries."

"No vaccine is not an option," Don groaned.

"Then I guess you better make sure the scientists and doctors are doing their jobs." Ruiz raised his eyebrows.

"Roger, that Captain." Don replied.

"Saying 'aye, aye,' might work better, now." Ruiz smiled.

"True." Don nodded. He took a moment to look out at the light green sea rolling before the bow of the *Iris*.

Vall Kuenen enjoyed a breeze and slight ocean mist on the deck outside. The moment of joy ended as 'Admin Glare' appeared at the top of the stairway next to her. Vall felt like a school girl caught outside the classroom. Don's typical, narrowed gaze didn't help. Yet, Vall knew she had no reason to spin in sick bay without patients. Plus, she hadn't seen an hour of free time outside of scant sleep since signing on to Emerald Tide. Vall assured herself she was guilty of nothing. She considered Don as he came down the stairs. He was relatively young. So was she. She hadn't thought of pairing up on this ship. She never had time to pair with anyone after the outbreak. If the plague couldn't be treated, the other carnage still needed stitching. As the living population shrank, Vall saw other women seeing pregnancy as a potential responsibility. If the vaccine worked, new humans would need to come from somewhere. Don was relatively attractive. Possible sex aside, he was also the best source of information on the ship and thus everyone's fate. Having his friendship would be a boon by itself. Vall took the initiative.

"Admin, good morning." Vall said.

"Same," Don answered.

Vall saw his stare as indication he thought she should be somewhere else, but he began to walk away as he left the stairs. She stepped back towards him. He stopped.

"Should I use the old form of address, or do we get new titles out at sea?" Vall smiled.

"My name 'Don' still works. Even rusting in this sea air."

Vall was surprised at his stab at humor. "It does smell differently, doesn't it?"

"As opposed to?" Don asked.

"Earth seas. They smell of salt. And on a beach, you can get a good whiff of drying seaweed."

"I've never been to Earth," Don said. "But I had to pull a lot of weeds back home. From dirt."

"Home?" Vall asked.

"Cayley," Don said.

"One of the old colonies." Vall nodded to herself in thought. "I'm sorry what happened there."

"It's happened here," Don said.

"Maybe they have a last hope mission, too."

Don looked to the deck and suppressed a sneer at the thought of 'last hope.' Yet he knew that was true.

"I hope so," Don said. He looked back at Vall. "Shouldn't you be working doctor?"

"I'm on shift." Vall raised her hands along with making a coy smile. "I'm medical, not research. So far, no one is sick."

"Can you help with the research?" Don asked.

"Yes. But tell that to Narren and Sast. They have a lid on their equipment and limit anyone just looking at it."

"I'll talk to Sast," Don said.

Vall wondered if she now had even more work handed to her.

"All right then." Don nodded to Vall and walked on.

Vall smiled as he halted for quick moments to steady his gait as the ship swayed. She allowed herself one more breath of sea air, and went back below decks, slowly.

Later, Vall sprinted back up. The medical staff had yet to elect their chief. Vall seized another opportunity when Don summoned division supervisors to the bridge. A crewman opened the hatch for her. Inside, Don glared at Narren.

"I asked for department heads!" Don barked.

"Well, not everyone got your order, admiral!" Narren shrugged and looked around. "We did, and Dr. Sast is sorry. She felt her research was—"

"All right!" Don waved him off and looked over at a preoccupied Capt. Ruiz.

"Don, what's going on?" Vall asked.

Narren raised his thin eyebrows over his glasses at Vall's informal address to the man who was presumably the highest official alive on Emerald.

"We have contact with other survivors out here." Don answered.

"Another ship?" Narren asked.

"Something that floats." Ruiz said. "We'll see. They had no current maps and drifted out too far. It should be coming into cam view." Ruiz pointed to his right eye.

All instinctively tapped their under-skin, sphenoid switches to see the images sent from a drone. A huge raft came into view. It looked as though a giant, water-logged mat drifted on the green ocean with small, decaying buildings torn free from a city and dropped among shipping containers. The faces of densely packed, desperate, but living people stared up from the raft at the circling drone's camera.

"We should help them," Don sighed.

"Um, ah, with what?" Narren asked.

"I'll put their captain on speaker." Ruiz said and taped at his keyboard flipped up from the lever panel. "It's on a separate radio frequency."

"Like I said," a man's voice spoke over static. "We've cleansed any infection. We're clear, Iris. Please assist. I repeat, we are adrift."

"What does that mean?" Narren shrugged. "Cleansed, how?"

"It's meaningless if they've been in contact with rippers." Vall said.

"Everyone here has seen rippers up close," Don looked over at Vall.

"That's true," Narren said. "But we were all cleared of the virus. Even if they currently have no signs of infection, they could be incubating the plague. We just can't afford contact with them."

"For all we know, we are they only ones that can help them." Don countered.

"For all we know, we could be they only surviving humans." Narren said.

"This disproves that." Don pointed out to sea in the raft's direction even though all saw it in feed from the drone.

"Maybe not." Vall said. "Dr. Narren is right. They may be already infected."

Don glared hard at Vall. She felt as though their budding relationship got pitched overboard.

"I'm sorry," Vall sighed. "We can't risk contracting the plague."

"Tell them we will sail to their location and asses if we can give aid." Don told Ruiz.

"Okay, Don." Ruiz gave a slow nod. "But we keep a safe distance and engines on." Ruiz double tapped the side of his head and spoke again. "Raft captain, this is the Iris. We will come to you and offer aid."

"Can't you take us onboard?" was the immediate reply over the static.

"Negative." Ruiz answered. "The best we can do is shuttle over supplies."

The only reply was static. Everyone refocused on the drone's images of the raft.

"Do you copy?" Ruiz said. "Come in."

There was another long moment of static, and then a reply.

"We read you." The disappointment was obvious even across the poor radio link.

"This will also put my people and ship at risk." Ruiz said.

More static crackled before the raft captain replied, again.

"I suppose if that's all we can get."

There was a 'click' as the raft cut the channel.

"This is a mistake." Narren said flatly.

"We need to know what's out here." Ruiz said and clicked off his drone video. "This is a recon as well as a mercy mission."

"I'd call it suicide." Narren smiled and shrugged. "But—"

"Okay. We made our points." Vall said to Narren as they all shut off the video feed.

Narren left the bridge with his hand fishing in his pocket. Vall looked over at Don starring out to sea.

"I'll check medical inventory," Vall said to Don. "Maybe we do have something extra."

Don nodded while still looking out. Vall turned with a nod to Ruiz and left.

The deck pitched at steeper angles as the *Iris* sailed towards the raft's coordinates at the fastest speed Ruiz dared. An hour later, the raft came into view of the starboard decks. Ruiz dared to sail within forty meters of the craft that caused both fascination and fear. It looked more pathetic rolling on the waves than in the drone's camera. Don stood with Ruiz on the starboard walkway along the bridge. People on lower decks called to the raft. Their efforts were lost in the distance, wind, and waves. Still, Don wondered if people were attempting to communicate with relatives or friends they thought were lost. Those on the raft seemed almost devoid of enthusiasm. Only a few waved toward the *Iris*. Don wondered how long they had been at sea. Perhaps they could tell them how to survive better. A scent of smoke drifted over the ocean. At first Don thought it was a lingered memory from the city's death. He was wrong.

"Captain!" The First Mate stepped from the bridge and called to Ruiz. Her voice has high and stressed. "They just radioed. They have a fire. Their screaming for help!"

"What caused the fire?" Don asked.

"They didn't say, sir!" The First Mate answered. "But there was shouting behind the voice on the radio, and then it—Geez!"

The First Mate pointed toward the raft. Ruiz and Don looked over. Flames shot like sudden, red fins between the decaying structures. Screams rose with greater intensity. People began leaping from the raft in the direction of the Iris.

"Back off! Back us off!" Don yelled in panic.

"Take us away from the raft!" Ruiz ordered.

The First Mate dove back into the bridge.

"Hit the alarm!" Ruiz yelled again.

A klaxon sounded as the ship lurched and her bow swung away from the raft. There were screams from the ship's lower decks. A few people that leaned too far over the rails fell from the sides and plummeted to the ocean. Ruiz grabbed the rail. Don fell backward, but someone caught him. He was shocked to see it was Vall. They both steadied themselves as the ship swung away from the conflagration and cries of the raft. The cam-drones stayed steady and shooting. The tallest structure of the raft fell. Flames exploded from its foundation. The raft split. Bodies were visible among the split structures. Many were burning. Some were motionless. Others displayed the unmistakable stagger of a reanimated corpse seeking flesh. Even as the raft burned and broke apart, the zombies lurched with purpose towards any living person still on each bobbing fragment. Some of the living pushed off biting attacks, even as the flames consume the deck. The same occurred as the ocean swamped the other half. It vanished from direct view as the *Iris* kept her swing away. The view on deck became empty ocean. The video feed was cut and the drones recalled. The raft and its people, alive or both forms of the dead, disappeared in the distance. Another group's last attempt at survival burned and sank. Those that fell were lost among the burning flotsam. The *Iris* sailed on.

"That was horrible." Vall said.

"Yeah. Again." Don added.

Narren entered the ship's laboratory. It had been a spacious cabin. Now, computer nodes, nanoscopes, gravi-fuges, and seemingly primitive syringes and pipettes were massed on almost every surface. The visual interface with their eyes spared them the need to take up more room with monitors. Narren took a beaker filled with green fluid from a lab table. He sat in a shockingly empty chair across from Dr. Nyla Sast. She rested on a small desk. Sast appeared to occasionally wave her hand at nothing and ignore Narren. The last part of her behavior was true. Images of the ship's manifest cross-referenced with each person's medical files occupied her apparent blank stare.

Narren watched her with a gaze that would make anyone uncomfortable. That was, if they cared they were being watched or about the watcher. Sast didn't care at all. Narren sipped the green fluid and continued to ogle Sast. He found her beautiful. She was the frequent object of his lustful fantasies. Yet he was intimidated by her, not from and inability to act on his attraction, but from the fact she was possibly smarter than he was. Much smarter. Sast was in control of their venture. Still, even Narren's sexual fascination and intimidation couldn't stop him from making his quirky smiles and gibes. He was far better socially aware than he let on, but liked to unsettle people as his own secret sport.

"Well, I wish I'd seen the raft completely sink." Narren sipped and allowed the awkward silence to become obvious. "All those people. All the potential data just ss-un-kk."

Sast took a deep breath. She sighed and answered, but kept her focus on the virtual information floating in her field of view. "I didn't see it at all. I didn't care."

"Too bad. It was a fairly interesting event."

"Interesting?" Sast queried. "How?"

"If the raft's population wasn't keeping an outbreak secret so we would come aid them, then the outbreak occurred after our communication."

"So you think the infection had no incubation." Sast finally clicked off her visual link, but still didn't look at Narren. "You theorize the reanimation was immediate."

"In-stan-tane-eeous." Narren said almost in song.

"Rubbish." Sast said. She darted a glare more cutting than Don's at Narren. "They obviously were hiding an outbreak. Occam's razor."

"But, if not?" Narren shrugged and smiled as he looked away. "We need to consider such a mutation. If it exists, it would further complicate our efforts, here."

"Wherever here is. We are always moving on this damn yacht."

"But this boat has all the equipment we need." Narren sipped his beaker again. "You have to tip the hat to our Admin for that." Narren raised his beaker.

"All I have to do is—no," Sast stood and took Narren's beaker away from him. "All you have to do is get to work. Look through the sequencing we already have and seen if such a mutation is possible. Now."

Narren clicked his visual link and began waving his hand in the air to move virtual screens of data. Sast looked at her own right hand, but not as a tool to flip invisible pages. She eyed the region between her thumb and index finger as if peering into her skin.

Vall's hunch was correct. Don stood holding the rail and looking out on the starboard deck. She walked over to him. Starlight lit his brow. His skin was showing a tendency to wrinkle. Vall knew that could mean he was in his seventies and just needed a quick trip to a cosmetologist. She sighed that no such place or perhaps even profession existed, anymore. Don turned to her. He nodded.

"Hello, Admin." Vall said and joined Don at the rail.

Don sighed to himself. "Even out here, we've left another cinder to burn."

Vall dropped her head for a moment as vivid images of the burning raft replayed across her mind without the need of recorded video.

"It was ominous," Vall said. "But I don't think it was an omen."

Don was quiet. The noises of waves breaking against the hull were heard bellow. Voices on lower decks also came to ear when the wave noise subsided.

"At least nothing is chasing us, or burning here." Vall said.

"True," Don nodded. "We live another night, and will see another dawn. I've seen a lot of dawns. I want to see a lot more."

The personal comment surprised Vall. She hoped that the damage done on the bridge by her agreeing with Narren was not permanent.

"It's a bit ironic that people now live longer than ever, but the ravenous dead are the biggest enemy."

Don was quiet for a moment. "The plague is the enemy. The dead are its victims."

"Well," Vall cocked her head while looking at Don. "I stand corrected, *doctor.*"

Don raised his eyebrows wide and slowly turned his head to face Vall. Vall playfully put her hands on her hips. Don pursed his lips. They suddenly became a smile. Vall smiled back. They drew closer and enjoyed the stars of an alien sky. Both knew the constellation that held Earth's star. In the past, that knowledge brought colonists comfort. Comfort now was in the quiet moment.

Several moments later, the dawn came and Vall was a physician in action. After cries for help and shouted orders, Vall knelt beside her patient. The 'hospital bed' was only a blanket thrown of the ship's inner metal deck in the cargo hold serving as sick bay. Small ovals detached themselves from the young man's naked chest. They floated to his left side and dropped to the defibrillator unit. Vall rested her fingers on the round housing of the vein-shunt attached to the man's right arm. The vital signs she saw were only flat lines. No pulse. No neurocerebral activity. Vall knew there was no use in wasting additional drugs. Her patient was dead. She resisted the impulse to bolt from the fresh corpse. The reaction made her nauseous, but it had become an understandable reaction to death.

"Should I detach the VS, Doctor?" Call's nurse asked.

Vall nodded affirmation to him, and stood. She clicked off her view of his vital signs. She folded her arms, and began the pathological examination in her mind. Vall had become an infectious disease specialist after the outbreak in addition to her specialty of internal medicine. Emerald was still a mostly alien planet. However, the disease was a well-known retrovirus. It was lethal if untreated, but it normally had a much longer incubation. It should also have been in his constantly updating medical files. An injected spy monitored everyone onboard. Something was wrong beyond this patient's odd death. She glanced at him again. He was still unmoving. She was almost ashamed that she was glad for that.

Days later, Vall grappled with stronger mixed emotions while looking up at a sort of layered sky. Clouds floated over the light green sea. Towards the horizon, thick cumulous clouds appeared to reach into the evening sky while tilting backwards. Vall was too tired to review the science of Emerald's terraformed atmospherics and their odd effects. She knew the layers had differing refracting qualities, but would one day resolve into a visually unified mixture. Then, clouds would float as humans thought they should from some shared memory of sky watching that spanned between stars.

If Vall had children, their sky would be different than hers. Terraforming meant children knew a different world than their parents. The grandchildren saw yet another one, until the visible changes were complete. Mere generations experienced a collection of seeming geologic ages. Vall knew physics and geochemistry remade a dying Earth into a habitable world. Yet, she wondered if the planet Emerald could think, would it feel simply altered or infected? Even so, she wanted the human changes to last. She wanted to live. However, her own life seemed to be at risk now on the ship than when she faced ripper hordes on land. Vall was at another funeral for another patient, and even more were becoming sick. She looked back down among the people gathered for the burial at sea on the aft deck. She wondered who to trust. Trust or betrayal was life and death.

Crew members lifted a rigid stretcher to slide the white-shrouded body overboard. The small crowd dispersed. Vall saw Narren walk to the rail and look to the sea as if following the body. Vall went and also looked over the rail. The body of her nurse was already several meters behind the stern. She expected it to be closer. The engines were off and the *Iris* was using ocean currents to save fuel. An odd, rotting scent wafted to her nose. She thought she saw a dark mass in the distance. It was hard to be certain from the white crests of the waves. The body was lost among them.

"I'm surprised we're not doing this more often." Narren said over the ripple of winds across ears.

"Why?" Vall asked and turned to him.

"You're a doctor. Of internal medicine, anyway. You know when people get densely packed, as on this boat, infection spreads rapidly. It's, well, natural."

"In that case, shouldn't it be spreading even faster?" Vall arched her left eyebrow.

"Well, we are a well-inoculated lot. Perhaps the pathogens are mutating at a slower rate without more susceptible hosts."

"An interesting idea, Dr. Narren. You've obviously been thinking about this."

"Well, I'm an interesting guy." Narren gave his characteristic look-away smile.

"How is your work?" Vall asked.

"Coming along well. Although there are days I think Sast will throw me overboard."

Narren waited as if wanting Vall to protest the imagery. She didn't. Narren gave a quick nod and focused back on the ocean. He gripped the rail as a thrilled child would do.

"I'm also interested in catching a glimpse of some indigenous Emerald life." Narren said. "At least life that's surviving the terraform process. We're moving into deeper seas. Some just has to be out here. I was hoping the light would last long enough while I was allowed on deck. I've caught glimpses of giant jelly fish, but those are seeded Earth alters. I'd love to see something truly alien!"

Vall glimpsed Don and Ruiz walking toward the super structure. She looked aft toward the dark mass. She couldn't spot it, but thought it might be useful to her.

"I saw something large behind the ship. Maybe if you look straight off the aft—"

"I will! Thank you!" Narren chirped.

Vall watched Narren almost sprint to the aft of the ship even as the deck pitched. She turned and saw Don and Ruiz talking by the superstructure. She carefully walked over to them.

"Doc." Ruiz greeted Vall.

Vall was silent. Her gaze was pleading but also one of confusion.

"What is it?" Don asked and waited. "You can tell us."

"I really have no one else to tell." Vall said. She paused and took a breath. "Okay. The deaths. They're not natural. The initial infection is a retrovirus. Like I told you. But it's been artificially mutated."

"And you asked Narren and Sast for help?" Don asked.

"Yes." Vall answered. "Sast said the deaths are caused by multiple pathogens. She's wrong."

"You're sure? They're supposed to be the best." Ruiz said.

"That's why I know the error is willful." Vall glanced to her sides. "I just needed them to verify my conclusions. But instead both added and obscured facts. Why?"

Don furrowed his brow and frowned so intensely his face muscles quivered.

"Could they be right?" Ruiz asked.

"No." Vall slowly shook her head. "I'm certain the reason these people died is due to the same initial pathogen. It allows other diseases to assert themselves once the patient's immune response is compromised. But the retrovirus—"

"Makes a good cover," Don interjected.

"Have you challenged them on this?" Ruiz asked.

"No." Vall said coldly. "I don't want to die."

"What?" Ruiz barked and then looked across the deck to ensure they were still alone.

Don eased his scowl and focused with intense interest on Vall.

"I don't know how they're administering the—" Vall began.

"Wait. Wait!" Ruiz nearly hopped as he spoke. "You're saying Narren and Sast are murderers?"

Vall and Don looked at Ruiz as if that conclusion was foregone and understood.

Ruiz threw his hands up. "Look, this is serious stuff!"

"I'm hoping it is them and not either of you." Vall sighed. "Like I said, I want to live."

"So do I." Don nodded. "So we keep this quiet."

"What? We can't—" Ruiz began.

"You want this ship to live?" Don asked, grimly. "Then we need to keep this wrapped until we can prove it. People are still

192

reeling from the escape. They still remember the raft. Now we have these deaths. I don't want a panic—a riot!"

Ruiz's eyes widened and he rubbed his forehead.

"We don't know how they're doing this." Vall said. "The method is very sophisticated."

"Okay. I get it." Ruiz said.

"Right now, we stop them." Don grated. "Gather some security officers and we go to their lab and tear it apart!"

"And their research?" Ruiz asked. "If they see us coming? They might burn it to spite us."

All three looked at each other for answers. All seemed to be swayed back and forth by more force than the roll of the deck. Finally, Vall spoke.

"I have an idea."

On land, Jaelen had been good at running. He knew to keep pace with any group of people while the rippers chased them. He always ran to the front as they got closer. He would then sprint out ahead with all speed his legs could produce when the screams and sickening sound of tearing flesh began. He was faster than most people. He knew groups of rippers always fell on one slower person just to get one mouthful of living skin instead of his whole sprinting body. Groups of people were his shield. Then he came onboard the *Iris*. Every space, even the latrines had a mass of asses and heads to wade through. He couldn't run anywhere. If a plague broke out on the ship, there wouldn't be a need for rippers to chase anyone. It would be like hitting the 'chop' button on a blender with dead teeth for blades.

Time outside the packed spam deck was strong enticement to follow Dr. Narren to his boss' quarters. He didn't know what Narren wanted him to do. He didn't care. Apocalypse wore away many taboos. Still, he was glad Narren sought his skills with computer systems. He was happy just to be in a small room with only two people. One of them, Dr. Sast, didn't seem to really be there as she focused on her work. How Narren knew he was a sapper, Jaelen didn't know. The term 'hacker' had been around for centuries, but fell out of favor because it also suggested someone who torn off parts of things. Or people. That was something rippers did, not smart people. They ran. Jaelen didn't really like the replacement term 'sapper,' but it was better than 'convict.' That was a title Jaelen removed from his current identity so he could get on the boat.

Jaelen knocked back the last of the vodka or whisky or whatever Narren had fed him. The room was hot, but his chair was comfortable. Jaelen whirled his fingers in the air as he worked a virtual screen. His eyes saw the red banner ACCESS DENIED almost as quickly as a strobe effect across various access screens. Jaelen sighed. His fingers finally rested.

"I'm sorry," Jaelen said. "I can't pop the seals."

Narren and Sast were silent, but Sast clicked her eye-feeds off and looked over at Jaelen. He found her narrow stare disturbing.

"Are you sure you can't do it, Jaelen." Narren asked as he crouched next to him. "I mean real-lee sure?"

"Yeah," Jaelen said. "The bio-spy OS has some security I've never seen. It wasn't part of the original security system. That looked as strong as steam. Pathetic. I guess whoever was hired to do amp the seals didn't look for sub-admin systems like you guys have. It was probably a machine. They're pretty narrow minded. Your keys let you give the sub-sys commands, but not alter the programming or data feeds."

"For that data we didn't need you." Sast sneered. "We want you to give real-time locations on individuals."

"Yeah. Sorry," Jaelen said with a quick shrug. "I mostly used a tool kit, and made a few tweaks. I didn't do much code writing. I mean. It was hard to keep up on new saps and seals running from rippers, anyway."

Sast stood and leaned over Narren. She spoke with a mocking impression of his quirky speech pattern. "And this is the best you could do, real-lee?"

Narren smiled and looked away.

"Can I go now?" Jaelen asked. "You guys are still going to pay me, right?"

"No and no." Sast said through clenched teeth.

"Hey—!" Jaelen started.

"Shut up!' Sast barked. "Narren, now!"

Narren reached over and tapped a button on a small key pad.

"What's that do?" Jaelen said and then felt a slight tingle in his feet.

"The devices we wanted you to access are in every person on this ship." Narren said. "I just blocked the feed for yours."

"Okay. Nice" Jaelen nodded.

"Yee-ah," Narren continued. "Also nice, the manufacturers make micro-med delivery vessels. Of course, those are supposed to release curative drugs." Narren looked away from Jaelen and gave a big shrug. "But they come in handy for other chems. Such as the paralytic released by the one you swallowed with the alcohol."

Narren looked back at Jaelen with a perverse smile. That would be bad enough for Jaelen without the weird spectacle things he wore distorting his eyes. Sast also glared at him. Jaelen felt uncomfortable having two weird people starring at him. The tingle had now reached his knees.

"I get that you guys don't really work for the Admin." Jaelen said.

"Nope." Narren replied.

"Who?" Jaelen asked. He noticed he had difficulty raising his legs, but wondered if he could work an angle with Sast and Narren's real boss. "I mean, everyone alive from corporate or government is one this ship. Right?"

"Not everyone," Narren smiled. "And not everyone is on Emerald. Or alive."

"Who? Where?" Jaelen shrugged with an effort. "Wait! Para-what?"

"Yes," Narren nodded with a quick, irregular head bob. "It is a-maze-ing. It's so concentrated it only requires a picogram to interact with—"

"Narren!" Sast shouted.

"He's noticed the effects," Narren said. "I'll bet you have an urge to run, but it isn't working out, is it?" Narren stood and fished his hand through his left pants' pocket. He withdrew a small white cylinder and laser scalpel.

"What are you doing?" Jaelen asked. His anxiety was rising but his heart was slowing down.

"Smoking." Narren lit his white cigarette with the laser, and exhaled the smoke at Jaelen. He offered the unlit end to Jaelen's mouth. "Would you like to try it? You can still inhale. For a few seconds."

"No!" Jaelen screeched and kept moving his face as if trying to propel himself by thrusting his cheeks forward.

"Just seeing if you wanted a new experience before you die." Narren shrugged. He pushed his glasses back up the bridge of his nose.

"What?" Jaelen screeched again.

"True," Narren said and took another puff. "It's a bit late for that. You might like it, and then what? Oops!"

"Don't torture him." Sast said with disdain to Narren. "Why are you even still talking to him?"

"I like a two-sided conversation." Narren said and flicked cigarette ash over Jaelen.

"But he's going to be dead." Sast growled.

"D-Dead!" Jaelen uttered as his body began to quiver.

"Yeah," Narren said to Jaelen, then flicked more ashes on him and focused back on Sast. "Well, then soon it will be like our conversations."

"P-puh—!" Jaelen now convulsed between Sast and Narren.

"You're getting to be a prick, Narren." Sast said with a sneer.

"A prick!" Narren chirped. "Good one. It's what I do for you without ever doing it to you."

"Juh-Geez," Jaelen managed to utter through violent spasms. Even in his altered state, it was obvious Sast and Narren had spent too much time together in too small a space. He could see that now their personal taboos were ripped away. "Yu-you guys should g-get—*KLAAGH!*"

Jaelen's eyes rolled back. Froth dripped from his open mouth and spattered against the floor.

"You should get a dose of respect, Narren." Sast said. "Fast!"

"You should get a towel." Narren jabbed his cigarette at Jaelen and then took a long drag.

Sast clenched her teeth and dove into the narrow closet that served as a lavatory. She leapt out with a small towel in her clenched right fist.

"Put that goddam thing out!" Sast howled and slapped Narren with the towel. "And *you* mop this up! Now! You've made one hell of a mess already you stupid, little man!"

"I did what—" Narren stopped and plucked the broken cigarette from his mouth and pushed his glasses back on. "I did what any rational individual would do. I'm a physician and a scientist. I acted to save lives."

"By killing more people!" Sast screeched and pitched her right hand backward to ready for another towel swat.

"There were too many onboard when we launched." Narren looked at his broken smoke and extinguished it on Jaelen's shoulder. "We've virtually eliminated the chances of a ripper outbreak. So, gradual reduction of non-essential population seemed logical. And the evidence all goes overboard after a cursory autopsy. I've already increased our chances by three percent with fewer mouths draining food and resources."

"But they don't need a whole body to link these death to a single, artificial pathogen, you idiot! They only need some blood. We only needed a few subjects for tests, not population control. If we can't hack the spy-bots, we won't know what the Captain, Admin, and security are doing behind us! Someone like Vall could piece together your little RNA-retrovirus. She has specialty in infectious disease!"

"Well, that wasn't in her personnel file." Narren shrugged.

"Well neither is the fact that you're now a serial killer, man-bitch!"

"You didn't tell me what you knew." Narren rocked his head back and forth as he considered his actions and what he should do now. "I mean, I shouldn't—"

"I shouldn't have to tell you anything!" Sast screamed. "You should just follow orders! I was the one assigned to infiltrate this project. I brought you in to work for me. But thanks to you, our employers—*my* employers—might cut us and this planet loose. How are we going to survive then? How?"

"Well," Narren lifted up his palms to the ceiling in an exaggerated shrug. "May-be, act-you-al-lee making a vaccine. Maybe a cure. Just an idea."

The towel hit Narren's face with enough force to knock off his glasses and send him to the floor. Jaelen's body rolled from the chair and fell across him. Narren stayed on the floor covered by the corpse as Sast slapped the walls, chair, and air with her towel bludgeon. He was there for a long time.

A room built as a small cantina for engine workers now served as a secret morgue. Plasscreen sheeting and bioseal on the doors trapped in any infection, and Don and Vall. Don stood in protective jumpsuit with clear cylinder for a helmet. He watched through the portal sealed between the kitchen and serving counter. He looked like a customer at a sterile but macabre café. Don thought there must be some irony or dark humor in the dead examined in a food service setting when a plague of zombies stalked over the planet. He was glad these bodies were motionless and he was not on the menu. Vall was alone in the kitchen area and sealed in her protective bio-hazard suit. She conducted a set of autopsies with technology in place of scalpels. One male and one female body pulled from the funeral rotation lay naked on separate tables. Vall observed the virtual feeds from her portable medlab console. From the small machine, Vall guided the scanner disks currently floating over the corpses, and the microscopic probes that roamed the still veins, arteries, and cavities of her subjects.

"You think all the evidence we need is in these bodies?" Don asked.

"In the blood," Vall said. "Or its residue. I just need to find the right glob for the right molecules."

"No small feat." Don said with a tight smile.

"Oh, 'the Glare' is a funny man, now." Vall said while still focused on data in her field of vow.

"Will you be able to pin the evidence on Sast or her team members?" Don asked.

"They might do that, themselves. I'm guessing anyone sophisticated enough to construct this virus from a lab will have an ego large enough to smile when confronted with the evidence."

"A smile?" Don said as he thought of Narren.

"Yeah." Vall looked over to Don through her face shield. "All I have to do is isolate the virus genome."

"There isn't any whole virus?"

Vall smiled. "You think it's like some little bug running around, but it's actually the genetic structure that plays havoc inside the host cells. The closest thing to a bug is when the virus is still contained within its capsid, a protein shell. A virus is not alive. They're sort of a natural molecular zombie. It just wants to make copies of itself, and without the awareness of an urge, or the sensation of an impulse. They can't even move on their own."

"But a ripper can." Don said.

"Yes. And they spread their virus. But its genome doesn't account for all the aspects of ripper reanimation. And we haven't detected a capsid that contains the virus. The genome doesn't contain information to make one. But it's too complex to not have a shield, or else it would break apart in the environment." Vall sighed. A puff of breath condensed to cloud her face for an instant. "That's why a vaccine has never been created. We need more information. For that we need more time. But the human population was so large, the plague spread faster than we could gather all the data to stop it."

"Do we know what causes the running around and biting?" Don asked.

"Yes. No." Vall answered. "It's the virus, but plus something we haven't detected. We are, or rather were getting close. The reanimation occurs after the victim is dead, so they don't make new antibodies to help us identify the agent. For that we need to scan an active ripper."

"So? Did anyone do that?"

"So, yeah, go ahead." Vall turned to face Don. "Scan a ripper."

"Point taken." Don frowned and nodded.

"I guess we will, someday, somehow." Vall refocused on her medlab's visual feed. "But I was hoping Sast and her team would get a viable treatment and render the need moot."

Vall suddenly turned to look at the female body and then jumped back from it.

"What?" Don asked.

"This, ah, body—" Vall halted and took a shallow breath.

"Is what? What?" Don yelled with concern.

"It has plague."

"The retrovirus?" Don asked.

"No. Plague. Ripper plague."

Don jumped back from the portal. Both of them remained silent as if not to wake the dead and be chased.

"Then why isn't it trying to eat us?" Don stepped back to the portal. "The plague isn't, ah, active?"

"No." Vall breathed. "It looks like the virus has infiltrated the corpse, but it isn't reanimating. Okay. Yeah. Weird."

"Are we safe?"

"I think so," Vall answered. "We aren't at risk of infection if we don't come in contact with its fluid or tissues. But this body has both the retrovirus and the plague."

Vall turned and cut her video feed. She stepped to the portal and looked straight at Don.

"Don, did you allow Sast to bring plague samples onboard Iris?"

Don was silent and stared passed Vall at the corpse.

"Don?"

Don took a deep breath. He looked at Vall. "No. Only virtual models. Not physical cultures."

"Well, someone either reconstituted the plague from those models or, more likely, they smuggled physical samples onto the ship."

Don was silent again. His plan to save the world and the human species had been doomed by lies, and for what he didn't know.

"So, we found the one-to-one relationship." Vall said. "The murder virus and the plague in the same body. We know who was working on the plague. Don, I know we need to do this carefully, but those people can't be allowed to be free on this ship. Or anywhere."

"Then we're dead." Don said with audible bitterness. "We just wait for the end, here, in the middle of an unknown ocean." He paused. "They were supposed to be the best minds to find a cure."

"Maybe they are," Vall said. "But they're still murderers."

Don clenched his right hand into a fist so tightly it felt as though his wrist tendons would snap. He stared at his gloved fist and watched it quiver.

"We're not done," Don said quietly, and then he yelled. "Damn it, we are not done!"

Darkness. At times it was a stench, not the absence of light. Orra looked out at the total black of the ocean night and smelled the other form. They sat in the sharp crease of deck steal that bonded to the aft bulkhead. Her children had never known another world. Orra wondered if they ever would. She knew they were tired, and now enjoyed the view from the aft passenger deck. She did, too. It let her think they were putting distance between themselves and the threatening land. Now she felt darkness chasing her at sea. It was time to move.

"Let's go." She nudged her son Jarren and nodded to his sisters beside him. "Now."

"What? Mom!" Jarren protested. "You know how long it took to get this spot."

"I know. But we need to move." Orra stood and gathered her pack. It was light and carried mostly objects for her children, and her own shiv cleverly hidden in the strap. "Come on."

Orra's children slowly moved aching muscles to follow their mother. She had lead her family across this world as rippers and vile forms of living humans tried to destroy them. Her children knew it was wise to follow her, even if their bodies followed their brains only reluctantly.

"I'm not going back in the spam deck." Jarren groaned.

Orra looked at her son as he stood. Soon he would be old enough to make tough choices on his own. Not today. The wind blew strongly across the ship's aft and carried the stench with it. Jarren turned to look towards the blackness. He reached down and quickly gathered his pack. He wasn't alone. Others were beginning to sense what Orra already knew and also collected what little they had. Something was coming close. Most of them had also fled death for so long that they didn't question the impulse to run, even if it was just the other end of a ship. It was time to run. Orra lead her family away from darkness, again.

Don and Vall entered the bridge. Ruiz had summoned Don, but was surprised to see Vall with him. Ruiz didn't know they were just pealed from protective suits and wondered why they were both sweaty. Normally that would have made him smile. Not today.

"Line 2." Ruiz said and pointed to the right side of his head.

Don and Vall clicked their sphenoid switches. A black expanse of sea was all they saw, but there was movement.

"This is live-wave LIDAR," Ruiz said.

Don and Vall felt sudden nausea and the impulse to run. The image of the black sea became a rolling field of horror. A collective mass of giant jelly fish and the planet's approximation of seaweed bound together bits of charred raft debris. The movement wasn't only from the roll of the waves. Arms legs and torsos bobbed. Some of them moved on their own. The mass was mostly reanimated human corpses. Rippers were floating in the waves. Some of them clung to and fed on the remains of shrouded bodies dropped into the ocean.

It's like a zombie Sargasso Sea that fell into the same current were using, and it's damn close.

"Speed up!" Don yelled.

"Oh, you think?" Ruiz snapped.

Don turned his head toward Ruiz and cut his video feed. Ruiz stared at him. Don waved his hands in a plaintiff gesture.

"Yeah. I'll gun the engines if it comes closer," Ruiz said. "But we've been traveling on the currents for a reason. I need to conserve fuel for the storm."

"Storm?" Vall said as she switched off the feed of the zombie Sargasso with a shudder.

"A big one," Ruiz replied. "It will overtake us, no matter our speed. I need the fuel to maneuver the Iris and minimize the impact. We're going to be hit with big waves."

"Will the ship be okay?" Don asked.

"Will we be okay?" Vall asked with a high tone.

"Oh, yeah." Ruiz said. "I'm too good and the Iris is too strong for this storm to sink us. But with this squeeze play of drifting rippers and approaching storm, I'm worried about what's going to go down onboard. Have you got the evidence you need to nail the killers?"

"Yes. We—" Don started to answer.

"Then if there's going to be a conflict, I want it on calmer seas." Ruiz cut in. "I don't want a loose killer running free, someone starting a panic, or even a damn poker game going on when I steering us away from one horror and through another."

"Poker game?" Vall asked. "What's with poker?"

"I like to play." Ruiz replied. "I don't want to miss out."

Vall cocked her eyebrows.

"Okay," Don said. "Let's get this done."

The ship was already pitching hard from the occasional large wave that rolled out from the closing storm. Even so, the warning signal Narren installed on the walkway to his cabin still worked. He enjoyed looking out passed the edge of the rail and at the waves breaking over dark green ocean. His was a choice, shipside view with a big porthole. He enjoyed it a little longer before he saw Ruiz, Don, and Vall approach. They were obviously coming for him. An unexpected wave of peace flowed across Narren's mind. He sat in a tattered but comfortable chair and placed his right hand on the handle of a large, upright cabinet once intended as a wardrobe. Narren wasn't sure of the occasional bumps of metal were from the roll of the deck jostling the cabinet or what was inside it. The ship made a lot of noises he wasn't used to. He felt life in general was an odd experience. He wondered how much longer his own would last. There was no knock. Ruiz unlocked the hatch and walked right in. Don and Vall steadied themselves as they followed him. Narren smiled and never released his grip on the cabinet handle.

"Welcome." Narren said. "Please make yourselves—"

"What's with the steel cabinet?" Ruiz asked.

"What, this?" Narren rattled the cabinet handle. "I had it moved up from the lab to store specimens. We scientists are always at work, where ever we are. Right, Doctor?"

Vall said nothing. Her focus was on the rumble inside the cabinet.

"So you found the retrovirus." Narren said and raised his eyebrows over his glasses as he focused on Vall.

"Yes." Vall said.

"Good work," Narren nodded. "I apologize for not thinking you had the intellect or knowledge to back trace my work."

"She's a doctor and you didn't think she was smart enough to do that?" Ruiz asked.

"Well, there's smart and then there's *smart*, Captain." Narren answered.

Ruiz raised his own eyebrows as he stared at Narren and wondered at what level of *smart* the odd, spectacled man placed him.

"We also found the plague." Vall added.

"But not a reanimate corpse. Neat, huh?" Narren smiled wide.

"No." Don said. "Not at all."

"Wait, did you say 'no'?" Narren questioned. "Do you have any idea what a technical feat that was?"

"You have any idea the trouble you're in?" Ruiz asked.

"Well, let us just see, mon cap-ee-tan." Narren gave a one-shoulder shrug while still holding the cabinet handle. "I'm on a planet overrun with zombies and on a makeshift ship that's about to be hit by a storm. Trouble? Yee-ah!"

"If I allowed weapons onboard, I just shoot you right now." Ruiz spat at Narren. He looked at Don. "Can we just throw him overboard?"

Don wrinkled his forehead in serious consideration of the act.

"Before you do," Narren slid his free hand into his pants pocket.

As Narren fished in his pocket, everyone tensed. Don expected Narren to put a cigarette in his mouth. Instead He pulled out a small data stick and handed it to Vall. She didn't take it immediately.

"What is it?" Vall asked.

"Well, safe for one." Narren said as he still held out the data stick with his left arm and gripped the cabinet handle with his right hand. "For another, it's the fulfillment of a promise."

Narren looked at Don and gave a nod free of sarcastic smile or physical quirks.

Don took the data stick. "Just, why?"

"The research. And that's it." Narren pointed to the data stick. "And to try and save us. Well, save the human race."

"You've got to be kidding!" Vall sneered.

"I know our methods are different." Narren raised the palm of his free hand at Vall. "But understand our work was not just for here on Emerald. Sast and I were working for interstellar concerns."

"The Inter-colony Commission?" Don asked. He handed the data stick to Vall.

"Nnno," Narren answered. He reached down to the floor and retrieved a brimmed hat. He propped it loosely on his head and smiled. Above the brim a motion-decal played a company slogan above its star logo in bright, friendly letters: From the Sun to every star. One purpose. Transit. UNI-SOL. "I stole this hat from Sast. The bitch."

"You're some kind of spy for a C-class shipping firm?" Ruiz said in disbelief. "That's an automated enterprise. It's a bunch of machines running machines!"

"Think about it!" Narren chirped. "Who needs humans more? A shipping company needs things to ship, and humans are a self-generating cargo that expands the number of places to ship things to. And if there are no humans—you get the point. We die, their function ceases. They aren't programmed for much adaptation."

"You actually work for machines?" Vall asked as her face pulled into a confused scowl. "Machines!"

"We all work with machines, of a sort." Narren countered. "This boat. Our medical equipment. You can describe it as *for* or *with*, but it's really all the same. We all fill a niche. That's all Sast and I did. We filled a niche. At least I still do."

"What do you mean?" Don asked.

The ship rolled. Ruiz stayed standing fast. Don and Vall grabbed each other to steady themselves. Narren pressed his arm against the cabinet's handle to keep it shut. A loud *THUMP* came from inside it.

"Weh-ell," Narren said. "Sast is toast. Expired. D-E-A-D. In capitals."

"You killed her!" Vall shouted.

"I wish!" Narren retorted. "But, no. She killed herself. It was actually quite funny. You see she had these microtubules in her hand that held plague samples. It's how she smuggled—anyway! She gets into a rage and starts whacking everything with a towel. Geez, she flipped. Anyway! She griped it so tightly she broke the tubules. Can you imagine?"

Narren broke into a spasm of laughter, but never lost his grip on the cabinet. The others watched him thinking a stretched mind now snapped.

"So, so the bitch killed herself." Narren wheezed. He composed himself and looked up at the horrified stares of Ruiz, Don, and Vall.

"Obviously we share a different appreciation for irony." Narren wiped his brow with his free hand. "See, she flew into a blind rage and—never mind. I hope you'll let me continue my work." Narren hoped his manic moment had gained him enough pity to press for lenience. It did not.

"With more killing?" Vall spat.

"Hey, wait—!" Don started to say and looked at the cabinet seeing it was large enough to house a person.

"We did that for the benefit of the majority." Narren said and adjusted his grip the cabinet handle. "I'm sure you can see the greater good once you read my research."

"I see you in my brig, jackass!" Ruiz shouted.

"I'm sorry, then, for you all. The incubation period is, doubtless, long over." Narren said.

Narren thrust his hand gripping the cabinet handle down. His hand just slid off from his sweaty grip. He dove from his chair to grab it again as Ruiz, Don, and Vall collided with each other as they rushed to grab Narren. They were one fraction of a second too late. The doors swung open. What had been the multiple PhD holding Nyla Sast hissed as the cabin light hit her dead eyes. The lack of muscle and skin elasticity kept her face pulled back as if stuck at high velocity. Her hair was already falling out. All she needed was her eyes and teeth. The teeth sunk into the back of

206

Narren's neck as he tied to push up from the floor. He screamed. So did Ruiz, Don, and Vall.

Don jumped up as Ruiz and Vall scrambled back from Narren on the floor. Don lifted Narren's chair and swung it into Sast's zombie. A tear on the back of Narren's neck spurted blood as his attacker fell back. The ripper bounced inside the cabinet and then fell across Vall's legs. Vall screamed, squirmed, and thrust herself to escape from it as it rose on its arms. A tooth-bared death mask looked up at her with strip of Narren's flesh between teeth. Don's heel smashed into the zombie's face. Narren gripped the back of his neck and rolled away. The zombie's violent flailing kicked his eyeglasses across the floor by. Don pummeled it with the chair amid undead kicks, clawing swipes, and frothing gnashes.

"Run!" Don shouted.

Ruiz and Vall bolted through the opened hatch.

"Come on!" Vall stuck her head back in and yelled at Don.

Narren stood while clutching his bloody neck. Don finally began to tire from his relentless beating of the seemingly unharmed ripper. He threw the chair onto it and ran. He hit Narren who also headed for the hatch. Narren fell against the bulkhead. Don leapt to the walkway and almost over the rail into the sea. Vall grabbed at his arms to pull him away from the hatch. Ruiz was gone. Klaxons sounded. Immediately all the hatches locked. Narren's hatch automatically swung closed and locked, just as he stumbled out with the ripper clawing his ass. Vall and Don bolted to the bow. Narren ran to the aft. The ripper chased its former colleague and partial meal.

Narren reached the top of the stairs onto the open aft deck. Sharp, cold wind buffeted him in bursts. They felt good against his neck wound. He looked up instinctively and strained to see the constellations. He wanted to find the one that held the Sun and thus Earth. There were only dark clouds.

Narren took the laser he used as an improvised lighter and cauterized his neck wound. The scent of burning flesh was horrid. He cried out and grimaced, but finished the job by feel and his unwanted experience as a field medic. The wound was fairly superficial. It alone would not be lethal. But he could feel the other pain of the changes unfurling inside his body. Inside him, recently reprogrammed surgi-bots slowed the plague's effects. The information he gave Vall would enable her improve on that programming and save him. That was, if he lived long enough and Vall cared to save a mass murderer. He wondered if he should push the laser to burn deeper. The hiss of the Sast ripper broke his macabre reverie.

Narren aimed the small laser at the zombie. A small piece of Sast's disfigured face began to burn. It slowed its shamble towards him. He once found that face attractive. Now he wanted her whole body to suddenly ignite. He smiled at the irony, but did not look away. A wave rolled the ship. The laser's power ebbed. Jaws opened wider as Narren struggled to maintain his balance and escape the ripper.

"Hey!" Don yelled.

The ripper turned. Vall and Don were crouched behind Ruiz and two ship's officers. All of them looked like they wanted to be on another ship or, better yet, another planet. Ruiz stood ahead of them all with a small cannon aimed at the monster.

"Just get down!" Ruiz yelled.

Narren hit the deck. The ripper turned to charge the fresh meat. Ruiz squeezed the trigger. There was a loud blast and an instantaneous cloud that engulfed the zombie. It froze as instant crystals jutted out from its mass and through it. It stood frozen as a jagged statue.

Narren pulled himself up along the rail. He took a deep breath and started to laugh. The deck rolled sharply. Narren felt his body rise from the deck and press against the rail. He saw the dark ocean as if the deck and the sea were at right angles. And then the wave struck him.

The sudden mass of sea across the deck slid Don, Vall, Ruiz, and the officers toward the superstructure. It rolled back and drew them toward the rail. The seawater spared them. It flowed back through the scuppers without taking any of them. Except for Narren. The wave washed him and the frozen zombie overboard. Don shook his wet head. He blinked and looked at Ruiz who somehow still held his small cannon.

"A rip-freeze?" Don said as they all began to rise back to their feet. "That's military tech. I thought you didn't allow weapons onboard."

"It's not a weapon." Ruiz said, and coughed. "It's a security measure."

"I like it," Vall added.

Clean and dry, Vall sat at her work station inside her small cabin that didn't have a nice view. She inserted the data clip from Narren into her computer that was no bigger than the clip and activated her video link. She stole her nerves at what she might see. It was indeed unsettling. Narren's face appeared in close focus.

"If you are watching this file and you aren't me editing it, again, then I'm out of the research picture." Narren's image said. "If I'm dead, then Sast probably killed me. Or, one of our research subjects somehow animated and ate us both. Of course, in that case you may also be dead from an outbreak. But, if you're not and can make sense of this data, allow me to proceed. Or you can shut me off. Whatever."

Narren's image smiled and looked away in his quirky style.

"Okay," he continued. "We were able to separate the elements of the plague. We dissolved the virus' DNA and analyzed what remained. This had been done before, but we had new screens, better computers, and a new perspective. We knew something had to be there, and not something typically correlated with a virus. We found it. It was protein. Dense protein. Yes, it was prions.

"These were a unique and undiscovered prion form. They were more complex and exhibited behaviors beyond just acting like an enzyme. In fact, you could describe these structures as prion-like, in that they are made from dense protein but work differently. I wanted to dub it Narrentien, or perhaps the prions Narrenoids. Cumbersome name, yes. But if I'm dead—dead, dead, I hope. Either way, indulge me.

"So the Narrenoids—oh, hell. The prions take the place of the virus capsid. Neat, huh? Explains a few things. The virus inhabits folds in the prions. The prion and virus is a commensal form. Both use each other to allocate resources and replicate. Mutual evolution in non-living forms."

On the video, Narren took a moment to shake his head. He looked at the viewer. Vall found herself also shaking her head in agreement and instantly stopped.

"Yeah." Narren's image continued. "The prion unfurls and releases the virus. The prions then begin to converting human proteins into the reanimatory structure, bonded to the corpse's nervous system. The re-ambulant corpse is then guided by impulses given to the brain and nerve tissues by the virus. Okay, at this point, you get it, you get it. If you do not, then why are you watching this? Find someone who does. But here goes, very, very basically: the prions make a spring inside the corpse and the virus gives it the direction to bounce. With teeth.

"In the past, we isolated the virus, but not the prion because we simply weren't looking for it. By the time it was active we were either blowing the corpse to pieces or it was ripping off our face. A pretty good hiding strategy. But it's over. Now we can, or I hope have, built on this data and created a cure.

"I don't know what you know about me. Just realize—oh, hell. Whatever."

The file ended. Vall switched off the visual feed. She began to analyze the data. She was certain all Narren's research could have been done without causing a chain of events that lead to his own death and cost many other lives. She recalled the ancient Hippocratic oath of physicians that bade them 'first, do no harm.' Obviously Sast and Narren forgot that, or didn't care. And they both died and left the final steps of the cure to be discovered and created by others. What did they think they were doing? Accelerating the research? Vall wondered. In truth, they only accelerated their own, horrible deaths.

Narren woke. The storm had passed and he rolled along gentle, emerald waves. He lifted his head and saw the smooth expanse of ocean stretch to the horizon. The *Iris* was far away. He was alone. His appreciation for irony came to a fine point when he noticed what he gripped to stay afloat. It was the plank with the ship's name carved into it. It must have ripped away in the same wave that took him off the ship.

He noticed a stinging pain, but not from his neck. That still throbbed, but this was a new burning pain in his legs. Large jellyfish floated around him. They were clear and not all seemed alive. His own flesh was still living, mostly. The plague was slowed by the microscopic machines at war with the prions in his tissues. Still, the virus lurked in his blood. He looked up at the partially cloudy sky. A breeze wafted the smell of rotting flesh. He turned his head and saw a large, dark mass floating nearby. He knew what it was. The engineered jellyfish would not be what killed him. Narren parted their membranes around him and looked into the deep but clear ocean. He hoped to see something truly alien before he died. He did.

It swam several meters below him. It was a long black spine with several, large cilia beating in rhythmic waves along its sides. Large, oval structures appeared to be like eyes before forward facing gills or a tiered mouth. A sloshing noise broke Narren's concentration. The dark mass was closer. He could see the zombies bob among the flotsam. They also saw him. Some left the dark mat and did an undead version of the dog paddle swimming stroke towards him. They were unlike any rippers he's seen. The elements and ocean had bloated and ravaged their bodies. But they still could move. They were obviously hungry, and heading for him. Narren imagined being ripped to pieces and the sea water flowing into his wounds and searing his insides. He hoped the alien creature was a predator. He dove down and wanted it to kill him fast.

Through stinging eyes, Narren saw what he thought were large cilia shoot way from the central, black spine. They darted towards him, but then just as quickly back to the spine. He wondered if they sensed he was something alien. He wondered what he saw. The cilia now looked to swim on their own. They reformed around the spine and resumed their synchronous rhythm. Was it a polymorphic form of life like jellyfish? Were the cilia actually young and the spine the mother? Or was it a form of life that somehow controlled its limbs without physical attachment? Perhaps it was some type of magnetic life. Maybe it was a machine. Burning lungs ended his theorizing. The creature dove into the depths.

Narren lost his hope of a swift death. He swam deeper and gulped sea water in an attempt to drown. Something grabbed his ankle. He wasn't as deep as he thought. A cold hand, certainly human pulled him up. Several other cold hands yanked him back to the surface. Narren felt teeth bite him from all direction. He tried to scream but only gurgled out seawater. His blood washed over him and colored the ocean dark red.

Don's hunch was right. He found Vall looking up at the stars as the *Iris* sailed into calmer waters and under clearing skies.

"Company?" Don asked.

"Sure," Vall smiled at him.

"Think we're alone?" Don asked as he joined Vall looking skyward.

"Odd how once that question was about alien life," Vall observed. "Now it's a question if humans still survive on other worlds."

"Maybe the other colonies are keeping silent out of fear the plague." Don said. "Maybe they won't once a cure is known to exist."

"It will," Vall nodded. "Soon. Various anti-prions were developed on Earth decades ago. He can do what they did on this ship. And no one needs to die."

"I'm glad," Don said and heard his voice quaver with the thought of his plan actually succeeding.

"We will turn the tide." Vall smiled and looked at Don. "But I don't think the journey ends there."

"Oh?" Don looked at her with curious eyes.

"This is still a changing world." Vall said. "We will also have to change to live in balance with it, and in balance with ourselves. We may be the last of humanity, but also the first generation that gives rise to new, intelligent life."

Don said nothing as he considered Vall's words. He felt the deck pitch as the *Iris* rolled with the alien ocean. Before they made landfall again, he knew they would need to travel out into deeper waters.

STORY NOTES

The stories "Amid the Deep," "At Peace," and "Underfoot" originally appeared in the e-book volumes and print edition of _Nightmares and Other Vices_. All other stories are first published in this book.

The character Joshua Grail, AKA Mr. Ice, has appeared in several magazines and the _Nightmares and Other Vices_ volumes. A collection featuring Grail stories is in the works.

ABOUT THE AUTHOR

Zombies may rule the world, but Bruce S. Larson is not dead. Some claim Bruce was born to write. He has been writing since birth. At least since he could hold a pen. Keyboard use came later. Then walking and speech.

Visit Bruce's website @ **www.thewritebruce.com** where living and undead can read free fiction, his irregular blog, and histories of alternate Earths.

In addition to zombie style Armageddon, Bruce wrote the epic novel *Beyond Apocalypse*. In it, several worlds end during a galaxy spanning war with Hell. His other works include the e-book Horror collections *Nightmares and Other Vices*, Volumes 1 and 2. Both volumes are published in a single Print Edition. Science Fiction and Fantasy combine in his collections *Within and Beyond: The Realms of the Sun*, and the following *Within and Beyond: The Storm*. Each is available in print or e-book formats.

More books are expected from Bruce, once he destroys the zombies attacking his farm house.

World Line One wishes him good luck, and you happy reading.

World Line One Press

www.ingramcontent.com/pod-product-compliance
Lightning Source LLC
Chambersburg PA
CBHW060920180626
46817CB00004B/1326